D0776282

HOLLYWOOD HILLS

Don't miss Holly and Alexa's other
scandalous escapades!

HOLLYWOOD HILLS

Aimee Friedman

SCHOLASTIC INC.

New York Toronto London Auckland Sydney
Mexico City New Delhi Hong Kong Buenos Aires

No part of this publication may be reproduced, stored in a retrieval system, or transmitted in any form or by any means, electronic, mechanical, photocopying, recording, or otherwise, without written permission of the publisher. For information regarding permission, write to Scholastic Inc., Attention: Permissions Department, 557 Broadway, New York, NY 10012.

ISBN-13: 978-0-439-79282-0
ISBN-10: 0-439-79282-7

All rights reserved. Published by Scholastic Inc.
SCHOLASTIC, POINT, and associated logos are trademarks and/or registered trademarks of Scholastic Inc.

Book design by Steve Scott

12 11 10 9 8 7 6 5 4 3 2 1   6 7 8 9 10 11/0

Printed in the U.S.A.
First printing, December 2006

For Martha Kelehan and Patrick Johnson, who make a girl feel at home on any coast.

*   *   *

A million thank yous to:

Anica Mrose Rissi, for her editorial superpowers and for always being just a phone call away.

Craig Walker, Abby McAden, Morgan Matson, Steve Scott, Kara Edwards, Rachel Coun, and everyone at Scholastic, for their invaluable contributions.

Rob Miller, for being my LA guru; all my fantastic friends, for their patience and humor; and my amazing family — especially Noah — for the everyday inspiration.

Ain't it a shame that all the world
can't enjoy your mad traditions.
— Rufus Wainwright, "California"

CHAPTER ONE
The Invitation

Gail Wilson-St. Laurent-Feldman,
Head Buyer at Henri Bendel,
Cordially invites you to a party in honor of Paz Ferrara,
A sparkling new talent in the high fashion world.
To be held at Ms. Wilson-St. Laurent-Feldman's home,
10 Charles Street, Apartment 1A, New York City
Monday, June 15, 8 P.M.
Stilettos optional.

Her ocean-blue eyes dancing with mischief, Alexandria St. Laurent accepted a cocktail napkin and a pen from Brian or Benjamin or whatever his name was. She knelt carefully in her white, wooden-heeled Tod's pumps, set the napkin on her mother's antique coffee table, and, her long, flaxen hair rippling over one shoulder, promptly scrawled out a fake phone number.

"Thanks, Alexa," Bennett or Barry gushed as Alexa stood up, adjusting the tulle hem of her peach-colored skirt. "I can't believe I lost my cell today." His beady brown eyes twinkled hopefully as he fiddled with his silk necktie. It was printed with tiny question marks, which gave Alexa a headache if she stared at them for too long. "But I'm glad I found *you* here."

"Well," Alexa murmured, her glossed lips curling up in a wry smile. The grand living room, its tall windows thrown open to offer a glittering view of the Empire State Building, was teeming with black-clad, diamond-studded guests. And, out of everyone, this winner — the son of some senator, or so he said — had skulked up to Alexa while her friends were off getting drinks. "My mother invited me, so I wouldn't miss it."

On cue, Alexa heard her frosty-blonde, oft-married mother give a high-pitched laugh from across the room. *Ugh.* In all-too-typical fashion, Mommie Dearest had actually *mailed* Alexa the friggin' invitation instead of picking up the phone, like any other parent with a functioning heart would have done. Alexa hadn't even planned to show tonight, but she'd felt so carefree after handing in her AP Biology final that morning — her very last exam as a high school senior — that she'd decided *some* sort of celebrating was in order. After all, her graduation from New Jersey's Oakridge High School was less than a week away — that coming Sunday, to be exact. At the thought, Alexa felt a rush of excitement that had nothing to do with the boy in front of her.

"One saketini for the mademoiselle!"

Finally! Alexa glanced over Bartholomew's shoulder with a grateful grin. Her on-again-off-again (currently on-again) best friend in the world, Holly Jacobson, was making her way across the room in her gold-beaded ballet flats, holding up two martini glasses filled with berry-colored liquid. Holly's boyfriend of over a year, Tyler Davis, trailed behind her, munching off of a cheese plate.

Alexa gave a silent prayer of thanks that she'd had the foresight to bring Holly and Tyler along tonight — though inviting Holly had been pretty much a no-brainer. Alexa and Holly had met in the second grade, right after Alexa had moved to New Jersey from her native Paris. After eleven years of whispered secrets, swapped lip liners, vicious fights, stolen crushes, and drama-filled trips to South Beach and Paris, the girls' friendship was stronger than ever. And no matter what, it seemed Holly was always there to rescue Alexa whenever Alexa needed her most.

Like right now.

"I'm really sorry, but my friends are waiting for me," Alexa swiftly told Boris, who offered a meek "I'll call you?" as Alexa hurried off into the buzzing crowd.

"You're a lifesaver," Alexa whispered, kissing Holly's freckled cheek. She took the saketini from her friend's hand, and snatched a sliver of Gouda off Tyler's plate. "That guy was hitting on me so hard he was practically breaking a sweat."

"Which guy?" Tyler inquired, his mouth full.

"You mean Bryce Thompson?" Holly asked, squinting her gray-green eyes in the direction of the boy Alexa had abandoned, and giving him a friendly wave. "But he's so nice! I chatted with him when we first got here. Did you know his dad's a senator?"

"*Bryce* — that's it," Alexa said, snapping her manicured fingers. She fought the urge to roll her eyes; only naïve, wouldn't-hurt-a-fly Holly Jacobson would fall for that senator line *and* bother to remember his name. Alexa had to love the girl for it, though.

"Hol, were you flirting behind my back?" Tyler teased, sliding one toned arm around Holly's waist and kissing the top of her head. Holly laughed, turning to peck Tyler on the lips, and Alexa sipped at her sour-sweet saketini in order to avoid gagging. Sure, she was happy that boy-shy Holly had snagged herself tall, golden-haired lacrosse star Tyler Davis as a boyfriend. Alexa had even moved past the weirdness she'd once felt about the relationship (back in ancient-history-junior-year, *she* had dated Tyler). No. It was just that Alexa had been breezily, brazenly single for the past three months — and, like any single girl worth her salt, disdained the kind of googly-eyed affection Holly and Tyler were always displaying.

Alexa couldn't even remember the last time she'd kissed a boy — okay, maybe she could, but he'd been this total French slimeball, so good riddance to that. Bryce Thompson was far from the first guy Alexa had given a faux phone number to; since declaring herself seriously single in March, she'd had offers from plenty of suitors, but had rejected them all. In May, she'd even gone to the prom alone, giving other girls' dates whiplash as she sauntered through the hotel ballroom in her backless black dress. And she looked forward to starting Columbia in the fall with zero romantic ties — very much unlike Holly and Tyler, who would doubtless be *the* athletic It Couple at Rutgers come September.

"Anyway, what took you guys so long?" Alexa asked, placing a hand on her slim hip, and effectively putting an end to the cuddle session.

"It was my fault," Holly giggled, removing her freckly arms from around Tyler's neck, and turning back to Alexa. "I stopped to check out those disgustingly ador- able baby pictures of you." Holly gestured toward the marble mantel, where a row of silver-framed photos featuring Alexa as a deceptively angelic blonde child were displayed.

"Oh, please," Alexa snorted, shaking her head. "My loving mom only trotted out the photos tonight to appear, you know, less evil than usual –" Alexa's stomach sank as she noticed Holly's face blanch. "She's right behind me, isn't she?" Alexa whispered.

"Um," Holly said, tightening her grip on her saketini glass as Tyler began to anxiously brush back his hair. "Good evening, Mrs. St. Laurent, I mean, Feldman, I –"

"Holly, honey, I've been begging you for the past eleven years to call me Gail," Alexa's mom drawled in her throaty voice, walking around Alexa to plant effusive kisses on the air near Holly's cheeks. "Besides, I'm getting too old to drag all those names behind me like a dead weight. *Hello*, Travis," she added, fluttering her false lashes in Tyler's direction. He colored but didn't correct her; as Alexa remembered it, Tyler had always been intimidated by her mother. It was kind of hard *not* to be. Even Alexa stiffened in her heavily perfumed presence.

"Alexandria," Gail intoned, running a hand over her sleek blonde bun and straightening the lapels of her silk pantsuit. Each time she moved, the chunky black pearls around her neck clunked together, and Alexa felt her teeth clench at the familiar sound. "I know you are *extremely* busy tearing me to shreds, but I wanted to know if you've had a chance to meet Paz."

"Yes, Mother," Alexa managed through her teeth. "You introduced me to her the minute I walked in, remember?" It was true; while Tyler was parking the car and Bryce Thompson was accosting Holly, Gail had shepherded Alexa over to Paz Ferrara, the petite, raven-haired designer of edgy/sexy bridal gowns who was known for her cutting remarks on *Project Runway*. Even in her broken English, the Portuguese-born Paz had come off as coolly dismissive, and, upon learning that Alexa wouldn't be needing a wedding dress anytime soon, stalked off in her thigh-high leather boots to chat up Michael Kors.

"Well, excuse me for forgetting," Gail replied, taking a hearty sip of her gin and tonic, which was clearly one of the many factors in her forgetfulness. Truth be told, Alexa was fully expecting her mother to conveniently "forget" her graduation on Sunday. At least her laid-back French dad, with whom Alexa lived, could be counted on to show up.

Gail cast her eyes over a silent Alexa, Holly, and Tyler, and cleared her throat. "So," she said, rattling the ice cubes in her glass. Alexa smiled; it was obvious her mom was groping about for something, well, motherly to say. "What are everyone's plans for the summer?" she finally asked, looking proud of herself.

"I know Alexa will be interning at the fashion department of *Vogue*. . . ."

"The *photography* department, Mother," Alexa put
in sharply. As deep as Alexa's love for fashion ran,
taking pictures was her true passion, and she couldn't
stand it when her mother conveniently chose to ignore
that fact.

"Oh, yes, that's right," Gail sighed, shaking her
head. "You and your camera."

Despite her annoyance toward her mother, Alexa
felt a shiver of anticipation. She planned to spend this
week before graduation getting lazy pedicures, but on
June 23, she'd move into Columbia student housing
in the city and start work at her favorite magazine.
Best of all, Alexa had gotten the plum job all on her
own, *without* her mother's fashionable connections.
Though it certainly hadn't hurt when she'd mentioned
Gail's name during the interview.

"I'll, uh, be a counselor at a sports camp up in the
Berkshires," Holly was saying in her soft, stiff, I'm-
speaking-to-a-parent-voice. Tyler, also eternally prim
and proper, reported that he'd be coaching the junior
lacrosse team in Oakridge. Then, resting a hand on
Holly's shoulder and flashing his toothy grin, he added,
"And tomorrow we're heading off to the Adirondacks
on a weeklong camping trip with the Jacobsons."

Holly's mouth twisted ever so slightly, and because Alexa knew Holly as well as she did, she understood her friend was nearing the intersection of Pissed and Annoyed. "Baby," Holly told Tyler, clearly trying to keep her tone neutral. "I thought we'd decided —"

"Camping. How nice," Gail replied, her upper lip curling, and Alexa met her mother's gaze in a rare moment of understanding. One of the few points mother and daughter agreed on (besides the fact that Keds, no matter what people said, were never coming back in style) was that tents, insects, and sleeping outdoors were gross. "Oh, look," Gail added, waving at someone in the distance. "I think I see Heidi. As in, Klum. 'Ta for now." With that, she marched off, pearls clanking loudly.

Alexa scowled at her mother's retreating figure, then turned back to Holly and Tyler, who were now in the middle of a quasi-fight. "But the other night you said you'd think about it," Tyler was murmuring to Holly, his brow knit. Holly was facing him, her shiny-straight, light-brown hair sweeping her shoulders as she shook her head back and forth. Alexa got the distinct impression that she was spying on a scene she wasn't meant to witness.

"Tyler, the last thing I want to do on my *one* free week is help my dad and brother, like, build a fire in

the middle of nowhere," Holly hissed, now having trouble keeping her voice level. "Don't we spend enough time with my parents?"

Score one for Jacobson, Alexa thought, finishing off her saketini. She almost wanted to jump into the fray and back Holly up, but she thought the better of it. This was clearly Couple Time. "Listen, guys," she cut in. "I'll let you finish up your lovers' spat without me." Before either of them could protest, Alexa gave Holly's arm a squeeze and promised to find them later.

Walking off, she could still hear their bickering. *Like an old married couple*, Alexa thought with a smile as she turned into the corridor that led out to the garden. She wouldn't be surprised if Holly and Tyler did tie the knot one day, and had even informed Holly last week, over glasses of homemade sangria in Alexa's backyard, that she fully expected to be the maid of honor.

"No — tell them I will *not* pose half nude with my maid of honor!"

Alexa froze, wondering if she'd heard right. She was pushing open the screen door to her mother's back garden — a place that was tucked away behind twisty-turny hallways, and which Gail kept off-limits to party guests. Alexa peered outside; enormous tea roses twined around a tall fence, and white patio chairs were grouped around a burbling stone fountain. A tall,

lithe girl with super-short, purple-streaked black hair sat in one of the chairs with her back to Alexa. She was clad in a strapless burgundy tunic over cropped fishnet leggings and pink patent-leather pumps. A fuchsia Helio Kickflip was pressed to her ear.

"I don't care if they're going to make it *classy*," the girl was saying, one hand toying with the long rope of metallic pink beads around her neck. Her low, throaty voice sounded incredibly familiar, but Alexa couldn't place it. "*Maxim* is never classy. *Vanity Fair*, I'd do in, like, a second, but never that sleazy frat-boy bible —"

Alexa hadn't even realized she was giggling until the girl spun around, her kohl-lined eyes narrowed in suspicion. In that heart-dropping instant, Alexa realized who she was, and her mouth fell open.

It was Margaux Eklundstrom, indie-movie princess. Just last week, Alexa and Holly had seen Margaux in the artsy black-and-white film *Grit and Gravel*, and yesterday, Alexa had read a posting on the website thesuperficial.com about the actress's upcoming zillion-dollar wedding to a hotshot young screenwriter.

Margaux was also the big sister of Jonah Eklundstrom, the impossibly dreamy, blue-eyed young actor who'd won an Oscar for playing a gay boxer — but was *totally* straight in real life. HOLLYWOOD'S FAVORITE SIBLINGS! the headline in Alexa's latest *Us Weekly* blared, and Alexa had admired the photos of a sassily dressed Margaux

stalking the red carpet and of a shirtless Jonah jogging at LA's Runyon Canyon. Yes, Alexa's mother had connections to celebrity designers and models, but what was someone like *Margaux Eklundstrom* doing at her party?

And, more importantly, had she brought her brother?

"I didn't know you were out here —" Alexa began as Margaux leaped to her feet, looking surprisingly sheepish.

"Elaine, I'll call you back," Margaux said into her phone, then flipped it shut. "Oh, God, I'm SO sorry," she told Alexa, her eyes — a darker blue version of her brother's — widening. "I wasn't sure if I was allowed out here or not, I kind of stumbled on it trying to get cell service, but if your mother doesn't want —"

"Wait," Alexa said, slightly amused at how rambly the hotshot movie star sounded. "How did you know I'm Gail's daughter?" She couldn't help the sharpness in her tone when she spoke her mother's name.

Margaux lifted one bare, moon-pale shoulder. "Number one, you look like a younger, prettier, and more natural version of her, and number two, I checked out those photos of you inside." She grinned crookedly, clearly pleased with her logical deductions.

Alexa felt a rush of affection; celeb or not, she liked this girl already.

"And sorry you had to hear me railing at my manager like a spoiled brat," Margaux added, sinking back into the chair and crossing her mile-long legs. "I'm getting married this Friday, and she's goddamn convinced that it can further my *career* somehow." To indicate her disgust, Margaux stuck out her tongue, which had a little round steel ball in its center. Alexa, who'd always wished she had the guts to pierce her belly button, was both impressed and jealous.

"I hate it when people try to foist their expectations on you," Alexa said, thinking of her mother, and how she'd always assumed that Alexa would pursue a career in fashion.

Margaux blinked at Alexa, her face lighting up. "Ex-*actly*," she said. "Hey, have a seat over here." She motioned to the empty chair beside her. "You smoke? They're clove." The tiny skulls on her white-gold charm bracelet jangled as she reached into the black seashell clutch at her feet. With a small jolt, Alexa recognized it as the Heatherette "Margaux," which had been designed in honor of the actress.

"No, thanks," Alexa replied as she settled into the chair. "I decided to officially quit after my last trip to Paris." Paris was also where Alexa had had her most recent brush with celebrity, so it was no wonder she was now able to feel chill around an A-lister like Margaux.

"Cool," Margaux said, lighting her cigarette and casting an approving glance at Alexa. "You seem like a girl who always does her own thing. I'm trying to learn how to be more like that from Kabbalah. I know Madonna's kind of made it passé, but *I* still think it's totally inspiring." She gestured excitedly to the red string tied around her delicate wrist. "You should stop by the Centre for Shabbat services if you're ever in LA."

"Um, sure," Alexa said, biting back a laugh; she found the whole Hollywood-Kabbalah obsession kind of funny. "What's it like, living in LA?" she added. "I was there only once, with my dad, when I was eight." All that Alexa remembered of the sun-splashed, plastic-fantastic West Coast city was putting her tiny sandaled feet inside Marilyn Monroe's dainty footprints at Grauman's Chinese Theatre. Even that brief visit had felt somehow enchanted. Alexa wanted to ask Margaux what it was like to be in movies, but *that* question would definitely be filed under "insanely dorky."

"It's nothing like living in New York, for one," Margaux replied, exhaling a perfect O of sweet-smelling smoke. She glanced up at the cloudy night sky and the blinking lights of tall buildings in the distance. "There's more . . . space or something. There's the desert, the blooming flowers, the hills. That's where I live – in Hollywood Hills. My wedding's gonna be at home."

I know, Alexa almost said, but she held her tongue again. She had seen the photos online of a pale blue mansion perched high up in the hills, a stone's throw from the fabled Hollywood sign. "Sounds divine," was all Alexa said, meaning it completely.

Margaux sighed and gave Alexa a rueful smile. "Yeah. I'm not *that* homesick, though. Everyone out there's kind of self-obsessed and faker than their boobs."

"Well, in case you haven't noticed, there's *plenty* of self-obsession in New York," Alexa replied, and felt a warm glow when Margaux burst out laughing. It was bizarre, but kind of thrilling, to be bantering with a girl Alexa had so recently seen up on a flickering movie screen. "Which leads me to ask," Alexa went on, feigning nonchalance, "what brings you to this gathering?" Imagining LA – the white sweep of beaches, the air perfumed by fresh oranges, the constant presence of movie stars – Alexa wondered why anyone would want to leave.

"Paz Ferrara designed my wedding gown," Margaux replied, rolling her eyes. "Had to show up to pay my respects – or so my agent said." When her Kickflip buzzed, she looked at the caller ID and grimaced, not answering. "Speak of the devil," she groaned. "It's only six in LA so everyone's getting their work done now. I'll tell you something," Margaux went on, waving smoke away from Alexa. "I'm fed up with the wedding gar-*bage*. At this point I'm sick of every soul who's involved with it, except for my fiancé, Paul, of course." She took a long drag off her cigarette, then tilted her head toward Alexa. "Hey, you want to come?"

"Uh, where?" Alexa asked, feeling as if she'd missed something.

"To my *wedding*, silly!" Margaux laughed. "This Friday — it'll be so fun."

Alexa took a deep breath, trying to quell the giddiness building in her. *She's probably joking, Lex. Calm down. She's insane.*

"I'm serious," Margaux insisted as if she'd heard Alexa's thoughts, and Alexa felt her stomach do a somersault. "I know it's not a *formal* invitation or anything — not that I believe in that old-fashioned shit anyway. Paul and I just made a podcast and mailed out iPods to everyone we love." Margaux shrugged, as if this were an everyday occurrence. "But I swear on a stack of screenplays," she went on, lifting her right hand, "I'd love to have you there. You could make a little vacay out of it. Why the hell not?" Speech over, Margaux crossed her arms over her chest and stared Alexa down — in a friendly way, of course.

16

"But . . . but it's kind of last-minute, isn't it?" Alexa asked when she finally found her voice. Her fingers had started to tremble, a sure sign that she was inching beyond nervous into fully freaked out. She wondered how to subtly pull her cell phone out of her clutch and start texting Holly. She knew how she'd begin the message: Promise u im not lying but —

"Sweetie-pie, nothing's last minute in La-La Land," Margaux chuckled, and opened her phone. "Just to confirm I'll call Vikram — that's my wedding planner, he's a genius — but in the end, I'm the bridezilla, so what I say goes, right?" She shot Alexa a devilish grin.

"Right," Alexa murmured as the full impact of what Margaux was saying began to sink in. Alexa, in the City of Angels. In a convertible, blonde hair flying as she zipped down Santa Monica Boulevard, past streams of green palm trees, toward the sapphire Pacific. Alexa, at a celebrity wedding: pastel satin sundresses rustling, pointy heels balancing on the grass, a surfer boy with sun-kissed hair offering her a dance . . . Warmth raced through Alexa like electricity. She felt the pull of the West Coast tempting her, seducing her.

"Hang on," Margaux was saying, frowning down at her cell. "The only possibly sucky thing is that the Beverly Hills Hotel, the W, *and* the Roosevelt are all

filled up with my social-climbing friends, and Paul's, like, two hundred relatives."

Alexa opened her mouth to say she'd be cool with sleeping on the beach – which didn't *technically* count as camping – but Margaux was already pressing a button on her cell and bringing the phone to her ear. "Jonah?" Margaux asked after a minute, and Alexa suffered a mini heart attack, clutching the arm of the bench for support. *The* Jonah? It couldn't be. Maybe Margaux knew others. Maybe Jonah was a popular name in LA. Then Margaux glanced at Alexa and mouthed, *"My brother,"* and Alexa nodded casually, her pulse pounding, as if the brother in question lived down the block or worked at the local Starbucks.

"Baby Bear!" Margaux was squealing into the phone. "I met this *amazing* girl in NYC. She totally has your sense of humor, and she's *blonde*, which I know you love." Margaux shot a wicked look at Alexa, who drew in a sharp breath. Jonah Eklundstrom *had* famously dated blonde-waif actress Charity Durst. Still, that didn't mean anything. "Anyway," Margaux went on. "I invited her to my big day – you don't care if she crashes at your guesthouse, right?"

Since Margaux was facing away from her, Alexa pinched the skin of her upper arm hard, just to be sure.

"Thought so," Margaux said, giving Alexa the

thumbs-up sign. "Uh-huh, I'll tell her about the party at The Standard, too. Down, boy. She's hot, but I bet she's picky." At this, Margaux winked at Alexa, who managed to smile back shakily.

I'm going to stay with Jonah Eklundstrom.

Clasping her hands in her lap, Alexa repeated this fact to herself, like a mantra. Fantasies of a Hollywood hook-up floated through her head — what would it be like to gaze into those deep blue eyes up close, to run her hand along that warm, rough jawline? — but Alexa knew they were just that: fantasies. She'd been burned in the past, after all. Gorgeous, famous, make-women-faint Jonah Eklundstrom probably had, like, a harem of girlfriends at his beck and call. And while Alexa knew she could compete with the sparkliest of starlets, realistically, she doubted she'd register as more than a blip on Jonah's high-end radar.

But maybe he'd flirt with her one day when she was coming out of the guesthouse in her orange-and-gold Shoshanna bikini.

"All right, Baby Bear — don't stay out *too* late tonight, 'kay? I know you have read-throughs all this week. I'll call you when I'm back tomorrow." Margaux clicked off, then turned to beam at Alexa. "Done, and done. Oh, and that party at The Standard downtown — it's

tomorrow night around six. My brother and I are throwing it for some industry friends. You should come, if you'll be in town by then."

If she'd be in town? Alexa was speechless. She had one whole, blissful week off before graduation — and she certainly no longer intended to spend it in Oakridge, getting pedicures at Suzy's Salon.

Cheesy as it was, Alexa let herself think it: *California, here I come.*

After Margaux had entered Alexa's number — Alexa made sure to give her real one this time — into her cell, she stood up, and Alexa rose as well. "I'll text you my brother's address from the airport," Margaux promised. "I'm headed to JFK now — I need to catch a midnight plane back home." She put her cigarette out on the heel of her pump, then glanced up. "How moronic of me," she added. "I'm Margaux." She stuck out her left hand, her ginormous pink diamond ring catching the moonlight.

Alexa shook her head, bemused. Clearly, they'd skipped a step in the let's-be-friends game. "Alexa," she replied, returning Margaux's handshake. "And I know who you are."

"I knew you knew," Margaux replied, her eyes sparkling. "But I appreciated your attempt to hide it."

Their high heels clicking on the ground, the two girls made their way back to the garden door, and the

sounds of the party drifted out toward them, as if from another planet. As a dizzy, elated Alexa was about to reenter the apartment, Margaux tapped her elbow.

"Hey, Alexa?" she said with a crooked grin. "If I didn't mention it, feel free to bring a date."

"A date," Alexa echoed. Her first, breathless thought was of Jonah, but she brushed off the ridiculous notion. Then Alexa had another idea. A brilliant one. She felt her face breaking into a smile. "Okay. I know exactly who to ask."

CHAPTER TWO
Holly Would

The best part about fighting with your boyfriend, Holly Jacobson had learned, was the insanely hot apology hook-up that followed.

"I'm sorry, sweetie," Tyler whispered, wrapping his arms around Holly's waist and drawing her down onto the bed with him. Alexa's bed, to be precise.

When their increasingly loud debate in the living room had prompted eyebrow raises from the other party guests, Holly and Tyler had snuck off to the only private place they could find: the all-white guest room that, Holly knew, doubled as Alexa's whenever she stayed at her mom's. But any hesitations Holly had about fighting — and fooling around — in there had melted away with one touch of Tyler's warm lips against her skin.

"Me, too," Holly murmured, tilting her head back as Tyler planted slow, light kisses all down her neck. To be perfectly honest, she wasn't *that* sorry, and she and Tyler hadn't even reached a real resolution. The thought of them camping with her family this week — her mother making them synchronize their watches before every hike, her younger brother, Josh, persuading Tyler to sneak slugs into Holly's sleeping bag — still irritated Holly. But she was okay letting the issue go for now. Even though she'd developed a slightly thicker skin of late, Holly still loathed confrontations. And besides, she'd much rather be kissing Tyler.

Sitting side by side, her slender legs stretched across Tyler's lap, Holly and Tyler kissed, their lips meeting with sweet, easy familiarity. Holly buried her fingers in Tyler's wavy, dark-blond hair and shut her eyes, letting the pleasure of her boyfriend's nearness and the familiarity of his clean, soapy scent course through her.

Through the wall, she could hear laughter and champagne glasses clinking, and she was grateful that she and Tyler had escaped. Though Holly considered Alexa a surrogate sister, she couldn't quite appreciate the more glamorous aspects of her friend's world. The simple pleasures of running track — well-worn Sauconys pounding the pavement, ratty T-shirt sticking to her back, high ponytail swishing — were what made Holly happiest.

Next to being alone with Tyler, of course.

Tyler slowly ended the kiss and drew back, his handsome face breaking into a tender smile and his amber-brown eyes brightening.

"I love you, Holly Rebecca," he murmured, brushing her bangs back to kiss her forehead.

"Right back at you, Tyler Maxwell." Holly grinned, swatting at his hand and then finger-combing her bangs back into place. "Even when you do that," she added teasingly. It still amazed her how far she and Tyler had come since their first kiss on a moonlit Miami beach in their junior year. After so many ups and downs, Holly finally knew what rock-solid love felt like: a pair of arms around you, a net below you, safety, certainty, peace.

And the occasional stupid argument over vacation plans.

"That's why I want to share stuff like family trips with you," Tyler explained, pulling Holly in closer toward his broad chest. "It's part of who you are. I love that, too."

Holly swallowed hard, her earlier anger mellowing. Meghan, Holly's second-best friend after Alexa, had recently called Holly in tears because her father and her brand-new boyfriend, Jeff, had gotten into an actual fistfight due to Jeff's saying "goddamn" at a family dinner. Holly knew she was extremely fortunate that her parents and boyfriend got along as well as they did. Holly's mom and dad were so fond of Tyler that Holly sometimes got the sense that, if given the chance, they'd gladly swap her for him.

"And since we'll be going to school nearby," Tyler went on, clearly aware that Holly was softening, "I thought it might be nice for all of us to – you know – bond or something." He shrugged and shot her a game, yeah-I-know-I'm-a-loser grin.

Giving Tyler a playful shove, Holly tried to dispel the image of herself, Josh, her parents, and Tyler singing "Kumbaya" around a campfire. Bonding aside, that fall she and Tyler *would* be starting at Rutgers, which was only a twenty-minute drive from Oakridge, and the university Holly – and her parents – had always assumed she would go to. But Tyler's deciding to join her there had been a last-minute surprise.

Holly thought back to that perilous, stomach-churning time in April, when skinny and fat envelopes from colleges had started to arrive in droves. One night, over the phone, she and Tyler had torn open each envelope in tandem, breathlessly relaying the score: Holly into Bucknell, Tyler rejected; Tyler into U. Mich, Holly rejected; Holly into UCLA, Tyler into Bowdoin; Holly into U. Conn and, finally, both of them into Rutgers. Somehow, by the time they reached Rutgers, neither could imagine going to college without the other.

"That reminds me," Holly added, steering the subject away from their camping conundrum. "My housing request form came this morning. I haven't looked at it yet but — "

Tyler's face lit up. "Awesome — I got mine, too! Come over tonight and we can fill them out together. That way we'll make sure we end up in the same dorm."

Holly nodded, smiling. She pictured herself and Tyler as next-door neighbors on a freshman hall: tiptoeing into each other's rooms after midnight, studying, listening to Keane's "Everything's Changing" on repeat, making out, making love. . . . Holly could only hope that they'd have understanding roommates.

"You know what else I was thinking?" Tyler said, lightly nuzzling Holly's ear. "Maybe after freshman year, we could get an apartment off-campus. I checked out some places online, and it's kind of pricey right near the school, but we could live somewhere closer to Oakridge. There's a townhouse on Beech Street that's renting the top room to a couple now."

"Um, yeah," Holly said, a weird sinking sensation in her belly. Beech Street was right around the corner from her parents. Wasn't the whole point of college to get some much-needed distance from home? "Let's focus on freshman year first," she suggested softly, smoothing down the collar of Tyler's maroon polo shirt.

Tyler frowned slightly. "Hol, it's totally better to plan these things out now," he reasoned. "We're going to get so busy once we're *in* college. And since you're going to law school afterward, and I'll be coaching lacrosse, like we decided, our lives are going to be *really* hectic."

Holly bit her lip as the future rolled toward her like a cresting wave. Was something wrong with her, that she didn't want her life scripted out just yet? Yes, she hoped to be with Tyler forever. She'd be lying if she said daydreams of a golden wedding day hadn't flitted through her head during some dull physics class or another. But those were vague, misty kinds of plans. And, in those daydreams, she certainly hadn't pictured herself and Tyler living out their romantic life in drab old Oakridge.

"What?" Tyler murmured, picking up on Holly's unease. He tipped his head so that he could get a look at Holly's wide gray-green eyes, which always managed to betray her emotions. "Something's bugging you."

"Oh, Tyler," she sighed, hoping to circumvent another quarrel. "It's just that . . ." Holly glanced down at her hands. She was *never* as articulate as she wanted to be, and she suddenly wished Alexa were there to offer her moral support. "I feel like my parents have always mapped everything out for me — you know, with ballet lessons and math tutors and curfews and all that. And now, I guess I . . . I want to leave a little room for . . . spontaneity?" She posed this last word as a question, but knew deep down that it was exactly what she wanted. After all, she and Tyler were only eighteen. They had plenty of time to make solid plans once they'd had their share of wildness and fun.

Tyler was silent for a long moment as he stared straight ahead at the shut door. Then he cleared his throat and turned to her, looking thoughtful. "Spontaneity, huh?" he repeated. "I know something spontaneous that we can do right . . . about . . . now."

"Tyler!" Holly shrieked, giggling, as he pounced on her and toppled her over onto her back.

"Well, I don't want to turn into a *boring* boyfriend or anything," Tyler joked, slowly but surely inching Holly's pleated black Mexx skirt up her thighs.

"This is crazy," Holly protested, but she was already kissing Tyler's jawline, which she knew got him hot and bothered.

After months and months of getting each other hot, last month Holly and Tyler had finally taken deep breaths and gone all the way. As Tyler pulled back to slip off his navy-blue blazer, Holly closed her eyes with a smile, remembering prom night. Their first time. They'd booked a room at the Oakridge Hilton, and Holly recalled the nervousness in her throat as she'd followed Tyler up the grand staircase. After a night of dancing, her light-green Betsey Johnson dress was sticking to her sweaty back and her beige sandals were squeezing her toes. Her mind had churned with questions. How would she know what to do? Were they rushing? Had they waited too long? Was prom night too cliché?

But once in their room — giggling over the actual DO NOT DISTURB sign they hung on the doorknob — every concern had fallen away as effortlessly as their clothes. Onto the queen-sized bed they'd dropped, kissing as if they'd never tasted each other's mouths before. Holly's heart had been racing, but for once her thoughts hadn't kept her from acting. And act she did, her trembling fingers helping Tyler open the newly purchased box of condoms. After that initial fumbling, everything had gone smoothly. Though it had been at once terrifying and blissful and painful and sublime, Holly welcomed every sensation. And Tyler was right there with her the whole way, his eyes locked on hers, their fingers entwined, professions of love whispered in the dark. Falling asleep in his arms later, Holly felt as if she'd grown several inches over the space of an hour — as if her limbs were literally stretching, and her mind expanding — to encompass this strange and thrilling new world she'd come upon.

For the rest of May she'd walked the school hallways, run the length of the track, and done her homework with the words *I am not a virgin anymore* resounding in her head, both tormenting and exciting her. It wasn't until she and Tyler had done it a few more times, and she'd had a good, long talk with Alexa (who was so experienced that she found Holly's obsessing hilarious) that Holly began to adjust to the idea.

And tonight, lying on this white, frilly, virginal bed, Holly felt surprisingly chill about the whole sex thing. She didn't intend to go too far with Tyler right then and there, but being close like this felt so good. As Tyler lowered his head to nibble on her ear, Holly began rubbing the back of his neck. *We should lock the door*, she thought dazedly, but then Tyler was kissing her again, and their breaths were coming quicker, and Holly was undoing the top buttons on his shirt . . .

And then the door to the bedroom opened.

"Oh, my God!"

Holly and Tyler started, separated, and turned to see who had exclaimed so loudly.

It was Alexa.

"Alexa — um, wow — I know this looks bad —"

Holly stammered, straightening the straps of her green Hollister cami while Tyler, his ears scarlet, sat up ramrod straight and began redoing the buttons on his shirt. Holly had a sudden flashback to an early morning in South Beach, when Alexa had walked in on Holly and Tyler cuddling in bed — and been none too pleased.

"You're *here!*" Alexa cried, closing the door behind her, then whirling back around to face them.

Holly felt a wave of shame color her face as she ducked her head and swung her legs off the bed. She and her boyfriend had been about to get it on in what was for all intents and purposes Alexa's bedroom. *That, my friends, is what we call "classy."* Preparing her apology, Holly glanced up at Alexa.

Who looked absolutely thrilled.

Her cheeks were as pink as if she'd gone for a run around the block, which Holly knew was highly unlikely. Her blue eyes were twinkling, her delicate-featured face was glowing, and she was clapping her hands together, her stacked wooden bangles sliding up and down her arm.

"Holly Rebecca Jacobson," Alexa began breathlessly, clearly not giving a damn about the makeout moment she'd interrupted. "Would you do me the honor of being my date at Margaux Eklundstrom's wedding at her Hollywood Hills home this Friday?"

"What?" Holly whispered. Her stomach jumped in disbelief. "Alexa, stop kidding. How —"

Alexa stepped closer to the bed and, her tone triumphant, recounted the magical meeting in the garden, Margaux's out-of-nowhere invite, and Alexa's ecstatic acceptance. And that, Alexa explained, gesturing to the white iBook on the desk, was why she'd busted into the bedroom — to look up flights to LA online. She wanted to leave the very next day, in order to attend the bash the Eklundstrom siblings were throwing, *and* to build in appropriate shopping time at Fred Segal Melrose, the Beverly Center, and Kitson. Alexa, Holly realized with a burst of excitement, was *not* kidding.

Glancing apologetically at Tyler, Alexa added that Margaux had specified that she could bring only one guest — meaning Holly.

"Okay, but who *is* Margaux Ekle-freak?" Tyler asked, tugging on his blazer and glancing at Holly with a frown. Tyler watched ESPN, not E!, so he was often clueless about pop culture. Plus, getting interrupted mid-hook-up had clearly put him in a grumpy mood.

"You know," Holly told him distractedly, still gaping at Alexa. "She was in that movie, *Grit and Gravel.*" Holly didn't add that she'd found the film, which Alexa had dragged her to last week, pretentious and boring as hell. "And she's . . ." Holly paused, and felt her heart leap. "*Jonah Eklundstrom's* sister." Though Holly dismissed most Hollywood celebs as fake, shallow, and scarily tanned, she, like every other straight female in America (including Holly's own mother), had a gargantuan crush on the heavenly-eyed Jonah. She was sure he was utterly pompous in real life, but he made for the most satisfying eye candy.

"Right," Alexa said, a dazzling grin spreading across her face. "And guess whose guesthouse my date and I can stay in this week?" Slowly, dramatically, she removed her Verizon chocolate phone from her purse and held it open toward Holly and Tyler. A text message on the screen listed Jonah's Malibu address.

Holly's head spun. "Jonah Eklundstrom?" she gasped, shakily getting to her feet. A sudden thought made her face flush with excitement. "Alexa! Oh, my God — hold on! The two of you are *so* going to get together. You're exactly his type — he dated Charity Durst, but you're *much* prettier —"

"Relax," Alexa said, letting out her tinkly silver laugh and shaking her head. "We are *not* going to get together — we'll probably barely get to see him. Besides," she added, with a toss of her pale blonde locks, "I doubt he could be as cool as his big sister. Margaux is, like, my new favorite person *ever*."

Holly nodded, some of her shock fading. Impossible, fantastical things were always happening to Alexa — whether it was a guy whisking her up to an orchid-strewn rooftop or a French tabloid snapping her photo — so her becoming BFFs with a crazily famous actress kind of seemed like the next logical step. "Still," Holly argued, grinning, "imagine getting to stay on his property, with all the gorgeous Malibu beaches right there. . . ." A couple of weeks ago, in between cramming for finals, Alexa and Holly had sacked out in Alexa's den and watched a *Laguna Beach/The Hills* marathon on MTV, eating sliced kiwi, braiding each other's hair, and completely losing themselves in the California surf-and-sun scene.

"I thought you hated the West Coast."

Holly spun around to regard Tyler, who had spoken quietly, his eyes on the white carpet. Holly bit her lip, feeling as if her boyfriend had brought her crash-landing back to Earth.

"Well, I've never actually *been* farther west than, like, Ohio," she murmured. But Holly also knew exactly what Tyler meant. Despite — or maybe because of — her interest in *Laguna Beach*, and the occasional episode of *Entourage*, Holly had always pictured LA as a sunlit wonderland of silicone, bleached teeth, and people screaming at their agents. In other words, the kind of place where down-to-earth, sporty Holly wouldn't fit in *at all*. True, the former captain of Holly's track team, Kenya Matthews, was a freshman at UCLA, and had been the one to encourage Holly to apply to the university. But even while e-mailing in her application, Holly had known she wouldn't want to live so far from home, and in a city so phony and weird.

Still, how many times in her solid, dependable New Jersey life would she be handed the silver platter chance of attending a wedding amid palm trees and paparazzi? The last wedding Holly had been to was her aunt Janet's tacky, all-pink shindig in Leonard's of Great Neck, a wedding hall on Long Island that resembled a pastry puff. Holly *wasn't* Alexa; the fairy dust of outrageous fortune rarely rained down on her (except, of course, when she was with Alexa). Her skin tingled as she thought of all the wild stories she'd have for the other counselors at sports camp, her roommates at Rutgers, and her starstruck mom, who would definitely overlook her no-traveling-without-a-guardian rule this one time.

But then Tyler looked up to meet her gaze, his expression sober, and Holly felt a wave of guilt mixed with clarity. *I can't go*, she realized, feeling neither disappointed nor upset — but simply resigned. *Only one guest*, Alexa had said. Whether they went camping or not, Holly and Tyler had counted on spending this week together. And Holly remembered all too well what had happened the last time she and Tyler had been apart for a stretch of time — when she'd gone to Europe and he'd stayed in Oakridge. She couldn't abandon him again. Not even for Jonah and Margaux Eklundstrom.

"So?" Alexa was saying, tapping one wooden heel on the carpet. "If you want to get yourself to those Malibu beaches, babe, let's go online and —"

Holly turned to Alexa and let out a deep breath. "You know what," she said steadily, feeling Tyler's eyes on her back. "There's no way I can leave Oakridge at such short notice, and my parents won't ever —"

"Oh, come on, your mom will *push* you onto the plane so that you can bring her back Jonah's autograph," Alexa cut in with a giggle, echoing Holly's earlier thoughts.

"But Tyler's right. I wouldn't feel comfortable in Hollywood," Holly argued, knowing it was true. "And," she added hurriedly before Alexa could protest, "this week won't work for me anyway. I'm sorry, Alexa. I just — I can't be your date." Holly felt a little flare of pride at how firm she'd managed to sound. She met Alexa's wide-eyed stare, silently challenging her friend — whom Holly had aptly nicknamed "Little Miss Bossy" when they were younger — to argue with her.

Alexa, her pouty princess mouth turned down at the corners, reached up to toy with the high neck of her sleeveless lacy white top. "Hol, did you forget?" she asked, her voice soft and plaintive. "Rodeo Drive?"

Rodeo Drive. Holly's stomach dropped.

What she'd forgotten was that Alexa St. Laurent was a master of persuasion. And, once again, she'd hit her bull's-eye.

As a precursor to their days of lazy *Laguna Beach*–watching, Alexa and Holly, when they were eleven, had loved nothing better than to sequester themselves in Alexa's bedroom and bask in the glow of a forbidden DVD. Because Alexa's father (whose philosophy was that *les enfants* shouldn't be too sheltered) never asked what they were watching, the girls imbibed *American Pie*, *Dirty Dancing*, and, one fateful Saturday night, *Pretty Woman*.

Though the she's-a-hooker setup went over their heads (or at least Holly's head), both girls were equally enraptured by Julia's sublime shopping spree in Beverly Hills. Later that night, sleeping bags spread out side by side on Alexa's pink shag rug, the girls had hooked pinkies and whispered a vow that one day they'd go to LA and make a pilgrimage to Rodeo Drive. Together. Holly knew that their *Pretty Woman* pact walked that fine line between sweet and dorky, but it was just one of those *things*. Only close-as-sisters friends could understand the power that silly, embarrassing oaths had in forging the deepest of bonds.

But Holly also had a bond with Tyler. She sat back down onto the bed beside him, and reached for his hand. "I'm sorry," she told Alexa simply. "You'll have to pay tribute to Julia without me." She tried to smile, but the lump in her throat and the deflated look on Alexa's face made it difficult.

"This is so wrong," Tyler murmured.

Alexa gave a noisy sigh and pretended to search for something in her clutch, which Holly knew was her friend's classic, I-couldn't-care-less gesture. "You know, Tyler, I *did* apologize about only being able to bring Holly —" Alexa began.

"No." Tyler shook his head. He thoughtfully turned Holly's hand over in his palm, then glanced at her face. "What's wrong is that you *want* to go, Hol, but you feel like you shouldn't, because of me." He paused while Holly held her breath. "And that's really stupid."

"It is?" Holly asked in a small voice. A bubble of hope rose in her chest. Alexa stopped rooting around in her clutch.

"Uh-huh," Tyler replied, giving her a reassuring smile. "You need to do this, Hol. Come on, Hollywood's named after you — maybe it's fate." He laughed at his own joke, a move that was so patently Tyler that Holly felt herself choke up. What had she done to deserve such a good, kind, caring boyfriend, one who knew her better than she knew herself?

"Sweetie," she ventured, stroking the side of his face. "What about camping?" As Holly spoke, she felt cautious joy building in her; maybe, just maybe, this was her passport out of the dreaded family jaunt. She didn't dare make eye contact with Alexa, who Holly knew was probably wearing a megawatt smile.

"I'll break it to your parents, if that will help," Tyler said, confirming Holly's happy suspicions. "There'll be other camping trips."

She squeezed his hand, speechless. "You're — you're awesome," she whispered, using his favorite word. She couldn't think how else to express her gratitude.

Tyler kissed her cheek, then stood and straightened the lapels of his blazer. "I don't know about you guys, but I'm starved," he announced with what Holly thought sounded a little like forced cheerfulness. "When you ladies are ready to head back to Oakridge, I'll be in the kitchen, making friends with the cheese tray." He chuckled, and left.

There was a beat of stillness after Tyler shut the door behind him.

Then Alexa and Holly looked at each other, and screamed.

"I can't believe it!" Holly burst out, leaping to her feet as Alexa practically jumped on her. "We're going to *live* Rodeo Drive!"

"I *knew* you wanted to come!" Alexa squealed, her words overlapping Holly's. "And I'm *so* glad Tyler is cool with it." The girls flung their arms around each other and bounced up and down, doing a slightly more mature rendition of the "oh-my-God-no-way!" dance they'd choreographed in the third grade.

"Do you think he *really* is, though?" Holly asked, pulling back and feeling a twinge of regret. "Before you came in, I mean, before we started – um – anyway," Holly tried to shake off her blush as Alexa watched her, clearly amused. "Tyler and I were talking about future plans, and I kind of told him I didn't want to make any, and now I'm leaving before we can . . ."

Alexa held up one hand. "Stop right there, Hol. I have three words for you: Movie. Star. Wedding." She raised one eyebrow. "You should be focusing on *that* future now. Tyler can wait. And he will. Trust me. Boys are like punching bags — they bounce back."

Holly couldn't help giggling. "Did you just invent that brilliant little simile on the spot?"

"Hey, and you wonder how I got into Columbia," Alexa teased, linking her arm through Holly's. "Now tell me," she began as they started toward the computer on her desk. "Do you have a dress that's appropriate for a party to end all parties in the Hollywood Hills?"

At Alexa's words, Holly felt a bolt of anticipation. No matter what happened this week — no matter how much she missed Tyler, or how many phony LA types got on her nerves — things would be, to say the least, eventful. "Um, I don't think so," she replied as Alexa sat down at the desk and turned on the computer. Holly pictured the fancier end of her closet back home: the black-and-white dress she'd bought in South Beach that *still* needed dry-cleaning; the frumpy gray jumper her mother made her wear to synagogue on the High Holy Days; the shiny mauve number she'd mortified herself in at her aunt's wedding. . . . "Though there *is* my prom dress," she added with a shrug, remembering the halter sheath that was the color of pale grapes.

"You can't *repeat* an outfit at Margaux Eklundstrom's wedding," Alexa protested, clicking over to the Expedia site. "That violates every law of fashion. And possibly nature."

"Well . . ." Holly rested her elbows on the high back of the chair, checking out the computer screen. "Can't you just lend me one of *your* zillion dresses?" Alexa was practically a walking wardrobe.

"Ha," Alexa snorted, typing Tuesday's date onto the website. "My best stuff got stolen in Paris, and remember when I went through that ridiculous phase of buying *vintage?*" She shuddered. "Rodeo Drive is definitely in order." She scrolled down the page, then clicked on a flight option. "Aha — *here* we go. Two seats on True West Airlines, leaving from Newark at ten A.M., with a stopover in Vegas, and arriving at LAX at two P.M. —"

"Hang on," Holly said warily, leaning even closer to study the screen. "Las Vegas?"

"Just for an hour," Alexa said, nudging Holly away. "We'll check out the slot machines in the airport, sip skinny iced lattes from The Coffee Bean and Tea Leaf . . ."

"All right," Holly said, laughing. As usual, Alexa's bubbly optimism — her ability to make even airport layovers sound glam — was catching, and Holly's heart thrummed. She focused back on Expedia, and soon the girls were off and running, selecting a return flight for Saturday morning (thus giving them a day to regroup before graduation) along with seats and payment options — all the minutiae that went into planning their last delicious adventure before settling into college, and the rest of their lives.

And *that* kind of planning, Holly could totally do.

CHAPTER THREE
Go West, Young Man

The Oakridge morning sky was a dark, thunderous gray, and fat drops of rain landed on Alexa's windshield with audible plops. Her shower-damp hair piled up atop her head, her almond-colored Prada platform wedges on her feet, and her approximately fifty-seven bags crammed into the backseat, Alexa flicked on her wipers and grinned. Each plop was like a small symphony. Alexa lived for rainy-day departures.

In recent months, Alexa had grown surprisingly fond of Oakridge. She loved that, as she was turning on to Holly's street, she knew exactly where the road would dip and curve, and that the wide plane tree to her left was where she and Holly had carved their initials the summer they were nine. But today she didn't feel the slightest bit bittersweet about leaving her hometown. Blinding desert sunshine, celebs sipping cocktails, pedicures by the pool with Margaux and Holly . . . all that, and more, waited out there, out west, and she'd be there soon enough.

Or as soon as she was able to steal Holly away from the chaos unfolding outside her house.

The Jacobsons' yellow Lab, Mia Hamm (only Holly would name her dog after a soccer player, Alexa reflected with an eye roll), was barking madly at Mrs. Jacobson, who was holding an umbrella over her head while attempting to cram a lawn chair into the backseat of the family Subaru. Holly's fourteen-year-old brother, Josh (Alexa estimated that he would turn out to be hot in approximately four to six years), was dribbling a basketball and listening to his iPod, ignoring whatever his mom was yelling at him. The trunk of the Subaru was open and a harried Mr. Jacobson — with the help of Holly and the family appendage, Tyler Davis — was trying to stuff two gigantic backpacks inside.

Alexa put her pink Jetta into park, briefly closed her eyes, and thanked the spirit of Coco Chanel that she didn't have the kind of family that took trips together. Then she rolled down her window and tapped her horn, peering out to wave at Holly. They were going to be late, but Alexa was woman enough to admit that it was her fault.

She'd awoken that morning, the gloom seeping in through her bamboo shades, and with a jolt of joy, remembered her destination. *Hollywood. Malibu. Wedding.* Alexa had bounded out of bed, flung away the outfit she'd laid out the night before — a striped Luella Bartley shirt, denim mini, navy-blue leggings, and flats — and replaced it with what she wore now: a clingy yellow Lela Rose sundress with nut-brown spaghetti straps. Sure, it wasn't too travel-comfy, but paired with the floppy straw hat and oversized Oliver Peoples sunglasses she'd packed in her carry-on, she knew she'd make quite a statement stepping off the plane.

Through the fog and drizzle, Alexa could see that Holly was in her standard Gap jeans, terry-cloth flip-flops, and shrunken olive-colored cotton hoodie over a white tank. Alexa honked her horn again, mostly out of annoyance; after all this time, had she taught her friend *nothing* about fashion?

"Coming!" Holly called, looking up from the trunk of the Subaru to see Alexa in the car, wearing her Impatient Face. Holly felt a giggle rise up in her throat, and she blew her sweaty bangs off her forehead. "The Diva has arrived," she whispered, turning to Tyler, who put his hands on her waist and laughed, warm and deep, in her ear.

The minute Tyler had shown up that morning in

his baggy cargo shorts and wrinkled Oakridge Lacrosse T-shirt to help her parents load up the car, Holly, who'd run out to greet him with a piece of toast still in hand, had known everything was going to be okay. On the drive home late last night, she and Alexa had whispered over lingering LA plans — did they need to bring Jonah a thanks-for-letting-us-crash-here gift, and if so, what did one get a guy who had an Oscar on his shelf and a mansion over the ocean? — while Tyler had silently gripped the wheel, the muscle in his jaw twitching. After they'd dropped Alexa off, there'd been no talk of Holly coming over to fill out student housing forms, and she'd assumed that the soft, quick kiss they'd exchanged outside her house had been their good-bye.

But now here he was smiling down at her, raindrops glistening on his dark-blond head while her father wrestled with the backpacks and muttered curses. Around Tyler, Holly never felt embarrassed by her often crazy, overly involved family. Tyler simply seemed to understand, and, though he was more laid-back than any of the Jacobsons, he fit in seamlessly.

"Think she can wait a few more seconds?" Tyler asked, nodding toward Alexa. He reached out and took hold of Holly's hand. "There's something I need to do before you go."

Holly's heart rate picked up; Tyler wasn't big on

surprises. But she didn't hesitate an instant before following him around the car, through the light rain, and up the steps to her house, where they turned toward each other under the porch awning.

"*Great,*" Alexa murmured, turning up the volume on her Teddy Geiger CD. For all she knew, Tyler was getting ready to drop to one knee — and she and Holly could *not* have any other weddings thrown into this week.

Since she now had time to kill, Alexa plucked her cell phone from her citrus-colored Bliss Lau handbag and text-messaged her former best friend, Portia, *just* to let her know where she was going, with whom she was staying, and who was accompanying her on her *grand voyage*. With her dark curly ringlets and permanent sneer, Portia was — as Holly had once insightfully put it — that worst of combinations: stuck-up and insecure at the same time. Portia wasn't a fan of Holly's, either; her favorite hobby, next to chain-smoking, was critiquing Holly's outfits with her henchwoman, Maeve. Alexa felt a small swell of triumph that she'd been able to brush off Portia's trash-talking and choose *Holly* over her.

Alexa hit send and fell back against her seat with a contented sigh. Last night, it had felt equally rewarding dropping the Hollywood bombshell on her mother; Gail had gone all slack-jawed at the realization that

Alexa, too, could make famous friends. Of course, if there'd been any chance in hell of Gail attending her graduation, Alexa knew she'd probably blown it. But, oh well. Her dad had been nothing but supportive that morning while waving good-bye to her over his café au lait. Smiling, Alexa glanced out the window again, only to see Tyler nervously handing Holly a small white box. *Uh-oh.*

"What's this?" Holly asked Tyler as she accepted the box from him, her hands quivering slightly. Back in May, for Holly's birthday, Tyler had gotten them tickets to a Yankees game ("Whatever happened to romance?" Alexa had sighed when Holly had told her). This gift felt different, weightier, even though the box itself was feather-light.

"I wanted to give it to you at graduation," Tyler replied as Holly, her stomach flipping, took the lid off the box. "But now is even better. You can wear it this week and think of me."

Nestled in the white cotton was a delicate golden ring with an intricate design at its center: a pair of tiny hands holding a single heart, topped by a miniature crown. Holly caught her breath, overcome; nobody had ever given her real jewelry before. Tears pricking her eyes, she glanced up to see a blurry Tyler watching her with an expectant smile. "It's a Claddagh ring," he said, tracing a finger over the design. "My Irish grandma once explained the different symbols to me. The hands mean friendship, the heart represents love, and the crown stands for loyalty. If you're in love, you're supposed to wear it with the heart facing toward you, and if you're single, it should face out." His cheeks reddened. "I know it's kind of cheesy —"

"Not at all," Holly breathed, removing the chunky silver ring she always wore and sticking it in her back pocket. Then she carefully slid on the Claddagh ring, making sure the heart pointed inward. "See? My heart's closed off — because it belongs to just one person." She lifted her face to Tyler, who was already lowering his head to kiss her. Holly felt suffused with peace and warmth; she hadn't slept most of the night due to a mixture of belly-fluttering excitement and worry. But Alexa had been right; boys *were* resilient. Now Holly knew she could head west with a clear conscience.

Which was convenient, because Alexa was sticking her head out the window of her car and shouting something unintelligible — but not too friendly-sounding — through the rain.

"I should go," Holly said, bending down to grab her duffel bag; unlike Alexa, she was a steadfastly light traveler. She bounded down the steps of her house and over to her parents, who began flinging warnings at Holly as they wrapped her in tight hugs. "Wear sunscreen, *please* don't get yourself on TV again, don't let Alexa talk you into anything. . . ." Trying to tune them out, Holly petted Mia, waved to Josh, kissed Tyler once more, and jumped into Alexa's car, squeezing the rain out of her ponytail.

The two girls glanced at each other, and at the exact same time, demanded:

"What are you *wearing*?"

"You *do* know we're going to be chilling with Margaux in, like, seven hours," Alexa added, giving Holly a haughty once-over while putting the car in drive.

Holly laughed and shook her head, paying no mind to Alexa's jibe. "And *you* know we're getting on a plane, not a royal cruise, right?" she retorted. Holly enjoyed poking fun at Alexa's princess-y tendencies, and Alexa could usually mock herself in turn. This time, though, Alexa cast a scowl in Holly's direction and slammed one suede platform down on the gas.

"Let's hope so," she replied, tearing away from Holly's house. "If we miss our plane, I'm forcing you to give me a piggyback ride all the way to LA so we can make the party in time." She was only half joking; Alexa couldn't quite articulate why, but she had the strong feeling — as sure as the pulsing of her own heart — that she *had* to be at The Standard bash.

"It's a deal," Holly muttered, raising her eyes sky-ward as the car zipped down the rain-streaked streets of Oakridge. She missed Tyler already, and was in no mood for what she secretly thought of as Alexa's PTS — Pre-Trip Syndrome. Before taking off on a journey, Alexa's high-maintenance side emerged full force.

"So is *that* what Tyler gave you just now?"Alexa asked, her eyes on the road as she gestured down to Holly's ring. "Couldn't he have sprung for something from Tiffany?" Alexa knew she was being mildly inap-propriate, but after all, she'd always been the love expert, and Holly the novice. Holly *needed* Alexa's wisdom on dating.

"You wouldn't understand," Holly shot back, shielding her hand. Sometimes she couldn't believe the giant gap that existed between her and Alexa. Despite their recent closeness, they were still so dif-ferent in so many ways. For one stomach-sinking second, Holly wondered if they would spend this week backbiting and sniping, as they had at the start of their South Beach vacation. Then the sudden *brring* of Alexa's cell phone brought her back to the present.

"I have a text," Alexa said, futilely pawing through her handbag. She felt herself tense up; what if it was Margaux, texting to say that the girls shouldn't come after all? "Can you check it?" she demanded, thrusting her bag in Holly's direction.

Still sour, Holly grudgingly pushed aside Alexa's tube of Paula Dorf Taffeta lip gloss, iPod nano in its lavender plush case, and sample container of Dolce & Gabbana Light Blue in order to find her cell. She flipped open the phone to see the incoming message:

Have fun, lucky bitches.

Holly, chuckling, read the text aloud.

"It's from Portia!" Alexa cried, cracking up as well. She felt her spirits lift instantly. "She's so jealous of us right now she's probably . . ."

"Chewing a hole through her best Tsubi jeans?" Holly offered with a snort, and the two girls broke into laughter. Alexa, her spirits lifting, realized she may have taught Holly something about fashion after all.

The girls' moods greatly improved by the time they reached the airport, and soared once they boarded their cross-country flight. They spent the plane ride sitting cross-legged in their seats, sharing the peanut-butter-and-quince-jelly sandwiches Holly's mother had packed them, and analyzing Jonah Eklundstrom.

"I hope with every inch of my being that he's shaved his beard," Alexa pronounced as they sailed over the Rocky Mountains. The latest photo that she'd seen of Jonah, online, had shown him sporting a mountain man look — still yummy on him, but Alexa *so* did not buy into the whole beards-are-trendy fad.

"You want him all smooth when you guys inevitably make out?" Holly teased, tucking her knees up under her chin. She was amazed at how relaxed she felt on the plane, as opposed to the freak-out she'd had on her first flight with Alexa, to Miami. Maybe because she'd developed a taste for travel, Holly's once-paralyzing fear of flying had diminished over the past year. Alexa, who adored being airborne, took full credit for the breakthrough.

"Would you stop?" Alexa giggled, lobbing her stiff pillow at Holly, who ducked and shrieked, provoking a glare from the family across the aisle, "I told you — just because we're staying with him does *not* mean I'm going to hook up with Jonah Eklundstrom!"

A hush seemed to fall over the plane, and Alexa realized how loud she and Holly were being. Across the aisle, two sisters — who looked to be about fifteen and twelve, and were decked out in matching striped tank tops and jelly bracelets — leaned over, eyes enormous. "Excuse me, *what* did you say?" the older one whispered in a southern accent, her braces-covered teeth snapping a piece of gum. On the younger one's lap, Alexa noticed, sat an open *Seventeen* magazine, and Jonah Eklundstrom's bearded face beamed up from the pages.

"You'll have to ignore her. She's delusional," Holly told the girls, while Alexa hid her face in her hands, her bare shoulders shaking with laughter.

"Nellie, what's 'delusional'?" Holly heard the younger one ask her older sister. Grinning, Holly turned back to Alexa, who was pulling a pair of sunglasses and an adorable floppy hat out of her tote bag. Quickly, Alexa undid her hair from its bun, let it tumble down her back in pale gold waves, and slipped on the shades and hat. "It's time to go incognito," Alexa whispered through her laughter, looking uncannily like a movie star avoiding the press.

Once the girls landed in the Las Vegas airport and bid farewell to the curious sisters, they were able to pick up right where they'd left off. "The point is, I'm *not* delusional," Alexa was saying, still in her hat and shades, as she and Holly strode past rows of blinking, beeping slot machines. Determined elderly ladies with pink-dyed hair sat before each one, tugging on the levers while their husbands waited nearby, most likely wishing they could drive off to the Bellagio and play poker. Holly half expected to see her plucky Grandma Ida with her new husband, Miles, among them, but she knew they were home in Miami.

"Ever since my, uh, incident in Paris," Alexa continued as the girls arrived at their connecting flight's gate, and were stopped short by a serpentine line, "my new motto when it comes to guys is 'be realistic.'" She nodded; the words sounded good to her. She wondered if she could get them emblazoned on her cell phone in Swarovski crystals.

Holly patted Alexa's arm supportively; she fervently wished that her friend would one day experience the love and devotion she deserved. The only problem was, Alexa was reckless and choosy at the same time — a dangerous combo when it came to finding the right guy.

Holding her sun hat in place and rising up on her toes, Alexa surveyed the never-ending line before them: a series of balding heads, and worried voices buzzing into cell phones. Lines — in addition to a pairing of plaids and stripes, elevator music, and chipped nail polish — were the stuff of Alexa's worst nightmares. They got in the way of her natural progression toward fabulousness. "What's going on?" she demanded imperiously, while Holly shrugged.

The stressed-out mom in front of them turned around, a wailing infant in her arms. "Apparently there's some kind of strike," she replied. "I don't know —" She was interrupted by the crackle of the loudspeaker overhead, and then a twangy voice announced: "*Attention, all passengers. Flight four twenty-*

eight, which just arrived from Newark, will be True West's last flight today. I repeat — due to an airline strike, all of True West's flights are grounded indefinitely."

Alexa and Holly exchanged a look of horror.

"Don't panic," Holly instructed. But from the set of Alexa's jaw and the rosy flush of her peaches-and-cream skin, she was beginning to do just that. Holly tried to keep calm for the both of them, but visions of spending the week in tacky Las Vegas — sneaking into casinos, driving past Cirque du Soleil billboards, getting hit on by slimy card sharks wearing gold chains — were already flashing through her head. "I'm sure every other airline here has flights to LA —"

"Passengers flying to Los Angeles International Airport, Burbank, or Long Beach, please be advised that all other airlines' flights to those destinations are booked until tomorrow. We apologize for the inconvenience."

"The *inconvenience?*" Alexa burst out in fury as the crowd collectively groaned. She glanced around, searching in vain for some official-looking person to yell at. Dread washed over her; they'd never make tonight's party now.

"Listen," Holly replied, holding up her hands and hoping she sounded more in control than she was feeling. Getting stranded *anywhere* terrified her. She thought about calling her parents, but she knew their panicking would only make the situation worse. "We won't get to LA today," Holly went on pragmatically. "So let's see if we can get a cheap motel room for the night, and I'm sure . . ."

"No." Alexa was *not* about to let fate decide her travel plans. She had a glitzy event to attend in downtown LA, a wedding to shop for, and a Malibu guesthouse to enjoy — and she'd be damned if some teensy detail like an airline strike stood in the way. "I have a better idea."

Holly bit her lip, looking apprehensive. "Alexa, whatever I said before, I am *not* going to give you a piggyback ride to —"

"Not that, you idiot," Alexa said affectionately. Scooping up her Paul & Joe owl shoulder bag, Alexa motioned to the Hertz car rental desk, where another line was already beginning to form. "There's a *much* more luxurious form of transport. LA's got to be — what? — an hour's drive from here? Totally doable."

"Try five hours," the Hertz guy told them a few minutes later, his tone flat and his gray hair illuminated by the fluorescent bulbs overhead. The laminated pin he wore on his shirt read GEORGE. "And can I see some ID? We don't rent cars to anyone younger than twenty-three, or twenty-one if you're willing to pay extra."

This time, the look Alexa and Holly exchanged

plainly translated as *we're screwed*. Though both girls had fake IDs, they didn't need to confer to know that using one at an airport would be glaringly stupid. The people in line behind them started to complain about the holdup — a soft grumbling that could quickly turn into a roar. Holly's hand instinctively flew to the Claddagh ring on her finger; she twisted it around and around, wondering if she should call Tyler. He'd probably urge her to come home, which she sort of wanted to do anyway.

"You must understand, George," Alexa was insisting, leaning over the counter and wishing that she, like Holly, had actual cleavage; maybe Mr. Hertz would give her a break then. "It's life-or-death *crucial* that we get to LA within the next few hours, and I'm happy to put you in touch with Margaux Eklundstrom if need be." The name clearly meant nothing to George, so Alexa, throat tightening with desperation, rebounded with: "Do you *know* who my mother is?"

"Sorry to interrupt." A male voice came from a few feet away. "But I need to get to LA, too." Alexa glanced away from George, to her right, to see a strikingly good-looking guy with floppy blond hair and black-framed glasses. He was sitting cross-legged on a nearby bench, balancing a notebook on his corduroy-clad lap; he'd been writing something, but he closed the notebook. "And," he added, unfolding his long legs and standing up, giving Alexa a full view of the rumpled Hot Hot Heat T-shirt under his tattered tweed blazer and the worn brown belt slung around his cords. "I turned twenty-one last week."

"Happy birthday," Alexa murmured, stepping out of line and whipping off her sunglasses. Skinny hipster boys weren't usually her thing, but there was something pulse-quickening about this guy's strong cheekbones and his tall, graceful frame. Behind her, she could feel Holly tense up, her classic reaction whenever there was a hot guy in the vicinity.

But Hipster Boy's response to Alexa's flirtation was a wry smirk as he cast his gaze over Alexa's outfit. Alexa could read his thought process plain as day: *Somebody please get this Top 40-listening, makeup-wearing, magazine-reading dumb blonde as far away from me as humanly possible.* She balled her hands into fists, pissed. Boys, all boys, were so *obvious*. And she couldn't stand being written off like that.

"So tell me," the boy said, his voice heavy with sarcasm. "Who *is* this world-renowned mother of whom you speak?" He pushed his glasses up on his nose, still smirking.

Alexa bristled, wondering how she'd ever found this guy attractive. "A buyer at Henri Bendel's in Manhattan," she spat, then shoved her shades back on, not wanting to maintain eye contact.

He nodded thoughtfully. "Should've guessed that from a mile away."

Alexa drew herself up to her full height, preparing a comeback, when Holly stepped forward and placed a hand on Alexa's elbow. "Uh, look," she said, addressing Hipster Boy. "About getting to LA. Do you have legit ID?"

Glancing at Holly, the boy's square-jawed face broke into a slow smile. Holly felt the strongest sense of recognition, of understanding, pass between the two of them, even though she'd never seen him before in her life. She tried to fight back what felt like the beginnings of a blush; why, *why*, did cute guys always do that to her?

"Indeed," the boy replied, removing his wallet and holding up a New York State driver's license. Holly felt a flush of relief. His name, according to the card, was Seamus Kerr, his address was somewhere in Brooklyn, and he was, in fact, newly twenty-one. She hadn't thought he was a liar — there was a sincerity in his bright hazel gaze that disarmed her a little — but it was nice to see proof. "So shall we?" Seamus asked Holly. "I don't mind driving."

"Splitting the cost three ways *would* be better," she reasoned, turning to Alexa, who looked seriously miffed. Holly wasn't sure why she was now the one pushing them toward LA — seconds before, she'd been ready to return to New Jersey — but something about Seamus's warm, easygoing presence made her feel like heading farther west was the best thing to do. If only Alexa would stop stubbornly shaking her head.

"To drive or not to drive — that is the question," Seamus intoned, putting a hand to his chest and grinning at Holly again. A businessman waiting in the Hertz line regarded Seamus as if he'd lost his mind. "Whether 'tis nobler in the mind to crash in Vegas for a night, or rent a Mustang —"

"Easy there, Hamlet," Alexa snapped; she had only so much tolerance for English-major types. "Holly, can I speak to you alone for a second?" She led Holly a few paces away from Seamus, where they positioned themselves behind a beefy guy in a cowboy hat. "Don't be such the naïve suburban girl," Alexa hissed the minute they were safe. "This guy's a complete stranger. How do we know he's not, like, a serial killer?" Alexa checked over her shoulder. Seamus was now standing at the back of the Hertz line, thumbing through a paperback copy of *Crime and Punishment*, his book bag at his feet. Alexa noticed what looked like a green plush toy peeking out of the top of the half-open bag. *Freaking weird.*

Holly groaned, putting her hands on her hips. "Alexa, give me some credit — don't you think my parents have made me sufficiently paranoid by now?"

She refrained from reminding her indignant friend that, on all her exotic travels across the globe, Alexa had full-on *made out* with her share of "complete strangers." But Alexa was an expert at conveniently forgetting things. Holly glanced at Seamus to see him watching them, and then quickly return to his book. She smiled to herself. "I think he's a good guy," she finished with a shrug.

Alexa rolled her eyes. If Holly was developing a crush on this Seamus person, Alexa did not want to be the one to clean up the mess. But the truth was, they really had no choice; she *did* want get to Malibu by tonight, and Seamus was their lone ticket there.

"Fine, but I need to collect my luggage from the baggage claim," Alexa sighed, turning away. "You figure out the car stuff with your new best friend, and I'll meet you guys outside."

"Holly mother of . . ." Seamus muttered twenty minutes later, his eyes wide behind his glasses. He and Holly were sitting outside the airport in the convertible Mustang they'd rented with Seamus's ID, watching in disbelief as Alexa wiggled toward them in her platforms. She was trailing a blush-pink wheelie suitcase that was about the size and shape of Alaska, and in her other hand she lugged several totes, her handbag, and the satchel containing her PowerBook.

The black camera bag in which she carried her big, professional Nikon swung from her free shoulder. That she was able to move at all seemed to Holly like a miracle.

"She's like the bag lady of Rodeo Drive," Holly murmured, observing Alexa with a mixture of amusement and sympathy. Her friend stumbled, sending one of her totes to the ground, and as she bent to retrieve it, the hot desert wind almost snatched her hat off her head.

Seamus laughed warmly, drumming his fingers on the steering wheel. "That's perfect," he told Holly. "It sounds like a short-story title."

This time, Holly couldn't help but blush — she hated how her face always gave away the slightest stutter of her heart — and then fiddled with her Claddagh ring. "I'm not much of a writer," she admitted. "Are you?" she asked, thinking of the notebook Seamus had been scribbling in.

"In a way," Seamus replied as Alexa finally made her way into the car, flinging herself into the backseat with a dramatic moan. "I just graduated from NYU, so I'm starting as an editorial assistant at *The New York Observer*."

"Alexa, did you hear?" Holly asked, turning around to her friend. "Seamus lives in New York —"

"I did, but I don't care," Alexa spat, sweaty and

achy as she plunked her camera bag on the seat beside her. Squeezing all her other bags into the trunk had been utterly traumatic. She removed her sunglasses and hat and ran a hand through her tousled hair.

"I'm not sure you packed enough, Alexa," Seamus commented with a smile in his voice, turning the key in the ignition. Alexa thought she saw him exchange a glance with Holly. *Ugh.* Why didn't the two of them just go off to a hippie commune where nobody cared about clothes and everyone carried their earthly possessions in, like, hemp pillowcases?

"Wow, that's hilarious," Alexa yawned, leaning her head back and shutting her eyes; the emotional turmoil of the day had drained her. Seamus slipped a CD into the player, and a jangly guitar and a bluesy voice poured of the speaker. *Whiny emo bullshit*, Alexa thought derisively. *Figures.* As they pulled away from the airport, she felt a flash of jealousy that *Seamus* got to drive; she loved to steer, to control the music, to navigate through either rain or sun. And it felt wrong being relegated to the backseat. But she also wasn't about to fight Holly for shotgun. Alexa got the distinct feeling that the dynamic duo up front had been mocking her, and was in no mood to speak to either of them.

"So you guys are friends from before?" Seamus was asking as he picked up speed. The convertible's top was down and a dry wind whipped through the car, carrying with it the scent of cactus flowers. Holly drew a deep breath, staring out the windshield at the flat landscape; everything seemed so immense here. Out of the corner of her eye, Holly saw Seamus looking from her to Alexa and then back again. "I thought maybe you'd met in the airport," he added, still sounding incredulous that the two girls could actually be acquainted.

Alexa cracked one eye open to monitor Holly's response.

Holly laughed, unzipping her hoodie and settling back into her seat. "We've only known each other for, hmm, most of our lives." Seamus laughed, too — the exact same way that Holly did, Alexa noticed — a low rumbling that exploded into genuine merriment and ended in a happy sigh. Alexa found Holly's laugh endearing, but she was inches away from forcing jolly Seamus into hitchhiking his way to LA. "We grew up together in New Jersey," Holly added, glancing at Alexa and shooting her a wink. As if they were actually still *allies*, Alexa fumed, glaring back.

"Jersey girls?" Seamus echoed, meeting Alexa's gaze in the rearview. "*There's* a real shocker." It took every ounce of self-control for Alexa not to kick the back of the driver's seat.

Holly knew Seamus was poking fun at Alexa, and

not her, but she held back her laugh anyway; she could tell Alexa was peeved, and she didn't want to provoke her friend further. It was obvious that Ms. Thing wasn't dealing well with Seamus's intellectual-boy vibe. "Yup, we're a long way from home," she replied instead, and as she spoke, she realized how true the words were. A melancholy tumbleweed crossed the road, and she thought of Tyler, wondering how he'd react when she told him about her impromptu road trip. "I wasn't even sure I wanted to go to LA," Holly went on meditatively, still thinking of her boyfriend. "But —"

"We were invited to the biggest celebrity wedding of the year," Alexa put in tartly, opening both eyes and leaning forward. "And we're staying in Malibu, at Jonah Eklundstrom's guesthouse." *Ha.* Maybe *that* would shut Seamus up once and for all.

"Alexa, he doesn't need to know . . ." Holly trailed off, embarrassed. The idea that she, ordinary track girl Holly Jacobson, was about to spend a week rubbing tanned elbows with people who made more money in a day than she'd have in, like, a lifetime, still awed and humbled her. Her levelheaded parents had barely believed her last night when she'd awoken them to breathlessly spill the beans, and her skeptical brother, Josh, had demanded that Holly return with autographs and photos as hard evidence. Holly hadn't even bothered telling her friends Meghan and Jess. They were stuck in Oakridge for the week, and Holly didn't want to make them feel bad by bragging. Better for them to assume that she was hiking up muddy trails instead of sunning herself by the Pacific.

"Celebrity wedding?" Seamus glanced in the rearview again, lifting one eyebrow. "Sounds intense." He didn't pursue the subject; again, his tone seemed bemused and again Alexa prickled.

"It wouldn't interest you in the least," she replied coolly. They were cruising down the Vegas Strip — past the lush, extravagant MGM Grand hotel, the faux Eiffel Tower, and countless casinos — which looked pale and bland in the daylight. Suddenly Alexa was psyched that they were driving to LA; it made her feel like a cowgirl, an explorer, journeying toward the next destination. She took out her Nikon D100, and managed to get a shot of the strip right as Seamus accelerated. She was grateful that he hadn't made some snarky remark about her snapping a picture. Alexa took her photography very personally, and things would have turned even uglier between her and Seamus had he gone there.

As Seamus turned the convertible sharply onto Interstate 15, a gust of wind blew everyone's hair back and ruffled the giant paper map Holly was holding in her lap; the Hertz people had given it to her when

Seamus had signed off on the Mustang. "Are you sure we take this to LA?" Holly asked Seamus worriedly, studying the squiggly red and blue lines. Holly had only recently gotten her driver's license and was still figuring out how to successfully read a road map. She hated the sensation of being lost, especially when she was unfamiliar with the terrain. Oakridge, she could manage; this wild western land of cacti and wide sky was something new.

"Hol, I'm the direction guru, remember?" Alexa spoke up, reaching over the seat for the map. "I'll figure out which route we need to follow." After a minute of reviewing the map, Alexa glanced up and announced that Seamus was going in a fatally wrong direction and that they would arrive in Mexico by nightfall. Holly's stomach dropped.

"I know I don't look it," Seamus said, ignoring Alexa's prognosis and changing lanes. "But I'm a California boy — born and bred." As he spoke, Holly took note of the slightly raspy tenor of his voice; the birthmark under his ear, half-hidden by a lock of blond hair; his scent of incense and soap. She wasn't *attracted* to him exactly but she hadn't sat this close to another guy, besides Tyler, in a while. "I spent a lot of high school driving all night from LA to Vegas," Seamus added with a grin. "So not to boast or anything, but I *think* I can find my way."

Ew! Alexa was too disgusted by this display of arrogance to even respond. So she handed the map back to a relieved-looking Holly, stretched her legs across the seat, rested her head on her folded hands, and announced that she was going to take a long overdue beauty nap. Drifting off proved impossible, though, because Seamus's music — "Band of Horses, they're gonna be huge," she heard him pompously tell Holly — was blaring, and he and Holly kept breaking into spontaneous laughter.

When they pulled up at a roadside McDonald's for a bathroom break, Alexa continued fake-sleeping; despite growing up in suburbia, she'd only been inside a Mickey D's once, a horrifying experience she didn't care to repeat. It was only after Holly and Seamus returned sipping Cokes, and Seamus drove on, the road humming beneath the wheels, that Alexa was finally able to sink into a dream about playing a slot machine while wearing a spangly black dress, a nameless, faceless boy holding her around the waist and laughing into her hair.

The dream filled her with warmth, and then she felt true, full-bodied warmth on her face, and all along her skin. The warmth of streaming sunshine.

Alexa let her eyes flutter open. She was staring up at a sky of such pure cobalt blue that it looked painted. But no, she realized, it was real. As real as the rows of tall palm trees with fat, shaggy trunks that she was riding by. Blinking, Alexa sat up, brushed her windswept hair out of her eyes, and felt a glow of pleasure as she took in her surroundings. To her left was the great sapphire swath of the ocean — waves sparkling, tiny surfers bobbing — and to her right were craggy cliffs dotted with green gardens and cream-colored houses, each one more magnificent than the next. The air blowing in through the open roof smelled of budding flowers and fresh oranges.

"Where are we?" Alexa asked, still sleepy. Seamus's music had stopped, but she could hear that Phantom Planet song "California" playing in her head: *We've been on the run, driving in the sun. . . .*

Holly glanced over her shoulder, her bare feet up on the dashboard. "Look who's awake," she sing-songed, and Alexa narrowed her eyes at her. Holly knew Alexa had only been pretending to doze for most of the trip, but she'd enjoyed the quiet too much to call her friend on it. She and Seamus had chatted easily about music and college, and then fallen into a comfortable silence, Holly composing an e-mail to Tyler in her head, and Seamus smiling at the open road, likely thinking up lines of poetry or something.

"We're on the Pacific Coast Highway," Holly explained to Alexa, quoting what Seamus had told her when they'd arrived oceanside. Holly had been looking in vain for the Hollywood sign, but Seamus had explained that it was in a different part of the city, one Holly hoped she would see later; *that*, to her, would make the LA experience real. But the unimaginable beauty of the coastline had caught Holly by surprise, as did the freeing sensation of tearing down that highway, the sounds of hip-hop and the Beach Boys floating over from passing cars, the energy both relaxed and relentless. California would definitely take some getting used to.

"PCH, to us natives," Seamus said, braking behind a silver Beamer and stretching his arms over his head. Alexa noticed he'd taken off his tweed wannabe-professor jacket somewhere during the drive, and now wore only his annoying band T-shirt. "And more specifically," he added, turning the car off the highway, "we're now in Malibu."

"You gave him Jonah's address, Hol?" Alexa asked, peering eagerly ahead; the car was inching its way up, up, up a steep, rocky path that was lined with lush green shrubbery. If she craned her neck, she could make out sprawling homes cropping out of the hills; Alexa imagined the various tennis courts, pampered puppies, and fur-lined slippers that were behind each gate. *This* was where she belonged. Alexa was still a little sore at Holly and Seamus, but she wasn't going to let them spoil this rapturous moment.

"Just go all-out Hollywood and call me your chauffeur," Seamus teased, and Holly felt a pang of guilt that he'd driven all this way to drop them off. He'd explained on the way that he was staying with his family in La Brea, which meant he'd have to loop back toward the city after leaving Malibu, but he'd promised Holly that he didn't mind. As a compromise, he'd suggested that he and Holly swap cell numbers so she could treat him to an iced coffee that week.

The dusty Mustang, having finally reached the summit, came to a stop in front of a tall, trellised gate hung with red bougainvillea. Behind the gate was a house that took Alexa's breath away. It was a pale, pale rose color, with a sloping Spanish-style red roof and a wraparound deck that faced out onto the water. It seemed like a place fit for a prince, Alexa thought, her skin tingling. A little beyond the gate, near a glittery blue infinity pool, was another house that looked like a miniature of the original. The guesthouse. *Their* guesthouse.

"Well, I guess this is it," Seamus said casually, as if he pulled up in front of Malibu mansions every day. He popped the trunk, a sure sign that he was ready to say farewell and get back on the road. "Maybe I'll see you girls again sometime — if you'll ever want to leave here, that is." Neither Alexa nor Holly was able to reply.

The gate opened, and out stepped an attractive, shapely young woman in her mid-twenties, with dark copper skin and black hair up in a tight bun. She was in all white, from her trim suit to the tiny cell in her hand to her razor-thin heels. As the woman made her way purposefully toward the convertible, Holly sat up straighter, clearing her throat. Had they come to the right place?

"Um, hi, we're looking for — " she began, her voice squeaky, but the woman cut her off.

"Mr. Eklundstrom was expecting you to arrive today," she announced in a soft, modulated tone. "I'm his assistant, Esperanza. Please follow me."

Her heart drumming, Holly turned in her seat to regard Alexa, whose lips were parted and eyes shining. For the first time since getting in the car, the two girls held each other's gazes for a long moment, and slowly, despite any bickering that had gone on before, their faces broke into simultaneous smiles. Holly knew they were thinking the exact same thing.

They were, in fact, lucky bitches.

CHAPTER FOUR

Starry-Eyed Surprise

"El Sueño," Esperanza said in crisp, flawless Spanish as the white-jacketed butler (who may or may not have been faking his British accent) set the girls' bags down in the entrance hall of the guesthouse. Esperanza nodded at him, and he noiselessly departed.

"Perdón?" Holly asked shyly. She'd been gawking out the window at their white-and-silver sundeck, but now she turned around, intending to put her limited Spanish to some use. But Esperanza shot her a look that indicated she shouldn't even try.

"'The Dream,'" Esperanza translated coolly, flipping open her cell phone to check something on the screen. "It's what Mr. Eklundstrom named this — his estate" — she gestured out the huge windows — "when he bought it last year."

"The Dream," Alexa echoed, walking in a slow circle around the sun-drenched entrance hall, her suede platforms silent on the cool marble floors. High luxury was nothing new to Alexa — she'd stayed at the starriest of five-star hotels on research trips with her architect dad — but *this* was absolutely unreal.

There were sheet-glass walls that looked out onto the shimmering Pacific, red-spotted koi swimming inside a bubble tank, an Xbox 360, and squishy lemon-yellow sofas the size of beds. On every free surface there were vases overflowing with fresh-cut irises, framed snapshots of Jonah laughing oceanside with Scarlett Johansson and Kristen Bell, and porcelain bowls piled high with fat, shiny Greek olives, which, Alexa had once read on a gossip blog, were Jonah's favorite snack.

One glance at Holly's incredulous expression told Alexa that her friend was also wondering if an alarm clock was going to *brring* at any moment, bursting the bubble of her *sueño*. The two girls grinned at each other, both trying to contain themselves in front of Esperanza. In the space of saying good-bye to Seamus and walking from the car to the guesthouse, Alexa and Holly had managed to put their long, grumpy road trip behind them. It was hard to hold a grudge in a place that felt like an episode of *Cribs*.

"You will find two bedroom suites, one in each

wing of the house," Esperanza was explaining, pointing left and right like a flight attendant while Alexa wondered in which bedroom Scarlett had stayed. "There are a host of other amenities for you to enjoy," Esperanza added formally. "And you can reach the main house at any time." She tapped one French-manicured nail against a white intercom beside the door. "With any request."

Seriously? Holly leaned against a wall to fight off a sudden dizzy spell, but that only made her feel as if she might fall through the glass and straight to the azure ocean below. Back home, Holly was constantly expected to scrub the dishes while her brother dried, straighten up her room on weekends, and even prepare dinner if her parents were staying late at work. She'd certainly *never* been pampered like this. Holly tried to breathe evenly. *I so don't belong here.*

"So," Alexa was saying to Esperanza, her blue eyes dancing. "You're saying that if we want, like, foie gras, hot stone massages, and a live Click Five show at three in the morning, we should press that button?"

Holly glanced at her friend in awe. Clearly, Alexa was having no trouble adjusting at all.

Esperanza, who, Alexa suspected, had left her sense of humor back in Assistant to Celebrities Training School, gave a brisk nod. Then the white cell phone in her hand vibrated, and she lifted it to her ear. "Yes, Oren, he's already at The Standard," she snapped into the phone. "It's Jonah's agent," she told the girls, covering the mouthpiece. "I'll let you settle in." Then, with a quick, dismissive wave, she turned and headed out onto the gorgeous grounds of El Sueño.

Alexa watched Esperanza go, wondering if Jonah's anal-retentive assistant *ever* loosened up. Then, realizing it was *her* time to let loose, she whirled around to face Holly, grinning. "Okay, where should we start exploring?" she squealed — and then her heart stopped.

Holly was sitting on the floor, her back against the wall, with her head in her hands.

"Hol!" Alexa cried, dashing over. "What's wrong? Do you feel sick?" Alexa couldn't stand to see anyone throw up, but she'd make an effort to be strong for Holly.

Holly looked up, her freckled cheeks splotchy and her gray-green eyes enormous. "It's just — " she whispered. "I'm not — this house — and Esperanza — and when we meet Jonah tonight — " She shook her head, her light-brown ponytail swishing from side to side.

Alexa patted her friend's back. Holly was an East Coast girl if there ever was one — practical, level-headed, a fan of zip-up fleeces and duck boots — so it made sense that she'd be overwhelmed by LA's sunny excesses and excitements. "Look, I'm sure Jonah will barely say hi to us tonight," Alexa said reassuringly, taking Holly's hands and helping her to her feet.

Holly blew her bangs up, feeling slightly calmer. Alexa, for all her histrionics, could be surprisingly soothing when she wanted to be. Then Holly remembered the one *other* person who could always ground her back in reality: Tyler. Though she'd briefly talked to her parents from the road (they'd gotten cut off thanks to awful reception at their campsite), she hadn't had a chance to speak to her sweet, reassuring boyfriend yet.

Holly was reaching down to retrieve her phone from her Vans tote when her stomach let out a noisy grumble. She and Alexa burst into giggles as Holly straightened up and clutched her belly. "*That's* why I'm freaking out," Holly laughed. "I'm starved." Like any respectable athlete, Holly had a hearty appetite, and that Coke she'd bought on the road hadn't been remotely enough fuel. "Maybe I should look for the kitchen, huh?" she added with a smirk.

"You scope that puppy out," Alexa said decisively, squeezing Holly's shoulder. She was hungry, too, but she wanted to soak in some of the house's other treats first. "I'll investigate the rest of our digs. Over and out, soldier." She shot Holly a quick salute, before bending down to unstrap her Prada platforms.

Slipping off their respective footwear, the girls took off at a run in opposite directions, excitedly reporting their discoveries to each other like explorers landing on an island.

"I found one of the bedrooms — it's light blue!" Alexa called, admiring the circular bed, plush rug, and walk-in closet that practically begged for newly bought designer goodies.

"Yeah, the other one's green — I'm totally claiming it!" Holly hollered back around a mouthful of olives.

Giddy, Alexa sprinted from the bedroom to a small orange-painted game room, which contained a vintage Pac-Man arcade, a robot dog, and other unnecessary-but-fabulous toys. "Okay, Hol, no joke — I'm looking at a trampoline!" she shouted, resisting the urge to give it a test-bounce.

"I believe you, because I just discovered a room with an indoor golf course!" Holly responded. "But I can't find the kitchen. . . ."

"Whatever — I'm in the bathroom, and we have one of those waterfall showers and — ooh! — Bumble and bumble seaweed conditioner in the cabinet!"

Silence greeted Alexa, and she frowned, examining a delicate tub of Crème de La Mer moisturizer. True, Holly didn't get as psyched about product as she did but that didn't mean she had to *ignore* —

An earsplitting shriek erupted from the other end of the house, and Alexa dropped the La Mer in the sink, her knees buckling. "Hol, you okay?" she called. *Shit*. Holly had probably collapsed again. Now Alexa would have to whisk her to Cedars-Sinai, the fancy LA hospital where Britney had all her babies, and call Tyler and the Jacobsons, who would all *completely* lose it . . . Holding her breath, Alexa flew out of the bathroom and in the direction of Holly's cry.

When she arrived at the kitchen – Sub-Zero fridge, granite counters, cool aqua-blue tiles – she found Holly very much upright. She was also grinning, and pointing one trembling finger to something on the nearest counter: a chilled silver champagne bucket, containing crushed ice, an unopened bottle of Moët & Chandon Nectar Champagne, and two glass champagne flutes. Propped up against the bucket was a piece of cream paper with a handwritten message:

Welcome to the 'Bu, Alexa and friend — a car's coming by around seven to take you to The Standard — in the meantime here's a little something to get you in the right mood

See you there — JE.

P.S. I'd suggest swimwear.

"Jonah," Holly whispered, her heart kicking. "He lives."

"What time is it?" Alexa whispered back, stunned by the surprise message. She had to admit that Jonah's gesture was pretty . . . sweet.

In slow motion, Holly brought her blue Swatch Skyball to her face and replied, "Six . . . forty . . . five."

The girls gasped, turned to leave the kitchen, then immediately turned back to each other, at a loss. "Where do we even start?" Holly cried, gesturing down to her ratty jeans. Though she wasn't as dizzied by the house's luxury anymore, *this* was a whole other brand of nervousness.

Alexa, a near genius when it came to the mathematics of primping-to-go-out, had already calculated that waterfall-shower-plus-full-makeup-plus-trying-on-different-bikinis would equal a big bad zero. They needed to proceed wisely. Which was why she set about uncorking the bottle of champagne and pouring two glasses for herself and Holly.

"To the most efficient fifteen minutes of our life," Alexa declared as they clinked their flutes, and Holly nodded grimly.

In a whirlwind, the girls managed to down their flutes of champagne, tipsily race to get their bags from the entrance hall, and sequester themselves in their rooms to change — Holly into the lime-green halter bikini that had been her good luck charm in South

Beach, and Alexa into her new orange-and-gold bandeau. Cover-ups and shoes were slipped on: a white American Apparel polo dress and flip-flops for Holly, and silk short-shorts, a strapless, flowy black top with a small gold skull in its center, and gold Polly mules for Alexa. When Esperanza buzzed them to announce that the car was outside, Alexa, brushing out her hair, didn't feel *quite* as model-glam as she'd hoped when making her debut at a Hollywood party. But then she reminded herself that she shouldn't care. *Be realistic. Be realistic.*

The "car" turned out to be a white stretch limo, complete with a capped chauffeur, a stocked bar, and a flat-screen TV. Pulses racing, the girls slid inside and, as the limo pulled away from El Sueño, Alexa opened the moonroof and convinced Holly to stand up with her. The girls poked their heads out into the early evening sea air, the wind wild, the scent of blossoms intoxicating. Alexa stretched her arms up as her hair blew out behind her like a blonde flag. This ride was certainly different from the one she and Holly had taken earlier that day.

"We are officially in Hollywood!" Alexa exclaimed, blowing a kiss to an SUV packed full of bronzed boys and their surfboards. They whistled and waved at her as they tore past, and Alexa hoped she might run into more of their kind later on in the trip.

Holly, meanwhile, was busy noticing the bill-boards. She didn't think she'd ever seen quite so many all in one place, all brightly colored and enormous, trumpeting movies, TV shows, and hot new cars. Then Holly noticed a slightly smaller one that made her jaw drop. "Look!" she cried to Alexa, pointing as they passed:

WEDDING BELLES ARE RINGING! EXCLUSIVE LIVE FOOTAGE OF MARGAUX EKLUNDSTROM'S WEDDING. THIS FRIDAY, ONLY ON E! — ENTERTAINMENT TELE-VISION.

"Well, I've died," Alexa shouted over the wind, shrugging her shoulders, "and gone to heaven."

"I don't know," Holly said, putting her hands on the moonroof so she could duck back inside. How would she explain it to her parents if she ended up on TV *again*? That one time in South Beach, when cameras had caught her winning a bikini contest, her entire family had gone into a tailspin.

As Alexa remained standing and saying her hellos to Hollywood, Holly sank down into the deep seats and flicked on the TV. Despite the latest E! revelation, everything else — the champagne, the limo, the way she felt in her favorite bikini — was conspiring to relax her.

Then Holly noticed what was on the TV screen, and she gasped. "It's destiny," she announced to Alexa's knees.

"What is?" Alexa asked, sitting back down and finger-combing her untamed golden tresses. She saw that Holly was watching the Civil War romance *A Captain's Heart* — a film that starred none other than Jonah Eklundstrom himself. He was on the screen now, passionately arguing with a colonel, and looking sexier than ever in uniform.

"I bet he's DVRed it so it's always on in the limo," Alexa scoffed, tucking her long legs beneath her and reaching for a packet of pretzels from the bar.

"You're so cynical," Holly laughed, changing the channel. Her heart jumped and the remote fell from her hands when *Pretty Woman* blinked onto the screen. "Okay," Holly demanded. "Believe in destiny now?"

"Maybe, maybe not," Alexa replied, her voice teasing. As the limo turned onto the 110 to take them downtown, the city skyline rose in the distance. *Let's see what tonight brings.*

Alexa had experienced her share of her dazzling rooftops, but The Standard's roof bar, where the concierge sent her and Holly upon their arrival, trumped them all.

Soaring glass and steel towers, turning peach and

gold in the setting sun, surrounded them on all sides. The bar was a bright, candy-apple red, and the orange plastic tables were all 1960s retro-funky. There were red waterbeds designed to look like space pods, and waitresses dressed in cheerleader costumes carried trays of summer-colored drinks and tiny hors d'oeuvres. A DJ in the corner was playing a mash-up of Bloc Party and Gnarls Barkley, and at the edge of the roof, almost floating in the pinkish sky, was a neon-blue pool. Ridiculously thin and trendy guys and girls were splashing in with shrieks, and hopping out to bum cigarettes and wrap themselves in fluffy white towels. Alexa thought she recognized Samaire Armstrong, and someone who'd been on *American Idol*, but couldn't make out either Jonah or Margaux amid all the beauty.

"Yeah, no," Holly said after a minute, turning to go. This was a bad idea. First of all, she hated heights. Second of all, the thought of stripping down to her bikini in front of all these celebrities — or at least people who looked like celebrities — was terrifying. Feeling very much like the timid Holly of last year, she rubbed her Claddagh ring with her thumb, her heart thudding. "How close is the airport?"

"Get a grip," Alexa whispered, catching Holly by the arm. "I want to introduce you to Margaux, and we *should* try to find Jonah. But let's gather our strength first," Alexa recommended, waving to one of the cheerleader-waitresses. "Could we have a couple of those mini-burgers?" Alexa asked, pointing to a passing tray.

The pouty waitress stopped, put her hand on her hip, and informed the girls that the burgers, like everything else on the menu, were vegan, and actually called tempeh patties.

Alexa sighed, wondering if anything in the world could possibly sound less appetizing than "tempeh patties." But Holly, who'd always had a secret thing for health food, began to ask the waitress exactly what was in those delicacies. Bored, Alexa piled her hair up on her head and started scanning the crowd for more celebs when she felt a tap on her shoulder.

"Let me guess — Alexa?"

The boy's voice was deep, slow, and so familiar that Alexa immediately went breathless.

Oh . . . my . . . God.

She let her hair fall and turned around.

The first thing she noticed was that he had, in fact, shaved his beard, leaving only a trace of stubble along his beautiful jaw. The second was that, up close — those famous pale blue eyes on hers, his dark hair messed up by the wind, and his taut frame clad in a loose gray Drifter Sea Monkey tee and khaki board shorts — he was about a thousand times hotter than he'd *ever* appeared on screen (*A Captain's Heart* included). Alexa swallowed hard. All she could think to say was *Wow*, but thankfully what came out instead was "How did you know?"

Jonah Eklundstrom's face lit up, and he flashed her a bright-white grin. "Margaux described you perfectly," he replied, and took a sip from the dark green drink in his hand as he held her gaze.

Alexa smiled, feeling the slightest blush flush her cheeks. Coming from any other boy, Jonah's words would have sounded completely sketchy. But from Jonah, they were simply sweet and straightforward, while still acknowledging that he was a guy, and Alexa a girl – an attractive girl, at that. It was masterful, really; no wonder he'd won the Oscar.

Don't forget he's an actor, Alexa told herself firmly, and casually extended one hand. "Thanks for lending us your guesthouse," she said, trying to keep her tone cool. "And for the champagne."

"Hey. Life is all about sharing, isn't it?" Jonah smiled, then took a step closer, ignoring Alexa's proffered handshake. "And, besides, any friend of my sister's is a friend of mine." At this, he opened his arms wide. "Here, give me some lovin'," he said, and swept Alexa up in a hug.

Pressed up against him – *I am touching Jonah Eklundstrom!* – Alexa hoped he couldn't feel the mad thumping of her heart against his chest. His neck smelled clean and summery, like oranges, and Alexa resisted the urge to bury her nose in it. She had *not* expected to react this strongly to the actor's off-the-charts hotness. Nor had she anticipated his mellow, down-to-earth vibe, which somehow seemed totally . . . sincere.

"Uh-oh," Jonah whispered, his breath warm on her ear.

"What?" Alexa asked. She drew back, certain that he was going to comment on the loudness of her heart.

"The girl standing behind you looks like she's about to faint," Jonah answered.

"Holly!" Alexa spun around to see her friend holding on to the waitress for support, her face pale. *Here we go again*, Alexa thought, reaching an arm out to steady her. Then, to Alexa's horror, Holly opened her mouth . . . and began to *speak*.

"Jonah — Holly — God — all your movies — fan — love — *A Captain's Heart* — limo — you." In Holly's head, the words made perfect sense. Sure, seeing Alexa hugging Jonah Eklundstrom had rattled her a little, but she could hold it together, right?

"Hey, thanks, Holly," Jonah replied with a friendly nod. "My agent told me that film would be on TBS tonight."

Alexa glanced at Jonah, impressed. *He understood*

her? It occurred to Alexa that the actor, forever fending off foaming-at-the-mouth fans, had probably seen much, much worse. *Whew.*

No longer mortally embarrassed by her friend, Alexa touched Holly's shoulder. "Holly's my date for the wedding," she explained to Jonah with a smile. The waitress, clearly miffed that Jonah wasn't paying attention to *her*, left without taking any orders.

Jonah raised his dark, heavy eyebrows. "Wait, as in, like, *date*-date?" he inquired. "I mean, you should know that I have total, total respect for all lifestyle choices, especially after my role as a boxer who —"

It took Alexa and Holly a minute to process what Jonah was implying, but then they turned to each other, cracking up. "*That's* a first," Alexa said through her laughter. Holly's face was turning crimson and she could only shake her head emphatically. "We're just best friends," Alexa finally replied, rolling her eyes. *Boys.*

Jonah shrugged, and his face broke into a smile. "Dude, this is LA. You have to ask." Alexa thought he looked relieved, but she didn't know if she was imagining it or not.

"New York City princess!" someone cried.

Holly turned to see a sopping-wet, lanky girl in a flesh-colored string bikini hurrying toward them through the crowd. Her short, purple-streaked dark hair was slicked back from her face, and at her side was a tall, skinny guy in swim trunks with a shaved head and a nose ring.

With a jolt, Holly realized the girl was Margaux Eklundstrom, and she watched in disbelief as the actress flung wet arms around Alexa.

"You made it!" Margaux exclaimed in her signature raspy voice. "*And* I see you met my brother," she added, shooting an exaggerated wink at Jonah, who, to Holly's surprise, actually reddened. Then Margaux cupped Alexa's face in her hands, and Holly tried her best not to gawk at the stupendous pink diamond on the actress's finger. "I'm getting a good look at you," Margaux told Alexa, her dark-blue eyes intense. "Because this is basically the first and last time I'll see you before the wedding."

"You must be nuts with last-minute planning." Alexa smiled understandingly at Margaux. It was wonderful to see her again; here in LA, the actress gave off an even wilder vibe, like an exotic plant in its native environment. But Alexa was also hyperaware of the other Eklundstrom standing beside her, feeling the friction of his arm lightly pressing against hers.

"Yeah, *and* tomorrow Paul and I are going to an ashram in Napa to meditate," Margaux replied. Alexa nodded and purposefully avoided looking at Holly, who was definitely either bug-eyed with shock or about to burst out laughing. "Which reminds me," Margaux was saying, gesturing to the quiet, punk-hot guy at her side. "This is my fiancé, Paul DeMille — you *may* have heard his name before."

"I wrote *Grit and Gravel*." Paul smiled proudly, showing off charmingly crooked teeth.

"Oh." The word escaped Holly's mouth before she could stop it, and her cheeks burned as everyone in the group turned to stare, as if noticing her for the first time. *That movie gave me the best nap of my life*, she thought, but then thankfully she gathered enough self-control to keep that sentiment to herself.

After Alexa had introduced Holly to Margaux and Paul, Margaux turned her attentions to Jonah. "Baby Bear," she said, her tone stern. "I hope you're treating your new guests well?"

"You doubtin' on me, sis?" Jonah shot back. "I'll tell Mom and Dad you're being 'difficult' again." He made quote marks with his fingers, then took another sip of his green drink.

Holly grinned at this ordinary display of sibling rivalry; she was reminded of herself and her brother, Josh. For the first time since arriving on the out-of-this-world rooftop, she felt her nervousness start to dissipate. Three bleached-blondes wearing denim shorts, bikini tops, and satin pumps walked by, speaking loudly about "auditions" and "Bruckheimer" and throwing curious glances at the little posse. Holly felt a swell of pride; she knew the girls were wondering who the Eklundstroms were making such a fuss over.

"He's been a perfect gentleman," Alexa insisted, avoiding Jonah's gaze as she felt her cheeks grow warm. God. She was getting into trouble with this boy. "Right, Hol?" Alexa asked her friend quickly; she could still feel Jonah's eyes on her.

"Right," Holly said, exchanging a knowing smile with Margaux and her fiancé. Holly knew better than anyone what it meant when Alexa blushed that deeply. And it was equally obvious, from the way he stared at her, that Jonah was smitten with Alexa as well. Holly didn't think that kind of attentiveness could be faked, even by a world-famous actor.

"Holly, assuming you have a bikini on under there, please remove your dress," Margaux requested, reaching for Holly's arm. "There's an entire pool waiting for you, and your first drink's on Paul and me."

"Um, great," Holly said, realizing she'd been craving a dip in the pool anyway. And Margaux and Paul seemed friendly enough. With one last glance back at Alexa and Jonah — who were now looking at each other in such a rapt, intense way, that it gave Holly butterflies — she followed Margaux and Paul toward the packed pool scene.

"That was subtle, huh?" Alexa asked, turning to Jonah with a teasing smile.

"What do you mean?" Jonah replied with a straight face, and Alexa laughed. She wasn't sure if he was joking or not, but she felt a thrill of excitement all the same. She shook out her long hair, letting it tumble over her shoulders, and remembered what Margaux had said to Jonah on the phone last night: *She's blonde, which I know you love.* . . . Alexa could sense her old confidence, the effortless ease she usually felt around boys, clicking back into place. So she practiced one of her favorite moves: She reached over to take Jonah's drink from his hand, her fingers conveniently brushing against his.

"Can I have a sip of your potion?" she asked, her voice breathy.

"It's wheatgrass juice," Jonah warned her. "I don't drink anymore, not since my trainer got me into yoga — I try to keep my body clean of toxins, you know what I mean?"

Alexa yanked her hand back. *Wheatgrass juice?* Though Alexa wasn't quite the party girl she'd been last year, she still loved sipping cool-sweet cocktails in glittering social settings. But she didn't want to make Jonah uncomfortable by ordering a *drink*-drink.

"How's the handsomest boy in Hollywood?" a

seductive female voice interrupted, and a curvaceous girl with long brown curls appeared at Jonah's side, wearing a bikini made up entirely of silver sequins. Alexa recognized the girl as a runner-up on the last season of *America's Next Top Model* and couldn't help but feel the tiniest flare of jealousy.

But if Jonah was at all intrigued by the model beside him, he didn't show it. "Loving life moment by moment, Meredith," he said breezily, flashing her a smile. "Listen, I'm sorry to bounce, but I was just about to show off the view to someone very special." As Jonah took Alexa's arm, leading her away from a fuming Meredith, Alexa tried to control the joy rippling through her. *Be realistic*, she thought, but the words seemed oddly faint and distant now.

She caught her breath as she and Jonah settled on a curved orange sofa, gazing out on an unobstructed stretch of nectarine-colored sky.

"I'd always pictured LA as all billboards and run-down movie sets and smog — I never thought it would be beautiful," Alexa admitted as she took in the glorious vista.

"It's all right," Jonah replied offhandedly, and, again, Alexa could feel his gaze on her profile. "There are definitely other, more beautiful things in this world."

Fighting to keep herself from melting, Alexa

turned toward Jonah and shot him an innocent smile. "So you're not such a fan of Los Angeles?" she asked. She couldn't get over his remarkable, otherworldly eyes: the center pale as crystal, and the rim a dark indigo.

"Man, I don't know," Jonah sighed, running a hand through his dark hair. "I'm so *used* to it." He gestured to the raucous party behind them, and Alexa turned to check it out.

A bunch of girls in skimpy bikinis were poised on the lip of the pool, laughing and cursing loudly as they prepared to dive in. Margaux and Paul were bobbing in the deep end, making out like teenagers. And then Alexa spotted Holly; she was floating on a red lounger, sipping a mango margarita and looking surprisingly calm in her hot little lime bikini. In a lounger beside Holly was a girl with sharp cheekbones and straight black hair whom Alexa recognized from the CW. *The Wizard of Oz* was being projected onto the side of one of the nearby buildings, and couples were kissing on the waterbed-pods. "It doesn't seem *too* bad," Alexa commented wryly.

"I was born here," Jonah said, and Alexa faced him again, feeling a now-familiar flutter at the sight of his flawless face. "My parents are producers, and I've been acting since I could, like, talk, so this is all I've ever known. I've traveled a lot on shoots and promos but you're always in your trailer and shit." He raised his broad shoulders, and Alexa nodded, trying to get a handle on what Jonah's make-believe existence must be like. "I mean, my best friend? He lives in New York City, you know? And his life seems so raw, so *real*." Jonah shook his head, and drank more of his wheatgrass juice.

"The city *is* pretty fabulous," Alexa replied, crossing her long legs. As much as she was relishing the Hollywood sparkle, a part of her missed New York's chic sophistication. So far, she was fairly unimpressed by the fashion she'd seen at this party.

Jonah stared at Alexa, his expression curious and intent. "Tell me about *your* life back east," he murmured, and Alexa felt her heart leap as he moved closer to her on the sofa. "I want to know everything."

Alexa was about to break the bad news that her New Jersey existence could never be classified as *raw* when she heard a loud "*Whee!*" behind her. She turned once again and saw the actress Charity Durst, wearing a strapless, saggy beige dress and strands of long beads, jump feetfirst into the pool. Spindly arms over her head, dirty-blonde ponytail flying, she sent up an enormous splash, causing everyone around her to grumble.

"She's such a weirdo," Jonah commented, but he was half smiling.

"Didn't you guys, um . . . go out?" Alexa asked carefully, not wanting to give away the fact that she'd been obsessively following their relationship via trashy magazines.

Jonah gave a bashful grin, rubbing the back of his neck. "Ages ago," he replied. "We just weren't . . . on the same path, you know? But it's all good now," he added with a nod. "In this industry, you can't really make enemies. I even invited Charity here, and to the wedding — I figured I'd extend the olive brand since we're filming a movie together now."

"You mean olive *branch*, right?" Alexa corrected him, giggling and leaning forward to examine the glass in his hand. "Are you *sure* that's just juice you're drinking?"

Jonah made a face — of course, he still looked insanely gorgeous doing it — and chuckled. "Oh, man. It's you. You make me tongue-tied, Alexa."

Alexa bit her lip, dying to take the flirtatious bait. If this were a movie, that would have been her cue to slide close to Jonah and kiss him, parting his lips with hers. *But this* isn't *a movie*, she told herself sternly. "It's hard with exes, though," she finally spoke, trying to keep the conversation more neutral. "I broke up with my last boyfriend over spring break, and then we had to sit next to each other on the seven-hour plane ride home." Alexa shuddered, remembering that one last time she'd seen Diego. It was ridiculous, really; of all people, a Tinseltown A-lister turned out to be a thousand times more sensitive than her ex had been.

"So you're single?" Jonah asked, clearly determined to keep things *not* neutral. His eyes shining, he reached down and took Alexa's hand in his, making her skin burn from his touch.

"Yeah," Alexa said softly, unable to look away from him. "Really single."

As Jonah began to trace a circle on her palm, Alexa wondered if she could resist him for much longer. Here it was, her Hollywood fantasy, blooming into a reality. Would she be insane to turn it down?

"Okay, it's insane — they're holding hands," Holly reported from where she was keeping watch in the pool. She was floating on a lounger alongside Belle Runningwater, the beautiful teen actress who played Pocahontas on the CW drama *Wild Land*. Margaux had introduced Holly to Belle, gushing that the girls would get along, before she and Paul had swum off to the deep end to grope each other. Belle's first words to Holly had been: "Don't tell them, but I hated *Grit and Gravel*," and so Holly had liked her immediately. Now the two of them were sipping their frothy mango margaritas and shamelessly spying on Alexa and Jonah.

"And I think his arm is around her waist now," Belle observed, finishing her drink and setting it on the side of the pool to be whisked away by a waiter.

Holly still couldn't get over how relatively normal this felt, one hand trailing in the cool chlorine while all around her the lights of Los Angeles twinkled, and people who she'd seen on TV laughed and chilled. When a sculpted, long-haired guy on the other end of the pool — a finalist on *American Idol* whose name Holly couldn't recall — flashed her an inviting smile, Holly didn't get too flustered or cross her arms over her chest. She simply smiled back. Of course, the margarita she was sipping wasn't hurting, but it was more than that — after being so worked up earlier that evening, Holly now felt surprisingly . . . at ease.

"Come on, let's not gawk *too* obviously," Belle was saying with a laugh. She slipped off her lounger — passing it along to a bikini-clad Alexis Bledel — and then hoisted herself out of the water, adjusting the halter of her white Eres swimsuit. Holly peeked back at Alexa and Jonah once more — they now seemed a few breaths away from kissing — grinned, and then pulled herself up, too, sitting beside Belle on the faux-grass carpet.

"There's only one downside to all this," Holly commented, peering up to watch as the wide sky slowly darkened into evening. "If Alexa hooks up with Jonah tonight, they're going to be attached at the hip. What am I going to do with myself for the rest of the week?"

"Are you *kidding*?" Belle asked, her almond-shaped black eyes growing big. "Holly, there's so *much* to do in LA! There's Zuma Beach in Malibu, which is perfect for surfing, and In-N-Out, which has *the* best burgers and fries you've ever eaten, and the Chateau Marmont, which makes you feel like you're in some Hollywood fairy tale, and all the Sunset clubs, which are kind of tacky but in a good way. . . ." Belle trailed off, smiling. "Am I completely overwhelming you?"

Holly shook her head. Everything sounded enticing, and unreal, and . . . she wanted to try it all. She figured it was the magic of the night making her feel this way, but she wasn't going to question it. "What about the Hollywood sign?" Holly asked Belle. After a full evening in LA, she couldn't believe she *still* hadn't seen it yet. "Where can I find it?"

Belle laughed, reaching for her velour clutch on a nearby chair. "I wouldn't go looking," she advised. "You'll probably just notice it one day when you're driving on Sunset or something. Listen," she added, taking out her Moto Razr. "I'm shooting *Wild Land* all week, but let's exchange numbers anyway — maybe we can hang out sometime."

Did I just make friends with a celebrity? Holly wondered in awe. After she punched Belle's 310 area-code number into her phone, Belle announced she was going the bar to get more drinks for them. As Belle sauntered off, Holly examined the cell in her hand, and realized there was someone with whom she wanted — *needed* — to share her exuberant mood. It was too noisy around the pool to place a call, so she began texting Tyler instead.

Hi, baby. H'wood is amazing. At a celeb pool party on a hotel roof & im not even scared — of the height, she meant, but also the celebrities, which she knew Tyler would get. A & I r staying in the sickest house — she paused, realizing she didn't want to get too carried away in her gushing, since Tyler was in Oakridge and all — & i know its cheesy but of course i wish u were here.

Tyler was notoriously quick at responding to texts, so she grinned expectantly when her cell trilled, and she opened it to see his reply.

H, thats awesome! U sound so happy. Glad ur having fun w/out me. LOL. Ill call u tomorrow. love.

Holly stared at the last word, her heart swelling. She had her boyfriend back home, and she had this time in California. What more could she ask for?

"Dude, sometimes I feel like, 'what more could I

ask for?'" Jonah was musing a few feet away, his arm loose around Alexa's waist. Alexa wondered if she'd lost the ability to breathe. They'd gotten to talking about relationships, or their recent lack thereof, and Alexa discovered that Jonah shared some of her disillusionment when it came to romance. Though, right now, that disillusionment had pretty much disappeared. Their faces hovered inches apart. The first pinpoints of stars had started to emerge above their heads, and Alexa could swear their glow was reflected in Jonah's huge eyes. "I have so much, and I feel so blessed," Jonah went on. "But then I wonder if I've ever really been in love. . . ."

The crazy thing was, Alexa didn't doubt that Jonah's words were heartfelt. That was the biggest surprise about tonight, she realized: not the champagne bottle, or the limo ride, or seeing all the gleaming celebs, but the surprise of Jonah himself. He *wasn't* the kind of guy who would DVR his own movie or hook up with a wannabe model. He was an actor who didn't put on an act. And suddenly Alexa knew why she'd had a premonition that she had to be at this party tonight. Holly had been right. Maybe it *was* destiny.

"Maybe you can still fall," Alexa whispered, her lips so near to his she wondered how the two of them *weren't* kissing yet. "This is La-La Land, after all. Anything's possible, right?"

"Well, I met *you* tonight," Jonah replied, reaching up to trace the Cupid's-bow shape of Alexa's mouth, which, in all the recent giddiness, she'd forgotten to freshen up with gloss. "And you're impossibly beautiful. Not like everyone else here. You're all natural."

Like wheatgrass juice? Alexa wanted to ask, but then Jonah Eklundstrom was kissing her.

His lips were hot and soft, his mouth tasted sweet and clean, and as Alexa began to kiss him back, she could feel, from the way he tightened his arms around her waist, how much he wanted this, wanted her. He was real, human, no longer a face on a screen. If she liked, she could reach up and feel the warm skin of his throat, his chin, which she did, slowly. She quivered with want. They tilted their heads from one side to the next, the kiss deepening, their tongues meeting. Alexa briefly wondered if Charity Durst and everyone else at the party could see them, but then decided she didn't care. Jonah's hands slid up above her waist, brushing the ribbon at the top of her shorts, over her strapless top, and Alexa's hands swept up under his shirt.

I'm making out with Jonah Eklundstrom, Alexa thought, stunned at the progression this night had taken. Then she decided to forget being stunned — and just breathe in the moment.

As Jonah's lips brushed against her neck, Alexa glanced up and let the shimmering skyline dazzle her eyes. *It's been so long.* She felt like a princess who'd been living under a kiss-less spell — which had now been broken by a dashing knight. When Jonah lifted his head to smile at her, Alexa gazed into his eyes and whispered what she hadn't spoken earlier. "Wow."

"Funny, that's what I was thinking," Jonah murmured. He brought his mouth down onto hers again, and Alexa closed her eyes. And despite her cynicism, despite her *be realistic* vow, she allowed herself the one thought she'd been trying to fight off all night:

It felt just like a movie.

CHAPTER FIVE

Blue Cruſh

"Hey, Alexa?" Holly asked, staring up at the moonlit ceiling as she and Alexa lay side by side on Jonah's trampoline. "Want to go to the Chateau Marmont?"

It was two in the morning, and the girls had been back in the guesthouse for an hour; to celebrate their amazing night out, they had finished the bottle of Moët Nectar, played an intensive game of Pac-Man, and then jumped up and down on the trampoline, cracking up the whole time. Now, they were lounging peacefully, listening to the quiet roar of the ocean outside their windows.

"I hope you're kidding, Hol," Alexa replied, her eyelids heavy and her lips still tingling from Jonah's insistent kisses. She stretched languorously, her black top inching up her flat belly. "Since when did you stop being a homebody?"

"I'm on vacation." Holly sat up, smoothing out the hem of her polo dress. Maybe it was jet lag, but she was feeling restless – in a good way. Belle's earlier description of the Chateau Marmont had sounded like such decadent fun that Holly was itching to visit its bar, to feel like a real Hollywood insider who knew to show up at hot spots after hours. "And," she admitted, smiling down at Alexa, "I guess I just don't want this night to be over."

In some ways, the night had kicked off for *both* girls when Jonah began kissing Alexa on the rooftop, and Holly had spotted the action from the pool (Belle had had to dissuade her from snapping a picture with her cell phone, because no photographers were allowed at the party). Margaux and Paul, who immediately started toasting the new couple with their Heinekens, had also clearly been pleased. The only person who'd looked decidedly unhappy was Charity Durst, and when Alexa and Jonah had noticed the actress's evil stare, they'd stopped kissing, hurried over to Holly, and asked if she wanted to escape with them.

The trio made their getaway in Jonah's black Aston Martin, which made Alexa feel like a Bond girl as she sat at his side, the city flashing by their rolled-down windows. Jonah seemed ready to return to El Sueño, but both Holly and Alexa, who'd both forgotten about their ravenous hunger until that moment, had clamored for food. Inspired by Belle's recommendation, Holly requested In-N-Out, and Alexa heartily agreed that real burgers sounded real good. It wasn't until the girls had settled in at the retro-chic, yellow-and-red In-N-Out in Westwood, and ordered their burgers, crispy fries, and tall vanilla milk shakes, that Alexa remembered that Jonah was vegan. He hadn't complained, though; he'd simply sat back in a chair with his baseball cap pulled low over his eyes, occasionally texting his agent, and looking on with a smile as the two of them devoured their midnight feast.

"I feel awful," Holly told Jonah at one point, taking a big bite of her mouthwatering lettuce-onion-and-special-sauce burger. She was surprised that she didn't feel at all like a third wheel around him and Alexa — *and* that Jonah seemed sort of like a friend now. Well, maybe not a friend. But at any rate, he was much more accessible than she'd expected, and she was no longer the girl who'd stuttered and stammered in his presence hours before.

"Dude." Jonah had held up his hands in a no-worries gesture. "*I* made the choice to give up meat. I guess watching my friends eat burgers is my plot in life."

"You mean your *lot* in life?" Alexa had snorted, playfully tossing a fry at Jonah. "You're not by any chance foreign, are you?" She'd heard similar malapropisms from her Parisian cousins.

"One hundred percent red, white, and blue," Jonah had replied, grinning at Alexa and taking her hand. "Though I did play an Italian count once," he'd added earnestly.

"I know, in *Venetian Valentine*," Alexa had responded, hoping she didn't sound too much like a crazed fan. But then a teenage girl with red hair, standing at the counter with two friends and undeterred by any silly baseball cap, had screamed: *"Oh my Gah you guys look I swear it's Jonah!"* and then the *true* crazed fans had swarmed the table, pleading and sighing, waving napkins and pens until Jonah scribbled his signature and responded kindly to declarations of love.

After their second escape of the night, Alexa, Holly, and Jonah arrived back at El Sueño, and Holly slipped out of the car, leaving Alexa and Jonah some time alone. They'd kissed again and again, and listened to the whispering of the ocean until Jonah whispered that he'd see her tomorrow.

Now Holly nudged Alexa, who looked as if she were sleeping on the trampoline, her long lashes resting on her cheeks. "Dreaming of your movie star boyfriend?" Holly teased.

Alexa smiled, keeping her eyes closed. "He's not my boyfriend," she protested, even as she recalled the feel of his lips against hers. "He's my . . . crush." That was a good word, Alexa realized. She should start using it more often.

"I don't know, Alexa," Holly warned, her words coming out in a yawn. Rolling off the trampoline, Holly thought about the hopeful way Jonah had watched Alexa all night. "*He* might feel differently." She rubbed her eyes, and started out of the living room, realizing that the Marmont — or any hot night-spot — was probably no longer an option. But she and Alexa would have plenty of time to go to the fairy-tale hotel before they left LA on Saturday.

"Stop fanning the flames of my delusions," Alexa mumbled, as she sat up and lifted the two empty champagne flutes off the rug. "Hooking up *was* incredible," she admitted, as her face flushed at another naughty memory: Jonah's nibbling on her neck while the windows of the Aston Martin literally steamed up. "But I doubt I'll hear from him again," she added, getting to her feet and blowing Holly a good-night kiss. "Not until the wedding, at least."

Six hours later, when each girl was fast asleep in

her circular bed, and the buttery Malibu sunlight was floating in through each set of drapes, the intercom in the hallway buzzed — loudly.

Groans and murmurs of "no freaking way" came from either side of the guesthouse as each girl stirred in her bed. Alexa pulled her fluffy pillow over her head, and Holly rolled onto her stomach. They were both wishing that they hadn't actually *finished* that champagne.

There was another, louder, more insistent buzz.

"It must be Esperanza!" Alexa huffed, finally throwing back her silken top sheet and sliding off the bed. Alexa hurried from the room in her black, lace-trimmed nightie, the house's central air-conditioning making her shiver. She was still sleepy and slightly hungover, but she also had that jumpy, Christmas-morning feeling in her gut, the feeling of presents to be opened.

"Maybe she knows we kind of trashed the place last night?" Holly called guiltily as she got out of bed, pulling up the strap of her worn-in Oakridge Track & Field tank top. She knew that the contents of the girls' purses — lip glosses, tissues, Listerine breath strips, and cell phones — were still scattered across the rug, and she was worried they might have broken the Pac-Man game.

Alexa passed by the startling ocean view outside, and then pressed the button on the white box by the door. "Good *morning*," she said pointedly, intending to make whoever it was feel bad for waking her.

"Am I speaking to Alexa?" As Alexa had expected, it was Esperanza's clipped voice that crackled out.

"Uh-huh," Alexa said, shooting a "what-the-hell?" glance at Holly, who'd stumbled into the entrance hall, wearing her tank and Tyler's plaid boxers, rubbing her eyes.

"I have a message for you from Mr. Eklundstrom," Esperanza said. "He is at Paramount all day, but would like to see you later. He's arranged for the car to pick you up at six and take you to Paramount. But Mr. Eklundstrom specifically asked me to inquire if you will be free tonight."

Alexa felt a surge of giddiness and wonder. How had she managed to find the one thoughtful, considerate celebrity in all of Hollywood? She let her joy course through her, and then focused back on Esperanza. "No, I'll be staying in and watching *Dancing with the Stars*," Alexa replied, rolling her eyes at Holly, who tried to muffle her laughter with her hands.

"Understood," Esperanza replied swiftly. "I will inform Mr. Eklundstrom that tonight won't be possible —"

"No, wait! Wait!" Alexa cried, pressing every button possible as panic rose in her. "I was joking! *Joking*. Of course I'm free. Please tell Jonah I'll see him then."

"Very well," Esperanza replied as Alexa let out the breath she'd been holding. *Mental note: Never use sarcasm on this woman.* "Oh, and Mr. Eklundstrom left you the keys to his Lexus Hybrid, which you are welcome to use during your stay," Esperanza added. "It's right in the garage."

Alexa waited a minute before releasing the button on the intercom and turning around to grin at Holly.

"Well," Holly said, putting her hands on her hips and feeling a spark of genuine excitement for her friend. Finally, Alexa had fallen for a boy who was equal parts hot and sweet. "I guess your movie star *crush* may be more serious than you think."

Alexa ignored the pulse-fluttering comment. "You know what this means, right?" she said, starting in the direction of the bathroom to wash up. "The need for serious shopping has just been increased to, like, the tenth power." Alexa felt the familiar sense of pre-shopping elation begin to build in her. "I didn't pack with a celebrity date in mind, and that must be remedied," she explained, ticking the reasons off on her fingers while Holly watched her with one brow raised. "We have to get our wedding dresses squared away pronto —"

"I'm wearing my prom dress," Holly protested, annoyed that Alexa wanted to bully her into an unnecessary purchase.

"You can still revel in Rodeo Drive," Alexa reasoned, giving Holly a huge smile and then humming the chorus to the song "Pretty Woman."

"I know," Holly laughed, and she felt a tremor of anticipation at the thought. "On one condition," she added, peering out the window at the flawless day. Now that she was more awake, she was glad to be up so early, and was eager to get outside and breathe in the fresh California air. "That we build in time for some sun-worshipping."

Alexa never needed convincing when it came to the beach, so, a half hour later, after checking MapQuest and zipping up PCH in Jonah's neat little Hybrid ("Of course he didn't give us the Aston Martin," Alexa complained), the girls were stretched out on white loungers on Zuma Beach. The deep blue Pacific soared and dipped before them, and they sipped the iced blendeds they'd picked up from Coffee Bean as the sun toasted their limbs.

"Remember the last time we were together on a beach?" Alexa asked Holly, once she'd finished rubbing Dior Sun Cream along her arms. She leaned back, adjusted the keyhole of her strapless paisley maillot, and let herself soak in one of her favorite views in the world: a gleaming blue ocean decorated with hot surfer boys.

"South Beach." Holly sighed with nostalgia, pushing her wraparound shades up on her head. "But don't you feel like LA's even better?" she mused, her eyes lingering on one of the surfers, a slender, fair-skinned boy with curly hair the color of oak. He was clearly the daredevil of the bunch; Holly watched him zigzag along a giant wave, riding it out until he tumbled off his dark blue board, laughing.

"That dude's, like, *bananas*," Holly heard a girl comment, and another reply: "Let him do his thing; I'm all about Zen philosophy now." The girls, wearing loose sarongs, flip-flopped lazily by Holly's towel and waved to the friendly-looking lifeguard. *That* was what she liked better about LA, Holly realized: the mellowness of a life lived under constant sunshine. South Beach had been high energy 24/7, but even at the upscale bash last night, Holly had picked up on a more laid-back vibe.

"Well, we're certainly *behaving* better here," Alexa replied, lowering her sunglasses and shooting Holly a knowing smile. "So far."

Holly smiled back and held Alexa's gaze, thinking about how much their friendship had changed since that trip. She felt as if they'd come full circle, from one beach to another. "Hey," Holly said softly. "Thanks for convincing me to come out here, Little Miss Bossy." What would she do without Alexa there to bring adventure into her life?

"Anytime," Alexa replied truthfully, reaching out to squeeze Holly's hand. Just chilling with her friend was helping Alexa keep a healthy perspective on the Jonah sitch; she was excited about tonight, of course, but she wasn't letting it consume her. Sometimes Alexa wondered what she would do without Holly there to keep her grounded.

Holly returned the hand-squeeze, and before she could get too choked up, rose from the lounger, taking off her shades. Watching the surfers had filled her with the craving to also ride those swells, to balance her feet on a board, to feel the salty spray on her face. Holly had done some surfing last summer, when her sports camp had spent a weekend on Cape Cod, but these huge, perfectly cresting Pacific waves were so much more inviting.

"I'm gonna find out where I can rent a board," Holly told Alexa, who nodded encouragingly, sipping at her iced drink; she'd never surfed in her life, and had no desire to break that streak. She was more than content to bake herself to a crisp while Holly went out there and foolishly risked her well-being with physical activity.

Holly was about to head toward the lifeguard, who

was still flirting with the sarong girls, when her cell phone rang from her Roxy beach tote on the sand. She reached for it and saw it was Tyler. "Hey!" she squealed when she answered.

"So you're still around?" Tyler asked, his voice warm and affectionate in her ear. "You haven't, like, been cast as an extra, and gotten all famous on me?"

"Wait, you mean you didn't see me on the cover of *Us Weekly*?" Holly teased, letting her toes sink into the hot white sand and listening to the familiar cadence of Tyler's laugh. "How was dinner at chez Davis last night?" she asked, shielding her eyes to gaze out at the water. Daredevil Boy had paddled out farther, and was motioning for his friends to join him.

"Oh, same old, same old," Tyler sighed. "My mom reamed me out for getting frozen peas instead of fresh ones, and . . ." he trailed off. "Sweetie, are you listening?" he asked. "Holly?"

"Sorry!" Holly gasped, glancing away from the ocean. "Alexa and I are on the beach, and I was thinking of going surfing —"

"Oh, surfing." Holly thought she detected a sour note in her boyfriend's voice. "Your *real* love. So I'm getting the shaft, huh?" He let out a low chuckle.

"No!" Holly cried guiltily, walking a few paces away from Alexa and lowering her voice. "I *want* to hear all about the dinner, Tyler, but this isn't the best time. Can I call you later?"

Tyler was silent for a moment. "Yeah. Of course," he said, and Holly bit her lip, wondering if he was miffed. "Just don't forget about me," he added, half teasingly.

"Never," Holly swore. After she said good-bye and clicked off, she was grateful for Tyler's unintentional reminder. She slipped her Claddagh ring off her finger and into her bag; she wouldn't want to lose it while surfing. Fixing the straps on her turquoise tankini, she waved to a dozing Alexa and headed down to where the ocean met the sand. The water was a cold shock at first, but as she waded in deeper, her skin adjusted to the feel of the silky waves. The salty breeze teased her loose hair and she shut her eyes, realizing she'd be perfectly happy to forgo shopping and stay here all day.

A chorus of shouts coming from farther out in the water broke into Holly's peaceful meditation. She looked over, squinting against the sun's glare. "Holy shit! I think he's out!" one of the surfer boys was yelling hoarsely as he and the others frantically tried to swim toward a bobbing shape in the distance. But they were obviously slowed down by their cumbersome boards. Holly realized with a stab of terror that the surfer in question — it had to be Daredevil Boy — had gotten into serious trouble. She didn't let herself think before plunging straight into the ocean, letting the current lift her body as she plowed ahead with smooth, sure strokes. The cool water filled her ears but she pushed out farther, feeling like a mermaid, oblivious to the shouts around her, and to the fact that she'd outpaced the surfer boys by a lot.

She surfaced, gasping, to find Daredevil Boy's board floating haphazardly on the waves, and the boy himself beneath it, one limp hand on the board, the rest of him underwater. Holly felt pure fear fill her throat. *Don't lose it, Hol. You have to help him.* As a camp counselor, Holly had received rudimentary lifeguard and CPR training, but she was mostly acting on instinct as she shoved the surfboard out of the way and put one arm around the motionless boy, hoisting all his weight onto her. Her heart kicking, wreaths of seaweed slapping her face, she mustered all her strength and began to propel them both toward the shoreline.

"Did you get Zach? Did you get him?" Suddenly Holly was surrounded by a passel of surfer boys, their hair plastered to their foreheads and their eyes frantic.

"Grab his board!" Holly shouted, trying to keep her mouth above water; somehow she sensed that

Daredevil Boy — Zach — would want it when he was okay. *If* he'd be okay.

One of the boys got on that, while the other three took some of Zach's weight, helping Holly carry him to shore. Holly heard the sharp scream of the lifeguard's whistle, and looked up to see him running into the water with his large red rescue board. The two girls he'd been talking to were standing on the shore with their hands over their mouths. Holly gave the negligent lifeguard a too-late! glare as the three surfers laid their fallen friend on the damp sand. Holly, still acting on automatic pilot, knelt down, the sun burning the back of her neck. Zach's eyes were closed, his fine-featured face was pale, and there was a telltale bump on his high forehead from where his board had hit him.

Holly was vaguely aware that a huge crowd had gathered around them — she heard Alexa calling her name — and that the lifeguard was telling her to get out of his way. But, with surprisingly steady hands, she held Zach's nose together, and when his lips parted, she tilted her head down, pressed her mouth to his, and gave two long, slow breaths. She kept one hand on Zach's still-warm chest as she continued the mouth-to-mouth, willing him to waken.

"Excuse me — that's my friend — Holly!" Alexa was crying, elbowing her way through the swarming crowd. She had been half napping on her lounger, mentally composing the ideal outfit for tonight's date — *Marc Jacobs Grecian sandals, Blumarine teal tube dress?* — when screams from the water had startled her. Alexa's first, horrifying thought had been that Holly was in danger, but as she scrambled toward the shoreline, she'd seen that Holly was, in fact, the hero. Alexa felt a rush of pride as she rose up on her bare toes to witness Holly pulling her head back from the unconscious surfer, who suddenly began to stir.

Holly, holding her own breath, barely dared believe it as Zach's long, wet lashes fluttered and he let out a series of small, gasping coughs. Then he opened his eyes entirely: They were a deep, pure brown, the color of bittersweet chocolate. They held Holly's gaze for a long beat before she felt the lifeguard's hands on her shoulders, moving her aside, and Zach began to cough hoarsely. Shouts of "he's okay" echoed through the crowd, along with a palpable wave of relief, and Holly stood shakily as the lifeguard tended to Zach. She was aware then of her hair sticking to her head, the water trickling down her back, the sogginess of her tankini, and the stitch in her side.

"Hey, you were incredible," one of Zach's surfer friends called to Holly. The others nodded in gratitude and a few onlookers standing behind her let out a smattering of applause. Holly felt her face flame and she ducked her head; was this what it was like to be famous?

"Oh, Hol!" Alexa tore through the crowd to wrap her friend in an effusive hug. "I can't believe you did that — you were so, so brave!" Alexa had always thought of *herself* as the bold one, and Holly the cautious wallflower. But Holly had looked so badass, confidently pulling that guy ashore, while Alexa knew she'd *never* have the guts — nor the swimming abilities — to attempt the same. More likely, *she'd* be the one in need of rescuing.

"I'm — I'm just glad he's okay," Holly said, her heart thumping as she watched Zach slowly get to his feet with the help of the lifeguard. And that *was* all Holly cared about right then. Though she couldn't wait to broadcast the news to her parents and Tyler.

Hmm. Maybe Holly didn't always need Alexa to make things adventurous after all.

"Let's go," Alexa suggested. Picking up on how overwhelmed Holly was feeling, she slipped an arm around her friend's waist and began to lead her away from the crowd. The girls were almost back at their loungers when they heard someone call out behind them.

"Wait up, guardian angel!"

Holly turned to see Zach, surrounded by his concerned-looking surfing buddies, making his way toward her across the sand. "How can I thank you?" he asked. His voice was a little hoarse, and the bump on his forehead was blooming into a bruise, but the naturally mischievous expression had returned to his face. His brown curls were matted and sandy, and Holly noticed a sprinkling of gold-brown freckles across the bridge of his nose.

Meeting his wide brown eyes, Holly felt the flush in her cheeks deepen. *I put my mouth against his,* she realized, her stomach somersaulting. Who was the courageous girl who'd possessed Holly in that moment? Now that her adrenaline — and her boldness — was wearing off, she wasn't sure how she'd done it. She shook her head at Zach, not with modesty, but with disbelief. "Don't worry about it," she told him, brushing her wet hair back off her face. "Really." She could feel her pulse ticking away in her throat, probably from her little swim.

"Listen," Zach said, undeterred, "I could get you in for free to see my band, Blue Dog Babylon, sometime —"

Alexa had never heard of Blue Dog Babylon — clearly one of those indie Cali bands — but she was definitely intrigued by the hottie Holly had rescued. She flashed him a smile, but before she could accept on Holly's behalf, Holly was abruptly leading her away by the elbow. "Thanks," Holly called over her shoulder. "But I'm just visiting LA for a short time." Alexa saw disappointment cross the boy's face, and then he shrugged and turned back to his friends.

"Why did you turn down that offer?" Alexa wondered aloud as the girls collapsed back in their loungers. "He's a musician surfer! He's, like, a California original. God. If *I* saved that boy's life, I would so have a crush on him," she added, passing Holly a bottle of Fiji water (El Sueño's housekeeper had stocked the guest fridge with them).

Holly had been vigorously rubbing her still-sopping hair with a towel, but she stopped and took a long drink of water. "It wasn't like that," she protested, her voice curt. Unlike Alexa, Holly wasn't a fan of the word *crush*; she felt like it implied something sort of serious. Instinctively, Holly reached into her beach bag to retrieve her Claddagh ring and slipped it back on. The whole rescue now felt so *random*, so bizarre. Holly knew what she needed was some normalcy to put her on an even keel again. Something mindless and trivial.

Alexa, observing her friend's sober expression, realized, with a prickle of guilt, how exhausted Holly must be after that intense experience. "Hol, I'm sure you want to go back to El Sueño and rest," she offered gently.

"Not at all." Holly swung her legs off her lounger, looking determined. "I want to shop."

And Alexa — who knew all too well what a rare occasion it was when *Holly* suggested retail therapy — decided not to fight it. "If you say so," she said, shooting her friend a grin. "Maybe you'll rescue someone out of their too-tight capris."

CHAPTER SIX
Rodeo Queens

Alexa had many pet peeves — pleated pants, bad kissers, the math section of the SAT — but chief among them were people who referred to that fabled strip of Beverly Hills high fashion as *ROW-dee-oh* Drive.

Rodeos, the cowboy kind, could be sort of sexy in and of themselves — all those cute, sweaty boys in plaid shirts, fitted jeans, and Stetsons — but the famous *Row-DAY-oh* Drive inhabited a world of glamour and class that had nothing to do with bucking broncos.

Unfortunately, when Alexa and Holly got lost en route from Zuma Beach to Beverly Hills and stopped to ask a passerby for directions, the woman turned out to be a tourist who committed the twin crimes of *not* knowing where the shopping paradise was and pronouncing its name all wrong. Sighing in frustration, Alexa rolled up the window and zoomed off, while Holly chided her for being so snobby.

"Not everyone *knows*, Alexa," Holly pointed out as the girls cruised down North Robertson Boulevard, passing The Ivy restaurant, which even Holly recognized as a celebrity power-lunch landmark. "The whole world hasn't traveled as much as you have."

Turning the wheel, Alexa felt herself mellowing as she realized Holly had a point. "*You* know," she argued feebly.

Holly shrugged. "I've seen *Pretty Woman*."

As Alexa giggled, Holly reached up to brush some stray sand out of her loose braid; she and Alexa had changed out of their swimwear in the Zuma Beach bathrooms, but even in her purple ribbed tank and drawstring white skirt, her skin soothed with Alexa's aloe hand cream, Holly felt gritty and still kind of shaky from her ocean escapade. To get her mind off the crazy adventure, she gazed out the window, noticing that the tree-lined sidewalks — blinding white in the midday sun — were empty, even though there were countless little shops and restaurants.

"It's kind of creepy, right?" Alexa asked, observing the same phenomenon. "Where *is* everyone, besides on the beach?"

"In their cars," Holly realized out loud, watching

as a fleet of Maseratis passed by, their trunks half open to accommodate bulging bags from boutiques. "People drive everywhere, shop, and drive back home." That notion didn't seem terrible to Holly right then; she was achy from her swim, and wasn't wild about the idea of doing too much walking.

Alexa, meanwhile, was ruminating on how much she loved to walk and window-shop — that was one of her favorite things about New York City. Once, last summer, she'd put on her leopard-print Miu Miu flats and walked all the way from Bloomingdale's uptown to Bloomingdale's SoHo, buying long necklaces, footless tights, and spiky heels as she went and breaking only to eat a hot dog. Alexa smiled at the memory, but her brief moment of New York nostalgia faded the instant she and Holly turned onto Rodeo Drive. At last.

"Lacoste!" Alexa exclaimed as she steered the Hybrid slowly between miles of slender palm trees. "Stuart Weitzman! Valentino!" She felt as if she were saying hello to old friends; it was rapturous to see them all in one concentrated place.

"You realize you sound like a lunatic," Holly teased, but when Wilshire Boulevard came into view, she gasped in recognition at the elegant, old-fashioned façade of the Regent Beverly Wilshire. "Isn't that —" she began.

"Yup." Alexa beamed up at the ornate VIA RODEO sign on the corner. In her big Oliver Peoples sunglasses, gauchos, and an aqua Michael Stars tank, she felt more than ever like a fashionable character in a movie. "The hotel from *Pretty Woman*. Don't you feel like, in this moment, you *are* Julia?" she added in all seriousness, twirling her hand through the air with a flourish.

"Except, you know, for the hooker thing," Holly remarked wryly.

The girls opted for valet parking, which neither of them was too familiar with. But in LA, valet was everywhere, and Alexa enjoyed the glam sensation of accepting the white ticket from the attendant as she handed over her keys. To kick off their shopping extravaganza, the girls strolled along an elevated cobblestone road lined with small shops, their arms linked as they pointed out familiar brand names and snapped photos, blending in with the throngs of tourists.

Their first stop was Burberry — all shiny blond wood and high ceilings — but the store proved a little too Northeast country club for their tastes. It was Alexa's idea for them to tie on silk head scarves printed with the distinctive red-and-black tartan design, and loudly call each other names like "Biffy" and "Muffy." Laughing uncontrollably while Alexa pouted into the mirror near the sunglass display, Holly reflected on how being with her friend could make her feel like she was twelve again — in the best possible way. She was reaching for a pair of aviator shades when a balding salesman in a cream linen suit strode over to the girls, frowning.

"Ladies." His tone was just this side of sharp as he cast a scornful eye over, Holly feared, her sand-speckled hair. "I must inquire if you are intending to purchase anything. If not, I will have to ask you to leave."

Holly and Alexa glanced at each other in shock. Then, stifling their laughter, they darted out of there and into Dolce & Gabbana, where the salespeople consisted of funky, multiply-pierced men who gave them no trouble at all. Holly tried not to curse out loud at the price tags — she always forgot what shopping with Alexa could be like — but Alexa, always willing to splurge a little, bought a short, poufy satin skirt decorated with pink-and-silver swirls. Then it was on to Theodore — a holy site, as far as Alexa was concerned, because the store had been among the first to sell Seven jeans. There, Alexa tried on a plum-colored dress that she decided wasn't fun or flirty enough for Margaux's outdoor wedding. Holly, for kicks, decided to try on her first-ever pair of dark denim Sevens, and the pricey designer jeans fit so well that she didn't resist *too* much when Alexa convinced her to buy them. When the girls decided that they'd sufficiently "done" Rodeo, they made a point of proudly marching past the Burberry window, swinging their shiny shopping bags, *Pretty Woman*–style.

"I can't believe I bought those jeans," Holly groaned as she and Alexa waited in the afternoon heat for their car. "I'm supposed to be saving money for sheets and a Supercool Fridge for my dorm room."

"And we're just warming up," Alexa declared as the Hybrid pulled up. "With God as my witness," she added dramatically, lifting one hand and channeling Scarlett O'Hara, "I will not go back to Malibu today until I've found my dream dress."

"But if you had no luck on Rodeo," Holly reasoned as Alexa tipped the attendant, "where do you imagine you'll *find* this one perfect dress?"

"Kitson, of course," Alexa replied, and the adorable, super-trendy boutique on South Robertson was the next stop on the girls' treasure hunt. But all Alexa came out of there with was a beaded silver Isabella Fiore clutch. And Holly, who had planned to repeat her beige prom sandals for the wedding, found an on-sale pair of strappy black stilettos that were surprisingly comfortable. Still, Holly felt another huge wave of shopping guilt as she and Alexa, like true Los

Angelenos, deposited their bags in their trunk and headed toward Melrose Avenue — their third and final destination.

Fred Segal, its name written in quirky blue-and-red lettering across the ivy-covered entrance, was, to Holly's surprise, not one big store, but a maze of interconnected small boutiques. She and Alexa dawdled in the jewel-like little shoe shop, where Alexa purchased a pair of peep-toe, pencil-heeled silver Jimmy Choos, and then found their way to a cozy room with butter-colored walls and a disco ball spinning on the ceiling. There, they came upon a wealth of sublime, summery dresses: strapless lavenders, creamy-pink halters, sky-blue empire waists. . . .

"Jackpot," Alexa sighed, picking out a daringly short, spaghetti-strap Jill Stuart that was a vivid aquamarine color. It reminded her of the ocean outside their windows in Malibu. Holly was pawing through the racks — "just to *see* what's out there," she insisted — so Alexa took her choice over to the fitting rooms.

As she posed in front of the full-length mirrors, she admired how the dress made her eyes even bluer and showed off her long, starting-to-get-tan legs. With the right smoky eyeliner and her new metallic peep-toes . . . then Alexa frowned, studying her hair. As always, it rippled over her shoulders. But seeing herself anew in this dress, she wondered if the same hairstyle she'd had all her life made her look a little . . . young. *Alexa in Wonderland*. She was thoughtfully twisting her hair up off her neck when there was a tap on her door.

"It's me," Holly said, her voice unmistakably excited, with a tremor of hesitation. "I want to show you something."

Alexa opened her door to see Holly standing barefoot, her cheeks flushed, and wearing an exquisite, papaya-colored strapless dress with a delicately ruffled hem. The bright color made her golden-freckled skin luminous; it was impossible to tell that she'd done impromptu lifeguarding just that morning. And there was something else about Holly, too, Alexa mused, her eyes flicking over her friend's face. It was like Holly had left her slightly uptight East Coast self behind to become freer, more relaxed — as if the short time she'd spent in LA had already transformed her somehow.

"It's not really my style, right?" Holly asked nervously, smoothing down the lightly embroidered bodice that hugged her curves. "I mean, it's so girly, and it's not green . . . and I didn't even want to *get* a dress today."

"But you look incredible," Alexa told her friend truthfully, grinning at her.

Holly chewed on her bottom lip, fingering the

cool, rich fabric. She knew Alexa was telling the truth. The dress made her feel almost regal — queenly. Wearing it, she realized that in her prom dress, she'd always feel like the old Holly. This deep orange-pink Catherine Malandrino dress seemed to bring alive a new Holly — one who was adventurous enough to buy the dress in the first place. But besides the general "green" issue there was yet another one: moolah. It was bad enough that Holly had blown most of her graduation money on airplane tickets, jeans, and new shoes. The dress was almost more expensive than all of those put together. But at the same time she wanted it so much her heart twisted a little, a sensation she didn't recognize when it came to something as basic as clothes.

"Are you going to take it?" Alexa prodded, leaning against the doorjamb with her arms crossed over her chest. "Need I remind you that E! will be filming the wedding?"

Holly sucked in a deep breath. Maybe it was the high of that morning's rescue still racing through her veins, or maybe it was the chill, go-for-it vibe of Los Angeles, but suddenly Holly made up her mind. Even though she'd told surfer boy Zach that she hadn't needed any sort of thanks, there was a part of her that *did* want a reward for her heroics — a karmic reward, in any case. Why not treat herself for once?

"Okay," she told Alexa, her cheeks growing warm and her stomach jumping. *Am I crazy?* "I don't care. Who needs sheets in college anyway?" Holly barely recognized this new recklessness in her, but she also . . . liked it. A lot.

Alexa's face lit up and she clapped her hands together excitedly. "Smart decision, babe. And won't you just be sleeping on Tyler's sheets anyway?"

"Oh, yeah." Holly laughed, trying to cast off any lingering doubts. Then she surveyed Alexa; Holly had been so caught up in her own dress drama that she hadn't noticed how model-esque her friend looked. "Speaking of hot . . ." she said. "Jonah's going to *die* when he sees you in that."

Right — Jonah! Alexa shook her head. What with the Zuma Beach 911, and the subsequent shopping bliss, all thoughts of the actor had sort of . . . slipped her mind. *Get with it, Lex.* They had a *date* that night.

"So what are you going to wear on your date?" Holly asked Alexa half an hour later, after they'd paid for their dream dresses and were lunching on the out-door patio of Urth Caffé, a hippie-chic place on Melrose. Holly was doing a surprisingly good job of not thinking about how much her dress had cost — sliding that credit card through the machine had been at once painful and liberating.

Alexa's faux snakeskin Vita bangles knocked

together as she stabbed at her salad. "I have no idea," she admitted, her heart leaping as she imagined the night ahead. Now that Jonah was back in her thoughts, she was remembering every detail of their kisses from last night, the way his warm lips had tasted, the way his voice had sounded in a whisper. . . . Heat made her skin flush. "You'll have to help me decide when we get back to El Sueño," she added, taking a sip of Pom to cool herself off.

"Okay, but then I'm going for my run," Holly said, popping a slice of avocado into her mouth. She knew that a quiet, twilight jog along the beach would help soothe away her buyer's remorse. At the thought of running, Holly felt a flash of inspiration. "*Or* I could . . ." she trailed off, setting down her fork.

Alexa raised one eyebrow as Jesse Metcalfe and Justin Long walked by their table, their famous faces half-hidden behind shades. "Go out to the Chateau Marmont and pick up eligible celeb boys?" she offered Holly teasingly.

"Alexa, I have a boyfriend!" Holly rolled her eyes, indignant, and made a mental note to call Tyler back later that evening. "Besides, I want to hold out and go to the Chateau Marmont with you. No, I was thinking I should get in touch with Kenya Matthews. Remember her? She's just finishing her freshman year at UCLA, so we could meet up tonight."

"Kenya Matthews?" Alexa repeated, leaning back in her chair in surprise. "You mean superathlete, super-student girl? Are you sure you want to rely on *her* for a fun night out?"

Holly shrugged, poking at a carrot on her plate. Knowing dedicated, dependable Kenya, she *might* actually suggest that the two of them go for a run — but at least Holly would have company. "Hey," she said, flicking a piece of lettuce at Alexa with a grin. "*I'm* not the one who's supposed to have the wild time tonight. That would be *you*, my dear."

"It would, wouldn't it?" Alexa grinned. Considering Jonah's kisses last night, she got the spine-tingling feeling that they'd pick up right where they'd left off.

Alexa glanced at her watch; suddenly, the afternoon couldn't go fast enough. She couldn't wait to be with Jonah again, to listen to his stories of behind-the-scenes drama, to study the depths of his long-lashed blue eyes, and, most important, to enjoy some serious kissing in the backseat of his limo.

Romantic Comedy

As the white limo slid through the famous, stately gates of Paramount Pictures, Alexa leaned forward to peer out the window, her coral-and-silver earrings tinkling. The car was gliding by low-hanging palm trees and a building marked STUDIO 4, and Alexa wondered if this was how old-time stars like Marlene Dietrich and Rudolph Valentino felt, coming to work every day. Though Marlene wouldn't have been wearing a brand-new, swirly D&G skirt, flat copper-colored sandals that laced up her ankles, and a light-pink, crochet LaROK cami, as Alexa was now. Alexa grinned at the thought; thank God she lived in the twenty-first century.

It was six thirty on a Wednesday, but the studio was bustling. Power-suited agents strode by, barking into minuscule cell phones, harried-looking assistants were carrying trays of coffee, and Alexa observed a gaggle of girls dressed in black-and-white nuns' habits, all clearly on their way to shoot a scene. Outside a squat soundstage, a ruggedly hot actor from a TV medical drama stood chain-smoking, his arm around a blond guy who had to be his real-life boyfriend. It was amazing – but also kind of weird – to get a glimpse at what went on behind the screen. Alexa didn't really like to have magic ruined for her.

Not far from the water tower bearing the Paramount logo, the chauffeur stopped the limo in front of a sleek modern building. When Alexa noticed that Jonah was not there waiting for them, she asked the chauffeur if she could pop inside and get him herself. The driver nodded, and Alexa eagerly hopped out of the limo with butterflies in her belly. She felt very Hollywood-official as she passed through the brightly lit lobby, but was disappointed when no one stopped her, framed their hands around her face and gasped that she was *the one* they'd been looking for. Alexa knew Holly would mock her for being so self-absorbed, but didn't *everyone* come to Tinseltown with the same silly daydream?

The read-through for *The Princess and the Slacker* – Alexa tried not to snort when the security guard told her the ridiculous title – was in a conference room down the hall. When Alexa arrived, she hovered outside the door, hiding; she wanted to spy on the action a little before she caught Jonah's attention.

Breathtaking in a black Theory dress shirt, his thick dark hair kind of sticking up in an adorable way, Jonah sat at the center of the long table, surrounded by several B-list actors Alexa recognized from random films and TV shows. Across from Jonah sat a bearded guy in a baseball cap who Alexa guessed was the director, and immediately next to Jonah was — *shit* — Charity Durst, clad in a white wifebeater (no bra) and size zero Chip & Pepper jeans. In front of each actor there was one thick white script and a cup from The Coffee Bean. Jonah was reading aloud from his script, his voice strong and sensual.

"Brianne," he was saying. "You have to forgive me. I know you caught me in your bed with your cousin. Fine. But that was last week. I was stupid then."

Alexa clapped her hand to her mouth so nobody could hear her giggle. She sincerely hoped that Margaux's fiancé, Paul, was not the genius behind this screenplay.

The director cleared his throat. "Let's try to get more passion in there, Jonah," he suggested. "Remember, this is Roger's big redemption scene."

Jonah nodded, then tilted his head all the way back and slowly rubbed at his temples with his fingertips, keeping his eyes shut. The rest of the room watched him with silent reverence, and Alexa held her breath, curious. After a minute, Jonah straightened up, shook his head a few times, and looked back at the script.

"Brianne," he said, and this time his tone was full of pent-up hurt and emotion. "You have to forgive me. . . ." As Jonah repeated the previous lines, his voice shaking, Alexa could have sworn she saw tears glimmering in those blue-blue eyes. Her heart seized up with worry before she realized: *He's acting*. She felt at once foolish, and then awed by Jonah's talent.

The director nodded emphatically. "Better," he said, making a notation on his legal pad.

"Prove it to me," Charity Durst suddenly spoke in her whiny voice, glancing from the script to Jonah and back again. "Not with words this time, Roger. But with —"

"With what?" Jonah asked, his voice still tearful.

"With kisses," Charity breathed. She glanced up from the script, shaking out her dirty-blonde hair while Alexa balled her fists together in annoyance. "Should we try it now?" Charity asked the director with a sly smile.

"Might as well." The director shrugged. "Let's get a sense of your chemistry."

Alexa watched in horror as Charity leaned close to Jonah, turned his face to hers, and planted an aggressive, sloppy kiss on his mouth. Jonah didn't respond, exactly, but he didn't fight her off, either, which Alexa would have greatly preferred.

"Terrif," the director said approvingly. "It'll look really natural on camera."

"Well, with enough practice . . ." Charity purred and Jonah lowered his head, blushing.

Ugh. That did it. Alexa moved into the doorway and waved at Jonah, who immediately raised his eyebrows and beamed. No matter what Desperate Durst tried, Alexa knew Jonah preferred *her*. Without a doubt.

Jonah got to his feet and apologized to the cast and crew about an important appointment, and Alexa took supreme satisfaction in the glare Charity cast her way as Jonah jogged out of the room.

"Hey, sorry about that," he whispered, taking Alexa's elbow and steering her into the hallway, shutting the door behind them. He turned to pull Alexa close, giving her a tender smile; it was remarkable how he'd been near tears only seconds before. But Alexa knew that the side of Jonah she was seeing now *wasn't* an act. She felt her anger toward Charity evaporate, and she leaned in to kiss his neck. She'd forgotten how good he smelled — like orange groves, like California itself. She breathed him in, reminding herself of last night.

"You know it's all fake, right?" Jonah added, his

voice concerned as he led Alexa down the hall. "I'm totally in the moment when I'm doing it, but once I'm out of there . . ." He snapped his fingers to indicate his effortless switch.

"Of course," Alexa replied; if she was going to date an actor, she'd have to get used to seeing him kiss other girls. "Fake as everything else in Hollywood," she added teasingly, and, in that moment, realized that maybe she didn't *really* want to be discovered. Yes, Alexa was a natural drama princess, but there was something weird about the act of . . . acting. Alexa knew she got too wrapped up in her emotions to see-saw between them so quickly.

"Alexa," Jonah said softly. He smiled and reached out to run his thumb along her glossy bottom lip. "That's why I'm crazy about you," he murmured, and Alexa felt her pulse quicken at the words. "You're so easygoing. Chill. Not high maintenance at all."

"I'm not?" Alexa asked, taken aback. "I am? I — I mean, thanks," she stammered. In all her eighteen years, nobody had ever called Alexandria St. Laurent "easygoing." *Holly*, in her ponytail and Adidas track pants, wasn't a high-maintenance girl; but Alexa knew that what with her designer makeup, fashion addiction, and fits of temper, she practically defined the term. She was flattered that Jonah thought otherwise, and hoped he'd continue to remain oblivious.

"Yeah, I picked up on that when I met you at The Standard," Jonah went on as he waved good-night to the security guards in the lobby. "I was all, 'This girl isn't behaving any differently around me.' Usually people get —" He grinned and rubbed the back of his neck as they walked out of the building. "Well, a little jumpy when they first meet me . . ."

Alexa smiled to herself. She'd made an extra effort to play it cool last night, and it had clearly paid off.

"And then there was your long blonde hair," he added playfully, and Alexa stuck her tongue out at him as Jonah held the limo door open for her.

"Third Street and Crescent Heights," Jonah told the limo driver as he slid inside. "I was thinking we could go to this really hot tapas place called A.O.C.," he explained to Alexa, who brimmed with joy; she *adored* tapas. As the chauffeur began backing up, Jonah turned to Alexa, looking suddenly bereft. "Oh, man," he sighed, putting a hand to his forehead. "I totally forgot."

"What?" Alexa asked, mildly alarmed; did he need to return to the studio and finish making out with Charity?

"To tell you how gorgeous you look tonight," Jonah said, his expression ardent as he lifted Alexa's hand to his mouth and kissed it. Alexa knew Jonah's words and gesture were absolutely sincere, but, strangely enough, she almost felt the tiniest bit like . . . *laughing*. He was just so earnest.

But still irresistible.

Alexa wriggled in closer to Jonah, feeling the warmth of his shirt against her skin. Jonah smiled, lowered his head, and began kissing her lips, his fingers slipping through the tiny holes in her crocheted top. Alexa opened her mouth to his, sliding one leg on up over his lap as the limo careened along the twisty streets of Hollywood.

Here it was, the limousine hook-up Alexa had hoped for. Jonah's lips were hot and insistent, and Alexa felt the same *I'm-kissing-a-celebrity* thrill that she had last night. But for some reason, maybe because she'd seen Jonah kiss Charity only moments before, their closeness didn't make her heart race *quite* as much this time. But as she and Jonah fell back against the leather seats, their arms around each other, Alexa decided not to worry about it. At all.

Not far from Paramount, around six thirty, Holly's heart *was* racing. But for an entirely different reason.

Because even though Holly Jacobson was no longer a *virgin*-virgin, she certainly felt like a driving virgin, especially here in LA. Her first time behind the wheel of Jonah's Hybrid, her palms were sweating like mad as she turned onto Hollywood Boulevard, passing seedy souvenir shops, secondhand music stores, and a painted mural of James Dean and Natalie Wood. Reckless LA drivers — trust-fund kids, skyrocketing celebrities, agents and managers surgically glued to their BlackBerries — swerved around her as if their million-dollar cars were big, shiny toys.

Just pretend you're driving to the Oakridge Galleria, Holly told herself as a neon-bright Scientology sign flashed by her window.

Yup. Exactly like home sweet home.

Holly was on her way to see Kenya, who had squealed with delight when she'd heard from Holly that afternoon, and had uttered an eloquent "no shit" when Holly had confessed what had brought her to LA. Kenya had then suggested that the two of them meet up at Musso & Frank Grill, a classic Hollywood restaurant. Which was all very well and good, if Holly could find the restaurant *and* make her way through the insane traffic alive. It was a challenge not unlike jumping hurdles at a track meet, Holly thought as she took a deep breath and braked slowly at the intersection of Hollywood and Highland.

She was wondering if she should pull over and call Tyler for emotional support, or Alexa for directional guidance, when she happened to glance out the window — and saw something that once again made her heart contract. Only this time, in a wonderful way.

There it was, smack-dab on one of the many rolling green hills that surrounded the city: the Hollywood sign. Holly felt herself choke up a little at the sight of those familiar raised white letters, standing out boldly against the gathering twilight. Finally, when she least expected it, she'd found what she'd been looking for. And, somehow, seeing that iconic sign, realizing that yes, she was really here, in this legendary land of palm trees and fantasy, eased Holly's fears. Newly empowered, she turned the car around. After all, she'd single-handedly saved a surfer from the depths of the Pacific that morning; she could sure as hell find parking on Hollywood Boulevard. Which she did, a few seconds later.

Musso & Frank Grill looked like a 1920s speakeasy, all maroon leather banquettes and framed black-and-white photos of movie legends. As Holly walked in, still glowing from her Hollywood sign moment, she half expected flappers in feather boas to Charleston past her with long cigarette holders, or a dapper Cary Grant to stop and ask her to accompany him to a lavish premiere. Instead — even better — she spotted Kenya Matthews at the bar.

"Jacobson!" Kenya cried as soon as she noticed

Holly. All smiles, she bounded over, her neat rows of dark brown braids swaying from side to side. "God, how long has it been?"

"Too long," Holly replied as she returned Kenya's embrace. Around this time last year, Holly had hugged Kenya good-bye at *her* graduation from Oakridge High; all the track girls had shown up in support of their tough-but-sweet captain. Holly well remembered Kenya's commands of "Give it your all, Jacobson!" when Holly had been a mere freshman and was taking her first baby steps on the track. Kenya had also been the one who'd promoted Holly to cocaptain in Holly's junior year, and Holly still credited a lot of her success as a runner to her.

"Let me see, let me see," Kenya was saying, holding Holly at an arm's length like a proud mom, her gray eyes sparkling. "Whoa. There's something *different* about you, girl. I mean, besides the fact that you're now best friends with Jonah Eklundstrom."

Holly laughed and fiddled with the shell belt she'd looped through her new Sevens, which she'd paired with a close-fitting, scoop-neck charcoal tee, dangly gold leaf earrings, and Alexa's gold mules. It wasn't a very Holly outfit — Kenya had probably expected her to show up in track pants. The thought of clothes reminded Holly of her fancy-dress splurge, and she felt a stab of guilt, which she tried to brush aside. If she *was* a changed Holly, then she shouldn't let that one irresponsible purchase nag at her.

"Well, um, I grew my hair out a little," Holly finally said, reaching over to tug affectionately on one of Kenya's braids. "You've changed, too, Matthews." Back in high school, Holly had always seen Kenya either in the library with her tortoiseshell glasses on, highlighting something in a textbook, or running up the track in old sweats, timing herself with a wristwatch. Now, clad in an adorable sky-blue tube dress that nicely set off both her cocoa-colored skin and trim, curvy figure, Kenya exuded playfulness and sass.

"It's this city," Kenya said with a confident grin, leading Holly over to two burgundy bar stools. "It changes everyone. Anyway," she said, clapping her hands as the girls sat down. "Before you tell me all about Jonah, fill me in on stuff back home. How are Meghan and Jess? Is Coach Graham still insane? Are you and Tyler still together? Are you actually friends with Alexa St. Laurent again? And where did you decide to go to college?" She let out a big breath and pretended to wipe her brow.

Holly laughed; Kenya's warm sense of humor had always bubbled beneath the surface in high school, but she'd been too busy being team captain to let it burst out. "Okay, here goes," Holly answered, sitting up straight. "Great, not as bad as before, most definitely, I am indeed, and Rutgers." Holly, too, paused for a breath; she knew Kenya would want more details, especially involving track team gossip, but Holly couldn't help feeling like her life back home was a little bland compared to Kenya's here. "Did I cover everything?" she asked, resting her arms on the polished wooden bar.

"Not even close," Kenya said, then turned to the portly, white-haired bartender. "Two cosmopolitans, please," she requested.

"*Kenya!*" Holly exclaimed, shocked. She would bet anything that, in high school, Kenya hadn't even known what a Cosmo *was* (and neither had Holly, until she'd reconnected with Alexa).

"Holly, relax." Kenya squeezed her arm. "They're virgin," she explained with a smile as the bartender chuckled, busying himself with the glasses.

"Virgin?" Holly echoed, feeling momentarily self-conscious. Then she chided herself; she knew Kenya was simply referring to a nonalcoholic drink. For a second, Holly wondered if Kenya was a virgin — she'd been too reserved to date much in high school, but maybe she'd found a boy worthy of her in California. With a twinge of anticipation, Holly realized that boys were a topic she and Kenya could discuss later.

"Naturally," Kenya was saying, crossing her toned

runner's legs and dangling one glittery flip-flop off her toe. "I have to drive back to campus later, and I was planning on getting up early tomorrow to run. Plus, that bartender knows me — my American Culture professor brought our class here last week."

"Your *professor* brought you to a *bar?*" Holly asked, feeling like a giant prude. God. California *was* laid-back.

"Well, obviously we didn't drink or anything," Kenya laughed. "But yeah, we were talking about the myth of the American West in class that day, and she wanted to show us a slice of Hollywood history. This is the oldest restaurant in town," Kenya explained, gesturing to the maroon booths behind them.

"That *is* pretty cool," Holly admitted, thinking of all the huge-name stars who had frequented the same bar she now sat at. "Do you ever see modern-day celebrities here?" she added, glancing over her shoulder as if Margaux or Jonah or one of their pals might be strolling in.

Kenya shrugged. "The whole celeb-spotting game isn't really my scene. Sometimes my friends will drag me to places like the Hyde Lounge, or the Polo Lounge at the Beverly Hills Hotel — which *can* be fun," Kenya said thoughtfully. "But I feel like those dyed-blonde, toothpick girls, and those chiseled, empty-headed boys all kind of look the same, you know? No offense to your buddy Jonah," she added with a wicked grin.

"I'm not really *friends* with Jonah, you know," Holly protested, smiling. "Alexa's the one who's going out with him." Holly wondered what her friend was doing on her date — something ridiculously romantic, she was sure.

"Alexa St. Laurent." Kenya tipped her head to one side as the bartender returned with their chilled cosmos. "She *was* always the type to have a Hollywood lover."

Holly laughed in agreement and reached for her glass. "So what *is* your scene, if not this?" She couldn't imagine that all of LA revolved around old Hollywood glamour and star-stalkers; there had to be more indie options for broke-but-trendy college kids.

"There are these cute, funky little cafés in Westwood, near campus," Kenya explained, lifting her glass. "And the neighborhoods Silver Lake and Los Feliz have the coolest nightlife, in my opinion. But *tonight* I wanted to take you to all the touristy spots. Cheers," she added, touching her glass to Holly's.

"Wait, *spots*?" Holly asked as she sipped at the tangy drink. "What else did you have in mind besides this?"

"Can't tell you," Kenya said with a wink, taking a sip of her drink as well. "Sorry."

"I'm sorry," the icy blonde hostess of the white-walled, super-chic restaurant A.O.C. drawled at Alexa. Wearing a tight black bustier and leather pants, the hostess spoke in a Valley Girl accent so stereotypical Alexa wondered if she was secretly auditioning for a role at that very moment. "Do you have a reservation?" she added snidely, motioning behind her to the bustling, candlelit bar area, above which several glistening bottles of wine were displayed. *Are you somebody important?* was the unspoken question in her narrow gray eyes.

"I'm sure we do. . . ." Alexa said, glancing over her shoulder to check with Jonah. But his back was turned; Mr. Polite Movie Star was holding the door open for another couple, and gamely agreeing to sign autographs for their twelve-year-old daughter back home.

Valley Girl raised one pierced eyebrow and looked Alexa up and down. "Well, what name is it under, sweetheart? In case you haven't noticed, we're a little busy tonight, and I can't exactly seat you in Mr. Spielberg's lap."

Before Alexa could explode — she didn't deal well with fake blondes, ever — Jonah finally turned around, placing his hand on Alexa's lower back. "Is there a problem?" he asked, as he glanced between Alexa and the hostess. "Oh man, I probably should have had Esperanza call ahead. I don't suppose you could find a table for us?"

Alexa felt a surge of triumph as she watched the hostess's jaw flap open.

"Mr. Eklundstrom — forgive me —" the hostess stammered as her face went scarlet. "Of course we have a table for you." She snapped her fingers at a pink-haired waiter, who shepherded Alexa and Jonah beneath swaying bamboo lamps, through the fashionable crowd, to an intimate table by the window. Alexa laughed lightly, linking her arm through Jonah's. The power!

If that didn't make her heart race, nothing could.

Practically bowing, the waiter seated them and placed bread sticks and a little pot of olive tapenade — Alexa's favorite condiment — on their table. "Shall I get you started with a bottle of wine?" he asked.

Alexa had grown up sipping French wine at dinner with her dad, but still felt unbelievably adult ordering it in restaurants. "Well," she said, glancing at the wine menu. "We could try the Pinot —" Suddenly, her stomach sinking, she remembered last night's wheatgrass incident, and she looked up worriedly at Jonah.

But he was already smiling and nodding at her.

"Please get a glass, Alexa," he insisted. "I'll have a mineral water," he told the waiter, and Alexa sighed, feeling slightly guilty regardless.

When Jonah excused himself to go wash his hands, Alexa glanced around, letting herself revel in her fancy-restaurant euphoria. A.O.C. was all shimmery, elegant, and Mediterranean: the exact kind of place in which Alexa loved to eat. And she could barely keep count of the familiar faces — including, yes, Steven Spielberg's — she spied at all the low-lit tables. As Alexa opened the menu and scanned the yummy options — small plates of cheese, artfully prepared salmon, gourmet Italian salami — she couldn't help thinking that it would have been fun to come here with Holly. The whole point of tapas was sharing them, and since Jonah was vegan, he wouldn't be able to indulge in all the foods Alexa was craving.

"Jonah, this place is to die for, but why did you pick it?" Alexa asked with genuine curiosity after Jonah had returned and was seated across from her again. "You can't eat — "

"I know." Jonah leaned forward, his expression serious. "But I chose A.O.C. on purpose. I wanted *you* to have an amazing LA night."

"Oh." Alexa felt herself melt. She reached out to caress Jonah's hand, and his bright blue eyes held only promise and commitment. Emotion welled up in

Alexa; all her life she'd waited for a boy as savagely beautiful as Jonah, who would also be as kind and caring — someone who'd manage to pull off the lost art of being a cute non-asshole. Suddenly Alexa remembered the dream she'd had on the way from Vegas, about a boy who'd filled her with warmth. Maybe, unlikely as it seemed, she'd found that boy here, in Hollywood, in Jonah Eklundstrom. "Thank you," she told him, her voice husky.

"The chef knows me anyway — he'll prepare me some vegan plates," Jonah said, flashing her a smile. "And, I can eat at any of my usual places whenever. You're only here for a short time." A sadness flickered in his eyes, and Alexa knew he was thinking, as she was, of their inevitable good-bye kiss after the wedding. Alexa felt the familiar pang of regret she always got when falling for boys on whirlwind trips.

"Hey, I meant to tell you," Jonah exclaimed, his face lighting up. "I'm shooting some scenes for *The Princess and the Slacker* in New York later this summer — I'd love to see you. . . ." He trailed off, his expression hopeful.

"That would be great!" Alexa replied. And she *did* feel excited, but for some reason her own words sounded a little wooden to her ears.

After the waiter had taken their orders, a silence fell over the table. Not an uncomfortable silence, but a lingering sort of quiet. Tracing a circle on her soup spoon with one finger, Alexa eavesdropped on the couple at the next table: "You're not understanding my *vision* — it's Kurosawa meets Woody Allen," the goateed guy was arguing in an impassioned voice while his model-pretty girlfriend sighed and checked her artificially plump lips in her hand mirror. Alexa felt a wave of annoyance; was *everyone* in LA somehow involved in the movie business? It seemed that was the only thing to talk about here.

"What's *The Princess and the Slacker* about?" she asked Jonah, glancing back at him. "I only heard that little piece of it. . . ."

Jonah sat up straighter. "It's a pretty incredible idea," he told Alexa, his eyes full of intensity. "And it's really been challenging my craft. I'd call it a classic romantic comedy about this guy, Roger, a stoner who's been kicked out of college. He ends up moving in with Brianne, this sophisticated magazine editor, and of course they hate each other at first."

"Of course." Alexa smiled as the waiter set her full wineglass down on the table.

"But then," Jonah said, leaning toward her with growing urgency. "They both eat some pot brownies that make them switch bodies, and you know . . . hysterities ensue."

Alexa took a big gulp of wine, swallowing down

her laughter. She didn't have the heart to tell Jonah that the expression was *hilarities* ensue, and that *The Princess and the Slacker* sounded like the worst idea in the history of film.

"My agent, Oren Samuels — you know him?" Jonah asked, cocking an eyebrow at Alexa, who shook her head. Agents weren't really covered in *Us Weekly*. "Anyway, he's the best in the business. He's the one who found this script and told me I should do it. That way, I'll have something a little lighthearted under my belt after, you know, the big award."

"Well, this movie certainly fits the bill," Alexa replied, patting her lips with a napkin, and hoping her tone wasn't as sarcastic as it sounded to her. What she really wanted to talk about with Jonah was the experience of winning an Oscar — she secretly suspected that the actors knew they were going to win, and just played up all the hyperventilating and back-flips and whatever. But Jonah seemed focused on *The Princess and the Slacker*.

"The thing is, it's *not* lighthearted," he was saying, gesturing with his elegant hands. "It's really about the growth of this guy, and I connected to the character's motivation the second I picked up the script. Even though he and I are totally different, in some ways *all* people are the same, you know? It's like this role has helped me to discover that, and it's kind of made me a more complete human being." Jonah paused to take a drink of his mineral water, and then his eyes crinkled up at the sides when he smiled at Alexa. "Does that sound crazy?"

"No way," Alexa lied, taking a deep breath. She wanted to say more, but Jonah's devotion to his craft was so hilarious (*hysterious?*) that she knew she'd burst into giggles if she tried. She struggled to relate to what Jonah had said, and wondered if she could tell him how photography made *her* feel complete in a similar way. But as she gazed into Jonah's big, earnest eyes, she suddenly knew — with the sharpest clarity — that he wouldn't really understand. All at once, Alexa felt that there was a chasm between her and Jonah, and she wasn't sure she knew how to bridge it.

As the waiter set their plates on the table, Alexa studied Jonah, marveling at how different he was from his sharp, witty sister. Remembering Margaux, Alexa felt a flush of relief as she hit upon the one topic she and Jonah could find common ground on.

"The wedding!" she exclaimed, reaching for her cheese plate with a grin. "Let's talk about the wedding."

Jonah chuckled. "You're so wacky," he told her affectionately, reaching out to stroke her cheek. Once again, *wacky* — like *easygoing* — was something Alexa was not accustomed to being called. *Wacky* girls collected cats and knitted baby booties and wore leg warmers over their jeans without trying to be trendy. Alexa decided not to mention her opinion on that matter.

"Are you all set for Margaux's big day?" she asked instead. "What are you wearing?"

But as Jonah began to describe the charcoal-gray suits and ties that had been designed for all the groomsmen by Oscar de la Renta himself, Alexa found her thoughts drifting. She gazed beyond Jonah's beautiful face at the darkening LA street outside the window. What was her *deal*? She was with the most desired guy in all of Hollywood, the guy who'd gone out of his way to make her happy tonight. Yet here she was, spacing out. She'd definitely have to analyze the weirdness with Holly later tonight.

Holly. Alexa cupped her chin in her hand. Even though she knew Holly was potentially doing something dull with Kenya, Alexa couldn't stop the bizarre thought that popped into her head: *I wonder if she's having a better time than I am.*

"Look — Tom Cruise!" Holly cried, pointing.

"Judy Garland's over here!" Kenya exclaimed.

"Who's Carole Lombard?" Holly asked. "She's right below me."

"Beats me," Kenya yelled back from down the

boulevard. "But I'm dancing on Ginger Rogers and Fred Astaire!"

Laughing, Holly glanced up to see Kenya twirling on the sidewalk. Over a big dinner at Musso & Frank, the girls had caught each other up, Holly filling Kenya in on the past year — "You ran away from a track meet to go to Paris?" Kenya had gasped while Holly shushed her — and Kenya opening up about her UCLA crushes, while admitting to not having found a serious boyfriend yet. "There are just too many options," Kenya had explained with a mock dramatic sigh. "I don't know if it's something in the water, but the boys in this city are damn nice-looking." Holly had nodded, remembering the sexy celebrities at The Standard and the cute surfers on the beach.

Now, with the sun setting behind them, the girls were strolling (and dancing) along the stretch of Hollywood Boulevard known as the Walk of Fame, where the sidewalk was covered in five-pointed stars, each imprinted with a different famous name in bronze.

"So is *this* the surprise destination you promised?" Holly called to Kenya, her mules planted firmly on Carole Lombard's star.

"No way," Kenya replied, crossing over several more stars to get to Holly. "We have yet to achieve tourist heaven. Allow me." Linking her arm through

Holly's, Kenya led her along Hollywood Boulevard, passing the sprawling Kodak Theatre — "Home of the Oscars," Kenya pointed out and Holly snapped a picture with her cell phone — before reaching a grand old movie palace designed to look like a red-and-gold Chinese pagoda. In front of the theater, celebrities' foot- and handprints were preserved in sand-colored cement. "Grauman's Chinese Theatre," Kenya pronounced. "I came here on my first day of freshman orientation at UCLA, and realized 'Okay, yeah. I'm in Hollywood.'"

Thinking of her similar epiphany when seeing the Hollywood sign, Holly smiled and joined the other tourists who were vainly trying to cram their Nike sneakers into movie stars' delicate footprints. With Kenya at her side, Holly glanced down and studied the inscription between Marilyn Monroe's and Jane Russell's prints: GENTLEMEN PREFER BLONDES!

"Bullshit," Kenya declared. "Everyone knows brunettes have more fun."

Holly glanced gratefully at Kenya. Tyler, Meghan, and Jess were all stay-in-and-watch-*Grey's-Anatomy*-on-iTunes-types, so back home Holly had always relied on Alexa for nighttime escapades. But now, it was kind of refreshing and, well, *fun* to be out on the town with someone other than Alexa, someone who was older and different and no longer lived in Oakridge.

"I'm so glad we got to meet up tonight," she told Kenya truthfully.

"Same," Kenya replied, bumping Holly with her hip. "You know, if Alexa is, like, having breakfast in bed with Jonah tomorrow morning, feel free to come meet me on campus if you want. I don't have class until the afternoon."

"I'd love to," Holly replied, nodding enthusiastically. "I don't know *anyone* in LA, so – " She was interrupted by her cell phone ringing in her clutch. Holly figured it had to be Tyler; she'd left him a rambling message about her ocean rescue before heading out to meet Kenya. But when she pulled out her cell phone, it wasn't Tyler's name flashing on the screen at all.

"Belle Runningwater?" Holly read aloud, and Kenya's mouth fell open. "I met her at a party last night," Holly explained hurriedly. She hadn't thought the super-busy actress would actually call, and she felt excitement course through her.

"I watch *Wild Land* every week!" Kenya whispered, grinning, as Holly flipped open the phone. Clearly, Kenya made exceptions to her no-fawning-over-celebrities rule.

"Holly?" Belle screamed into Holly's ear; reggae music was blaring in the background, along with high-pitched laughter and someone shouting, *"Call my agent to discuss that!"* Holly strained to hear what Belle was saying. "I'm — at — the Cabana — Club — with friends!" Belle managed to yell into the phone. "Come — meet me!"

"Where is it?" Holly yelled back as Kenya raised her eyebrows.

"On Ivar — off Sunset — right behind — Amoeba Music!" Belle replied. "DJ — amazing — oh, God — just saw Lindsay — Lohan — she hates me — gotta — run — " And then Belle was gone.

"Are you familiar with the Cabana Club?" Holly asked Kenya as she snapped her phone shut. Belle's garbled directions hadn't made much sense to her.

Kenya stared back at Holly, her expression incredulous. "I thought you didn't know anyone in LA."

Minutes later, Holly was back in the Hybrid, following Kenya's car down Sunset Boulevard. By now it was deep nighttime, and the windswept strip was alive and glittering; Holly was transfixed by the bright, blinking lights of the House of Blues and Whisky a Go Go, and yes, the glowing red sign pointing to the castlelike turrets of the Chateau Marmont. Three girls in teeny sherbet-colored dresses and skinny heels, followed by a lanky guy who looked suspiciously like Topher Grace, crossed the boulevard to get to a club, and a bouncer unclipped a velvet rope for them. Holly rolled down her windows and breathed in the scent of evening jasmine, and she felt a sudden, overwhelming rush of possibility. It felt, she thought, almost a little bit like falling in love.

After Holly and Kenya had turned their cars over to the Cabana Club valets, they walked across the outdoor patio. There was a reflecting pool, lit-up palm trees, a giant waterfall, and huge beach balls that bounced around among the sleek guys and girls. Holly decided that the atmosphere felt more casual, beachy, and less celebrity-obsessed than The Standard had last night, and she felt herself relaxing. She was even surefooted enough to tell the bouncer that she and Kenya were here to see Belle Runningwater, and her manner must have seemed assured, because he nodded and let them pass.

"Okay, I'm your biggest fan," Kenya said as she and Holly made their way through the gold-and-brown interior. "You handled that better than an LA *native*."

"I don't know how," Holly admitted as she scanned the dancing crowd for Belle's long black hair. "I'm usually such a baby about that stuff." *But am I?* Holly wondered. Maybe she didn't give herself enough credit for how much she'd grown over the past year — or even the past day.

She and Kenya came upon Belle on one of the elevated dance floors, shaking her slim hips to Matisyahu. Belle immediately enveloped Holly in a hug, greeted Kenya warmly, and introduced them to her group of friends, none of whom Holly recognized from television. In fact, the girls, in stovepipe jeans, leggings under skirts, and long, beaded necklaces, seemed fairly . . . normal. Holly realized she'd hit it off with Belle last night because she *wasn't* the kind of girl who necessarily befriended other celebrities.

"I'm going to text some of my friends and tell them to meet us here!" Kenya called to Holly over the music, then hurried off the dance floor toward one of the mocha-brown booths. As Holly felt Belle tug on her wrist to draw her into the dancing circle, she was flooded with a startling sense of . . . belonging. The sensation was unfamiliar; Holly hadn't exactly been an outcast in high school, but she'd never felt as if people had clamored for her attention, either. Yet here, in social-climbing LA, the most un–Holly Jacobson place on earth, she felt as if she'd managed to find a group of people who were on her wavelength. She felt like she was exactly where she wanted to be.

Before Holly could dwell on that surprising thought, her cell vibrated in her clutch. Taking a pause from dancing, she removed it and smiled when she saw that it was Tyler.

"Are you at a concert?" Tyler shouted in her ear when Holly picked up. Over the din, she could make out that he sounded a little annoyed. "I can't hear you!"

"I'm at a club near the Sunset Strip!" Holly cried in response, taking a few steps back from the flailing, sweaty crowd.

"Tell — amazing — surfing — story —"

Holly could only make out Tyler's every other word. "Let me call you back," she said, snapping her phone shut. She told Belle she'd be back, then turned and elbowed her way out onto the patio. Holly fanned her flushed face with one hand and leaned against a palm tree, not far from a group of hyper girls in belly-bearing Juicy sweats who were flirting with sloppy-looking guys in sideways trucker hats ("*so* 2004," Alexa would sneer if she were there). "I'm pitching my script to Wes Anderson," one of the boys was crowing, while one of the girls was boasting about a callback she'd gotten for an under-five on *Veronica Mars*.

Holly smiled at all the LA-speak; she actually found it more funny than irritating. She was opening her phone to redial Tyler, when the cell buzzed in her hand. Distracted by her entertaining neighbors, and the blur of color and light, Holly answered without checking the screen.

"Tyler? Honey?" she asked.

"Uh, no."

It was a boy's voice — deep and slightly raspy. Holly froze, her automatic reaction whenever a guy she didn't know called her. She let her hair fall back to her shoulders. "Who is this?" she asked, feeling a tremor of recognition.

"It's Seamus," the boy replied. "Seamus Kerr? I know that what happens in Vegas, stays in Vegas, but I was kind of hoping I wouldn't fall into that category. . . ."

"Seamus!" Holly cried, pleasantly surprised. But why was he calling? "Oh, my God — I owe you an iced coffee, don't I?" she gasped, upset that she'd forgotten. Holly was excellent about paying people back; Alexa, meanwhile, owed her, like, five hundred dollars after eleven years of gas money, chewing gum, and ice-cream bars that had never been reimbursed.

"No, no, don't stress about that," Seamus said, laughing his warm laugh. Suddenly Holly heard the beep of her call waiting, and knew it was Tyler. But she wanted to hear what Seamus had to say first. "I was calling for another reason," Seamus added. "To see if you'd be around tomorrow afternoon . . ."

"What are you doing tomorrow afternoon?" Jonah whispered to Alexa, twining his fingers through hers as they meandered up the flagstone path of El Sueño.

Night had fallen, and the estate was shrouded in darkness, but tiki lamps on the main house's deck illuminated the way. The fragrant smell of bougainvillea was even stronger in the darkness, and crickets hummed overhead. All this, combined with the delicious glass of wine she'd had with dinner, had lifted Alexa's spirits considerably. Her moment of boredom at A.O.C. was in the past. Now she felt tingly and flushed, and much warmer toward Jonah.

Or, rather, hotter.

"Because," Jonah added when Alexa didn't answer right away. "I get off early from rehearsal so I thought maybe —"

"Shhh," Alexa whispered, wheeling around, and putting her hands on Jonah's shoulders. She rose up on her toes and kissed him.

Jonah didn't argue; he pulled Alexa tight against him, running his hands up and down her back, his breath quick and his tongue teasing hers. In that moment, Alexa understood how fully and completely she *had* this boy. Jonah may have been the one who could get them a table in a restaurant, but *Alexa* was the one with the power now. It was a familiar sensation to Alexa — the moment when a guy completely gave in to her. Boys were *simple*, she'd realized at a young age, even boys like Jonah, who could have any girl they wanted.

"Hot," Jonah was murmuring into Alexa's mouth,

drawing back a little. "Hot tub." He cleared his throat. "I have a hot tub on my sundeck," he managed. "Meet me back out there?"

Breathless, Alexa turned toward the guesthouse to change, when Jonah called after her.

"Hey," he said, lifting one arm. "Do you want some herb?"

"Um," Alexa replied, surprised. *Jonah smokes pot? What the hell?* "I thought you didn't like, uh, toxins," she finally said. Despite all her daring when it came to boys and breaking rules, Alexa had never tried pot, and didn't have much interest in doing so.

Jonah shrugged and gave her a winning smile. "It's organic."

As Jonah went to go change — and possibly roll himself an organic friend — Alexa flew into the guesthouse. Weirdly, Holly wasn't home yet, and Alexa wondered what her friend was up to with Kenya.

After she'd slipped on the Shoshanna bikini that Jonah hadn't had a chance to see last night, Alexa hurried outside, her dark brown Havaiana flip-flops thwacking the ground, and made her way around the sundeck of the main house to find Jonah. He wasn't smoking up, only waiting, shirtless, in a sunken hot tub. The water was bubbling around him, and his broad shoulders and chest glowed in the moonlight as he rested his arms on the tub's sides.

Hooray for Hollywood.

Smiling, Alexa dipped one toe into the scalding water and slowly eased herself in until she was chin-deep. *Ahh.* The jets pulsed against her skin, the water almost too hot to stand. Above them, big, hazy stars sparkled, and the roar of the ocean below them was hypnotic.

"I want to photograph this," Alexa murmured, glancing down the mountain to see the Pacific, black and foamy. Her fingers tingled for her camera, back in the guesthouse.

"What for?" Jonah asked, reaching over to pull her close. "A million other houses have this same view." His wet chest pressed against hers as he held her waist underwater. "Now *this* is a view," he added, rubbing his thumb along Alexa's cheek.

Alexa, her skin flushed from the water and Jonah's nearness, closed her eyes and lifted her mouth to his. There was something about kissing a boy in a hot tub that made any other kind of kissing seem almost unsexy. Jonah's hands moved down to her hips, and Alexa slid her arms around his shoulders. Within seconds, they were kissing deeply, their hands growing bold, their legs entwining underwater, their breaths mingling. . . .

And the whole time, Alexa was remembering.

Hysterities. My plot in life. You're so wacky.

The words wouldn't leave her head. The more she and Jonah kissed and touched, the more Alexa remembered.

Challenging my craft. It's organic. You know it's all fake, right?

As Jonah backed her up against the side of the hot tub, kissing her neck, Alexa remembered how her heart *hadn't* palpitated in the limo, how she'd realized Jonah wouldn't understand her photography, and how he made her want to laugh — but for all the wrong reasons.

And, in the middle of Malibu, with her lips against a movie star's, living out every sane girl's dream, Alexa St. Laurent came to a simple realization:

She wasn't that into Jonah Eklundstrom.

The thought was so startling that Alexa literally gasped and pulled away. She swept her eyes over Jonah's confused face, wondering if she was going insane. But no. The realization held. This wasn't right for her. *He* wasn't right for her. Jonah raised his brows at Alexa, his hands still lingering on her hips, his fingers tickling the skin beneath the waistband of her bikini. Alexa knew that this was the classic cliff-hanger moment between guy and girl, when things could either go in the direction of lights, camera, action . . . or not.

"Cut," Alexa whispered, and Jonah's eyes grew round; that language, he understood.

"Do you not want to — you know — out here?" he asked. "We can go inside. . . ."

Alexa shook her head, taking Jonah's hands and guiding them off her hips. She didn't want to "you know" out here, *or* in the house. She didn't want to with Jonah. Period. Yes, he was dizzyingly hot, hotter than the water that burned up her skin. Yes, he'd been nothing but attentive and kind — which, of course, only made him sexier. But for maybe the first time *ever*, Alexa understood that true passion *couldn't* be faked or acted. She couldn't make herself fall in love with Jonah, even if she wanted to.

Alexa put her hand against her chest to feel the rhythmic thumping of her heart. She wished it would listen to her sometimes, but it always seemed to have a mind of its own.

"Is everything okay?" Jonah asked, sounding anxious. Alexa realized she'd been motionless, her hand pressed to her heart. "Am I moving too fast?"

Alexa almost wished Jonah would stop being so sweet; it was going to make what she had to do that much harder. She shook her head and backed up a few paces in the water. "No, you're fine," she told him. "You didn't do anything wrong."

Jonah's brow creased. "But you're not acting like yourself," he observed.

"Maybe I am," Alexa murmured. "Maybe that's been the problem all along." Jonah *didn't* know her, Alexa realized. Anyone who thought she was easygoing didn't know her in the slightest. Margaux had predicted that Alexa and her brother would get along — and they had. But Alexa didn't want a boy she got along with. She wanted someone who would understand her so well that he'd challenge her between every kiss.

"What are you doing? I don't understand," Jonah sputtered, shaking his head in frustration.

Holding his gaze, Alexa reached out to run her damp hand along the side of his face, knowing she owed him an explanation.. "Jonah, I'm so sorry," she said truthfully. "I know it's sudden, but . . . this isn't what I want right now."

Jonah frowned at Alexa. "It's about Charity, isn't it? The kissing scene today? I promise you it's all phony, Alexa." He caught her hand and held it against his stubbly cheek. "I know you must have doubts about me, about us, because I'm an actor, and I'm all famous and shit, but I —"

"Jonah, it's not that. Honestly." *I don't care that you're an actor — I'm just not* feeling *it with you*. Alexa wondered how, or if, she could phrase that sentiment tactfully. But it was true; although the thought of

Charity Durst still got under Alexa's skin, Alexa realized she wasn't — and had never been — that jealous of the actress.

Especially since Alexa knew she was about a thousand times cuter.

"I just can't," Alexa said. Hoping she wasn't making the biggest mistake of her life, she withdrew her hand from Jonah's face and turned to pull herself out of the hot tub. But Jonah's hand on her arm stopped her. His face, devastatingly handsome in the starlight, was etched with disappointment.

Alexa braced herself for his rebuttal; after all, Jonah was Hollywood royalty — he could do and say whatever he wanted. He could easily send her away from his estate or disinvite her to Margaux's wedding. If there was any moment for Jonah to shed his nice-guy image and flaunt his inner asshole, this was it. Alexa bit her lip, but to her surprise, Jonah's expression softened.

"Total, total respect, Alexa," he said, nodding at her. "You're your own person, you're on your own journey, and I'm just grateful that I got to . . ." Jonah paused, running a hand through his wet dark hair. "Spend a part of that journey *with* you."

As always, Alexa was a little unclear as to what Jonah was talking about but she decided a soft "Me, too" was a safe response.

The corner of Jonah's mouth lifted. "And maybe you'll change your mind before you leave LA. But that's entirely up to you."

Clearly, Jonah Eklundstrom didn't *have* an inner asshole.

Alexa gave him a grateful smile, and then got out of the hot tub, shivering as the cool ocean air hit her damp skin. "Thanks for understanding," she called softly, walking backward.

"I'll see you tomorrow," Jonah called back, but there was a question in his voice.

Alexa turned away from the hot tub and began to cross the soft grass, her flip-flops in her hand and the moon sailing the sky above her. Once again, she felt as if she were part of a scene in a movie. But, Alexa realized as something that felt suspiciously like relief rose up in her, the movie wasn't a drama. It was a romantic comedy. That was what she and Jonah had been trapped in — a bad romantic comedy, with clunky dialogue and not-great chemistry between the leads.

And, somehow, as she slipped back inside the guesthouse, shut the door, and took a deep, steadying breath, Alexa sensed that this wasn't the end of the film just yet. LA, in all its wildness and glamour, still waited out there, and so did Jonah.

Who knew what else might happen before the final credits rolled?

CHAPTER EIGHT
Grin and Bear It

"I can't believe you dumped Jonah Eklundstrom," Holly declared the next morning as she and Alexa sprawled across lounge chairs on the guesthouse sundeck, watching the ocean's turquoise surface glimmer through the ficus trees. Lingering jet lag had awoken both girls early, but they'd been too wiped out from their respective nights out to do more than pull on bikinis and collapse in the sunshine. Birds were twittering brightly and El Sueño's friendly gardener, Miguel, was humming as he trimmed the nearby hedges, clearly listening in on the girls' juicy conversation.

"I didn't *dump* him," Alexa argued as she adjusted her sunglasses on her face. "It's not like we were ever officially together."

She sighed and glanced across the estate's

sprawling grounds. According to Miguel, Jonah had left for Paramount at dawn, and Alexa was grateful that she didn't have to see him that morning. She was sure that the eternally laid-back Jonah wouldn't make things awkward between them, but Alexa herself felt a little uneasy about what she'd done. She knew she needed to hash out her decision with Holly before she could feel one hundred percent about it.

"Still, you blew him off," Holly argued, but she grinned as she said it. After her eventful night, she'd slept fitfully, imagining herself going bankrupt because of her new dress, and remembering the somewhat strained conversation she'd had with Tyler outside the Cabana Club ("Maybe you should just call me back when it works for you," Tyler had said, his voice distant). But Alexa's riveting Jonah story had taken Holly's mind off her fatigue. "Only you, Alexa St. Laurent. Only you would decide that a gorgeous, millionaire Oscar-winner isn't, you know, *good enough*."

"Oh, shut *up*." Alexa laughed in spite of herself, and swung her foot out to poke Holly's bare leg. "So sue me. I have high standards."

"That's why I love you," Holly replied, resting her head back on the chair and smiling fondly at Alexa. As surprised as Holly was, she was also secretly impressed; the Alexa she'd always known would never have turned down a guy like Jonah, no matter the circumstances.

What was it Kenya had said last night? *It's this city. It changes everyone.*

Remembering Kenya, Holly sat up straight, checking her watch. "Could I take the Hybrid this morning?" she asked Alexa. Driving home last night along the dark Pacific Coast Highway, listening to the ocean, and singing along to pop songs on KIIS FM, had been strangely freeing – and Holly was eager to get back on the road. Wait until she told Tyler that LA was turning her into a driver.

"Sure, but where are you rushing off to?" Alexa asked, straightening her Noir gold anchor necklace against her collarbone.

Holly swung her legs off her chair. "Well, I'm going to stop at Fred Segal and return my dress before I meet Kenya at UCLA, and *then* guess who called me –"

"Whoa, whoa," Alexa cut in, whipping off her sunglasses. "Why on earth are you –"

"Because I *have* to," Holly interrupted, her shoulders slumping. "I thought about it all of last night, Alexa. There's no way I'll be able to pay off that credit card bill and *still* manage to buy stuff for college." Holly was sorrowful at the thought of giving back the pink Catherine Malandrino, but she knew in her gut that it was the right, responsible thing to do. The *Holly* thing to do. "My prom dress is pretty cute, after all," she added defensively.

178

"Okay . . ." Alexa said slowly, tilting to her head to one side. "But that wasn't what I was about to ask. Why are you going to *UCLA* today?" Alexa couldn't believe it. Was Holly actually abandoning her in her hour of need? Alexa had been hoping to rehash her Jonah experience at least two more times, as was her and Holly's custom when discussing boy issues. And she was curious to hear all about Holly's seemingly exciting night with Kenya, which Holly hadn't time to get into because, well, Alexa had been talking nonstop since they'd gotten up.

"Oh, right." Holly bit her lip, feeling a pang of guilt. "I assumed you were gonna be, uh, *busy* this morning, so I told Kenya I'd meet her before she went to class."

Alexa scowled and flopped back against the chair, her loose golden bun bouncing. "No, I'm not busy this morning. And I'll probably never be *busy* again." Alexa thought of the fake nuns she'd seen on the Paramount lot yesterday; since she'd passed up her chance to hook up with the most beautiful guy on earth, Alexa figured she might as well join their ranks. *Get me to a nunnery.*

Alexa's pay-attention-to-me expression sent a flash of annoyance through Holly. She knew that Alexa wanted her to cancel her plans with Kenya, and tell Alexa that of course she'd get busy again, of course she hadn't ruined her love karma by ditching Jonah, and of course everything was going to work out for the best. But Holly didn't know if all that was even true. And maybe, for once, she didn't want to be the one to pull Alexa out from beneath the undertow of her own drama.

"We'll talk about this later, okay?" Holly said, feeling proud of herself as she leaned over to peck Alexa's cheek. Miguel continued to clip the hedges around the sundeck, filling the morning air with the pungent scent of fresh grass.

"When later?" Alexa asked petulantly, squeezing a dollop of sunscreen into her palm. "Aren't you and Kenya going to spend all day, like, stretching together or some crap?"

Holly got to her feet, shaking her head in annoyance. "No. If you'd ever let me get a word in edgewise, I was *going* to tell you about my conversation with Seamus last night."

"Who?" Alexa looked up from the sunscreen she'd begun massaging into her legs.

"Seamus — the guy who *drove* us here, remember?" Holly clarified, rolling her eyes, but she felt a pleasant tickle of warmth remembering her chat with Seamus outside the Cabana Club.

"Unfortunately, I do," Alexa replied. Did Holly think that news of Mr. Hipper-than-Thou was going to put Alexa in a better mood? And why had *he* decided to rear his obnoxious head?

"He called and asked if we wanted to meet him late this afternoon," Holly continued with a smile. She'd thought it very generous of Seamus to have included Alexa in his invite, considering there was clearly no love lost between the two of them. "At the Getty Center," she added, checking her watch again. "He said it's some kind of museum up in the —"

"Santa Monica mountains," Alexa cut in, nodding. She'd read about the Getty in the travel section of *Vogue* last month. The museum supposedly had a kick-ass photography collection — including an incredible exhibit of Diane Arbus, one of Alexa's favorite photographers — along with stunning white terraces, lush gardens, and winding streams. Since Holly generally found museums dull, Alexa had been hoping for a chance to sneak away to the Getty alone. But now, she had absolutely no desire to join Holly and Holly's new soul mate there; Alexa recalled the agonies of sharing a car with them all too well. "Give my regards to the know-it-all," Alexa added coolly as she busied herself with her sunscreen once more.

Holly remained where she was, her irritation growing by the second. "Alexa, you're not going to come? You love museums. Even *I'm* looking forward to going."

"I think I'll pass," Alexa replied, plucking at the strap of her Petit Bateau navy-blue polka-dot bikini. In that instant, she decided she'd spend the day shooting photographs of Malibu beaches. She'd gotten the craving for it last night, in the hot tub with Jonah, and she wasn't one to be deterred. "There's something else I'd *much* rather do."

"God, I'm really flattered," Holly snapped, anger flushing her cheeks. She rarely raised her voice to Alexa, but something — the fact that she was running late to meet Kenya, or perhaps the slightly bitter aftertaste from last night's talk with Tyler — was putting her on edge. "You know," she added, certain she would regret the cruelty in her voice a second later. "Maybe Jonah's lucky that you decided to ditch him. You're so *difficult*, Alexa. Don't worry — you won't stay single forever. But I feel bad for the poor guy who *is* gonna end up with you one day."

Then Holly put her hands to her mouth. She hadn't meant to say *all* that. Or had she?

Alexa heard her own breath as it caught in her throat. Holly hardly ever criticized Alexa in such a blatant — and ballsy — way. And this time, instead of reacting instantly, instead of firing back, Alexa remained still in her chair and wondered if what Holly had said was true. Maybe she *was* difficult. Too difficult to fall in love, and too difficult to be a truly good friend. As difficult, perhaps — dare she think it? — as her mother. The thought was so depressing that Alexa felt a lump form in her throat.

"Glad to know you feel that way," she finally responded, fighting to keep her tone cold and steady. She slid her sunglasses back on, the better to hide what she suspected was a wounded expression in her eyes. Then she tilted her face up to the sun, silently willing Holly to disappear.

Holly tapped one flip-flopped foot against the sundeck, surprised that she didn't feel more guilty about her blowup. Equally surprising was Alexa's silence; in the past, her friend would have surely retorted with some bitchy remark about Holly's lack of boy experience, which would have then led to a full-on snipe-fest. Now, only awkwardness lingered between the girls, thick as the heat. Holly tried to slice through the tension by looking at her stony-faced friend and speaking again. "So maybe we'll see you at the Getty later?" she offered, her voice softer.

"Uh-huh," Alexa muttered. She reached down for her frosty-cold Fiji water as Holly flip-flopped off noisily, almost colliding with Miguel. Alexa watched her go, then took a sip from the bottle. She felt she'd made it sufficiently clear that her showing up at the

Getty Center later was about as likely as her mother showing up at Oakridge High's graduation.

"I can't wait to graduate from Oakridge," Holly announced, apropos of nothing, as she and Kenya walked down the wide stone steps of the Ackerman student center, holding ice-cream sandwiches wrapped in waxed paper. After Holly had successfully driven from Malibu to Fred Segal — returning the dress with only a small pang of regret — she'd made her way to Westwood Village, pissed at Alexa the whole time. But meeting Kenya at an adorable off-campus ice-cream shop called Diddy Riese had cheered her up. Savoring their unhealthy breakfasts, the girls had then headed on to UCLA's campus, where they now stood, at the foot of the student center's steps.

"What prompted this declaration?" Kenya laughed around a mouthful of espresso ice cream, tucking her books under her free arm.

"I think being *here*," Holly replied, gazing around at the sun-soaked, bright green campus. The winding paths, grassy hills, and old-fashioned academic buildings were bursting with student activity. A group of girls in tank tops, with multi-colored boogie boards under their arms, flip-flopped past, sipping Jamba Juices and discussing a politicial science class. And clusters

184

of tanned, mellow-looking students lounged on towels in the grass, reading Descartes and Virginia Woolf. Something about the vibe made Holly's pulse spike, made her look forward to college in a way she never had before. Rutgers was perfectly pleasant, but visiting the campus had never quite been a thrilling experience.

Now, she was feeling pretty differently.

"In high school," Holly elaborated, taking a bite out of her cookies-and-cream sandwich. "It's like you hardly have *any* choices. But this place . . ." Holly gestured around. "Seems like it's all about being able to pick and choose what's right for you. Or am I imagining things?"

"No, it's true," Kenya said thoughtfully, brushing a stray braid off her cheek. "Even that first step of choosing the best school for yourself is kind of amazing, and all the rest . . . just gets even better."

Did I choose Rutgers? Holly wondered, feeling a heartbeat of hesitation. The fact that she would go to school there had always seemed preordained — now that Holly thought about it, there *hadn't* been much choice in the matter. But if she could have, would she have selected differently?

"For instance," Kenya was saying as she and Holly started down the nearest path. "I have to say there's something *really* nice about being kind of far from home . . . knowing that my parents are only a plane ride away, but that they're not keeping tabs on me every minute."

"Okay, you basically just described my fantasy," Holly joked, imagining a life beyond her parents' reach. Holly felt a swell of excitement, and pictured herself alone, independent, wandering across campus with her books in her arms and the sun lightening her hair. . . .

"Wait," she said suddenly, grabbing Kenya's arm. "Is that a *bear*?"

"Right on," Kenya said as she and Holly arrived at the statue of a bronze, roaring grizzly. Kenya grinned and proudly patted the bear's side. "He's the mascot for our sports teams – the Bruins, of course. California's big on bears," Kenya added wisely. "Just check out the state flag."

"The Bruins," Holly echoed as she and Kenya started walking again. Holly cast a smile back at the bear, which now seemed a little friendlier to her. She remembered when UCLA's track team coach had called her back in January to recruit her, and had told Holly about the Bruins' impressive records. "So what's the track program like here?" Holly asked Kenya, swallowing the last of her ice-cream sandwich. Earlier, Kenya had taken Holly past the gorgeous, crimson-colored Drake track — which had practically invited

Holly to go for a run. It was funny how easily she was able to picture herself on this campus.

"Well . . ." Kenya said, as if she were stalling. She took another bite of her ice-cream sandwich and straightened her red Timbuk2 messenger bag across her chest. The girls were heading down Bruin Walk, a tree-lined path along which students shouted about political petitions, free movie tickets, and upcoming concerts, all while waving bright yellow flyers and blue-and-gold Bruins pennants. Holly felt another rush of appreciation for the energetic, college-y feel.

"Okay, Jacobson," Kenya said after a long moment. She wadded up her waxed paper and tossed it into a nearby garbage bin. "There's something I need to tell you — I didn't have a chance to bring it up last night because of all the dancing and stuff. . . ." Holly held her breath, curious and a little nervous. "I stopped running track last semester," Kenya finally said, holding Holly's gaze.

"You *what*?" Holly asked, studying her friend in shock. Holly couldn't for the life of her imagine Kenya Matthews existing *without* running.

"I know, I know — random, huh?" A smile tugged at Kenya's lips. "But, Holly, UCLA has *all* these incredible sports programs, and I guess I wanted to try something . . . different." She shrugged as a cute, long-haired guy on a skateboard careened past them. "Earlier this semester I joined the intramural tennis team," Kenya went on, her voice full of genuine enthusiasm. "And next year I want to look into water polo. There's so much else out there to love besides track. But don't tell Coach Graham I said that," Kenya added with a grin, and then glanced worriedly at Holly. "You think I'm nuts, right?"

Holly didn't answer right away; she processed Kenya's news as the girls climbed a hill toward the quad. "Not at all," Holly finally replied softly. In a way, Kenya's radical change made perfect sense: She *had* reinvented herself out here, out west. Why shouldn't she sample all that this new world had to offer? Holly felt a prickle of envy; even when she started at Rutgers, she'd still be in *New Jersey*. Tyler would still play lacrosse, she'd still run track, and the bunch of other Oakridge kids making the pilgrimage to Rutgers with them would still see her as shy, sporty Holly Jacobson. No wonder the gray Rutgers campus had never filled with her a sense of anticipation. Over there, everything would be the same.

"Jacobson?" Kenya's voice broke into Holly's moment of introspection, and Holly glanced over to see her friend smiling at her. "Thinking about college, huh?" Kenya nodded understandingly, her necklace of round purple beads knocking against her pale yellow tee. "No worries — before you know it, you and Tyler will be all set up in your love nest in Rutgers."

"Uh . . . right," Holly said, feeling a pang of anxiety at Kenya's words. *But what if that isn't what I want?* she wondered, before pushing the thought aside. Kenya gave Holly a quick hug, announcing that she was going to be late to her anthropology class, and the girls promised to be in touch before Holly left LA.

With Kenya gone and some time to kill before meeting Seamus, Holly roamed through the quad, feeling the warmth of contentment. Holly knew it was unfair to compare the two, but the Rutgers campus would never measure up to this school. There was something exciting about knowing that the dazzle of the Kodak Theatre and the Malibu beaches waited beyond the college gates, as opposed to, well, the Oakridge Galleria. And when Holly came upon a serene sculpture garden, she felt suffused — as she had last night — with a sense of belonging. Smoothing out her drawstring linen capris, Holly sat on the warm surface of a black marble fountain, and took a deep breath, forgetting Oakridge, forgetting Alexa, forgetting everything that bound her to the past.

Then Holly noticed a girl sitting across from her on the grass, right below an abstract metal sculpture. Her light-brown hair was in a high ponytail, she wore a plaid, empire-waist sundress, and she was peeling an orange, a textbook open in her lap. She looked absolutely at peace, and Holly thought: *That could be me*. Holly *had* gotten into UCLA, after all — the track coach had actively recruited her — and her destiny could have gone in a very different direction had she sent back the acceptance form with the YES box checked off. For one dizzying second, Holly caught her breath and wondered if there was still time — if she could take action — look up the track coach here — reverse the course of her life. . . .

No.

Ridiculous.

Be realistic, Holly told herself, channeling Alexa. There was no need to blow a simple visit to UCLA out of proportion. So what if she'd seen the campus and found it, in a word, awesome?

Tyler. Holly retrieved her cell phone from her bag, her Claddagh ring glinting in the sun. Of course it had been difficult to talk to her boyfriend last night, she reasoned. It had been late, the Cabana Club had been noisy, and she'd been eager to get back to Kenya and Belle inside. Now, when she was feeling all chill and blissed-out, and Tyler was probably whiling away the afternoon shooting hoops outside his parents' garage, seemed the perfect time to call back.

"You sound so . . . California," Tyler declared as soon as Holly greeted him. Holly could picture him standing outside his house, the front of his T-shirt stained with sweat, a basketball under his arm, and the Oakridge afternoon gray and humid around him.

"*Dude*, what do you mean?" she drawled, doing her best stoned-surfer-boy impression. Tyler didn't laugh, but Holly figured it was because he didn't really know LA. She slipped off her green jelly flats and tucked her bare feet up under her. "I'm on the UCLA campus, the sun is in my hair, and I just had ice cream . . . so maybe *that's* why I sound 'California,'" she added, giggling. The brown-haired girl in the grass looked up and smiled at Holly, as if she understood.

"I – you're – awesome," Tyler replied, but his voice sounded broken up and distant.

Holly pressed her cell phone tighter to her ear, as if she could press Tyler closer. "Sweetie, I think we're breaking up," she said, getting to her feet and feeling like she was in a Verizon commercial. "What did you say? Are you there?"

"I'm here." Tyler's voice came through clearer now, and Holly thought she detected a flicker of impatience in his tone. "I said, 'I know you're having an awesome time.'"

"Oh . . . yeah. Yeah. I am," Holly admitted, gazing up at the arc of blue sky above. Who would have ever guessed she'd feel so strongly about the city she had dismissed as shallow and strange? She considered telling Tyler that only a moment before, she'd imagined withdrawing from Rutgers and coming *here*. But talking to her boyfriend now and thinking of Oakridge only reinforced how crazy that daydream was. She was on *vacation*, that was all, and La-La Land often filled people's heads with stupid notions. New Jersey — Tyler, her parents, Rutgers — was reality.

"That reminds me." Holly heard the faint dribble of Tyler's basketball on the ground as he spoke. "I went to the mall this morning — my mom *forced* me to go to Nordstrom to get a new tie for graduation — and I ran into Meghan and Jess." Holly smiled at the mention of her friends, but her smile froze when she heard what Tyler said next. "I told them all about your LA adventures, and how you —"

"Tyler, you didn't!" Holly cried in exasperation as she leaped to her feet. The girl in the grass glanced up, and Holly tried to lower her voice. "They weren't supposed to know I was here," she hissed. She hadn't had a chance to tell Tyler to keep her trip on the down-low, but she'd hoped he would've had the common sense to figure that out. But now, thanks to his spaciness, Meghan and Jess would be all huffy with Holly when she got back. *That* would make graduation fun.

"Look, Holly." Tyler's tone was surprisingly short.

"I didn't know it was some kind of secret. If we were able to talk for more than two seconds this week, you *could've* filled me in on that situation."

Holly's jaw dropped; just as she hardly ever reamed Alexa out, it was a rare occasion when Tyler told *her* off. Usually, both Holly and Tyler tended to back away, their hands up in surrender, with no resolution reached. Now, though, Holly felt annoyance shoot through. "It's not *my* fault you always call me at a bad time," she spat.

"Every time is a bad time," Tyler retorted instantly, and Holly could tell that his resentment on this topic must have been simmering for a while. "You're always busy, always at some club, always about to go surfing. It's like you're avoiding me or something —"

"Tyler, you know that's insane!" Holly gasped, startled by the turn the conversation had taken.

"Like even now," Tyler went on. "You're probably calling because you have some small window of time, but in a second you'll have to run off to meet, like, Jonah or Seamus for drinks at the Hollywood sign. Right?"

"No one's actually *allowed* to go to the Hollywood sign," Holly snapped, rolling her eyes at Tyler's ignorance; Kenya had filled Holly in on that fact last night. Then, with a jolt, Holly realized that Tyler was half right; she *was* due to meet Seamus at the Getty soon, and if she didn't get back in the Hybrid now, she'd be late. But of course Holly didn't tell Tyler that; she only informed him, in a cool, clipped tone, that she'd have to call him back later.

As Holly slid her feet back into her jellies and marched toward the north campus exit, she was trembling a little, but she was, once again, amazed at how she'd managed to hold her own in an argument. True, she'd had some practice with Alexa that morning, but overall she knew she'd become quite adept at the art of bickering with Tyler.

Even, it seemed, when there was no apology hook-up on the horizon.

Maybe I've had too many hook-ups, Alexa mused, her heart squeezing as she stood barefoot on the pearl-white Malibu beach, her sun-streaked hair whipping in the wind. *And now I've lost the capacity to fall in love. For the rest of my life.*

Alexa never thought small.

Sighing, she lifted her Nikon from where it hung around her neck, careful not to get it tangled in her gold anchor pendant, and brought it to her eye. Surfers, their shadowy forms outlined against the bright horizon, rose and dipped on their boards. Alexa, wondering if the surfer Holly had saved yesterday was out there among his brethren, snapped one picture, focused the lens, and snapped another. Ordinarily, photography could lift Alexa's spirits no matter what was happening in her life. But today, after the sharp words she'd exchanged with Holly on the sundeck, and Alexa's subsequent nosedive into self-reflection, nothing seemed to buoy her dark mood.

After Holly had stormed off, a sour Alexa had asked a sympathetic-looking Miguel how to get to the nearest beach, and he'd told her where it was possible to cross the Pacific Coast Highway on foot without getting killed. The whole time Alexa had felt a storm of emotions — about Jonah, about Holly, about boys, and about love — coursing through her. Had she been too rash in turning down Jonah last night? What was wrong with her in the first place, not falling head over wedge heels for a boy as perfect as the blue-eyed actor? Maybe, after so many different guys, so many fleeting kisses, and her recent spring break heartache, Alexa St. Laurent was through with love — and love was through with *her*.

Alexa frowned, zooming her lens in on another group of surfers, and Holly's words echoed in her head: *I feel bad for the poor guy....* Perhaps Alexa would be doing the male world a favor by retreating into a shell forever, like Botticelli's Venus on rewind.

A seashell poked Alexa's toe, and as she glanced down to see its coral-pink whorls in the sand, she felt a rush of inspiration. She knelt on the sand, brought the camera close to the shell, and took a very tight picture, knowing it would come out well. Alexa imagined the photo inside a frame, with her name printed on the wall beside it in bold letters: an exhibit of her work. Alexa's cheeks warmed and for a minute she forgot all about her sad romantic fate. With her *Vogue* internship around the corner, Alexa had been feeling more and more like a true, professional photographer; she'd begun to entertain images of herself taking photos on African safaris, changing her film on a run-down city street, or standing in a darkroom with her sleeves rolled up and her hair piled up on her head. There was so much in the world to examine, to investigate and record. At the thought, Alexa's heartbeat sped up in a way that Jonah could never prompt.

The next thought Alexa had, almost in spite of herself, was of the Diane Arbus exhibit at the Getty. Alexa knew that a real photographer would never let a disagreement with Holly or a dislike of Seamus stand in her way of seeing great art. And Alexa sensed that communing with art would help get her mind off her boy troubles. Her decision made, Alexa got to her feet, brushing sand off her knees, and took herself and her camera back to *El Sueño*, where a quick intercom-buzz to Esperanza resulted in the "car" pulling up to take Alexa to the Getty.

By the time the limo dropped her off, and Alexa had ridden the weightless, white air tram up a snaking road into the craggy mountains, she was feeling a little calmer about everything. And, when her red Faryl-robin straw wedges stepped onto the Getty's gleaming white stone terrace, Alexa saw that Holly and Seamus weren't among the people admiring the staggering mountain view, or the white-domed buildings of the museum. Maybe, Alexa thought with a flicker of hope, leaning over the terrace's railing to take a picture of the emerald-green garden below, she'd even missed the two of them altogether.

But as soon as she entered the airy, sun-splashed exhibit hall, she saw that her momentary luck had run out. In between the murmuring art-lovers and strolling security guards, there stood Holly and Seamus, right in front of Alexa's favorite Diane Arbus photograph: an intense black-and-white shot of identical twin sisters. Alexa noticed that Seamus, one hand pushing back his floppy blond hair, was intently focused on the photograph while, Holly, who was hanging back, looked a little distracted. Alexa wondered if she could duck behind a security guard and avoid running into them, but then Holly turned her head and gave Alexa a tentative wave.

Damn it.

Then Seamus glanced her way, and anger swelled

in Alexa when she saw his mouth curve up in a smirk. In his cuffed jeans, slip-on Pumas, faded Sound Team T-shirt, and pin-striped blazer, he looked just as Hipster Boy annoying as he had in the car ride from Vegas. She noticed that he also appeared a little tired, as if he hadn't been getting enough sleep. *Probably up late writing shitty poetry.* She scowled back at him, and Seamus's smirk blossomed into a full-blown grin. Alexa once again got the sense that he was silently laughing at her, especially as she walked toward him and Holly, her head held high.

"So you've decided to join us mere mortals," Seamus said, crossing his arms over his chest and then glancing at Holly. "What do you say? Should we genuflect?"

Alexa couldn't believe it when Holly actually giggled. Gritting her teeth, she fought back the urge to snap at them both; instead, she marched over and positioned herself in front of the twins photograph, telling herself to remain civil. After all, if she wanted to soak in all this inspiring photography, she'd have to simply grin and bear Seamus's and Holly's attitudes.

Well, maybe she didn't have to literally *grin*.

"Why *did* you change your mind?" Holly asked, sidling up to Alexa. Though Holly was still a little sore toward her friend, she was pleased that Alexa had deigned to show up. Though Seamus had been considerate and thoughtful as ever, he'd also been far too absorbed by the boring photo exhibit, and Holly knew she couldn't confide in him about her exhilarating morning at UCLA — *or* her sudden sparring with Tyler. Only Alexa could help Holly make sense of the confusing, clashing emotions that the fight with Tyler had stirred in her.

"Well, it wasn't because of either of you," Alexa responded icily, turning to glare at Holly and then Seamus. She about-faced and studied a photograph of a giant towering over his parents. "I spent the morning taking pictures on the beach, so I decided to come see how another photographer — one that I love — sees the world. Okay?" Alexa paused, surprised at the words that had come rushing out of her, almost without her own accord. She was rarely so candid about her thoughts on photography.

"Ah, then let us not disturb the artiste's concentration," Seamus stage-whispered to Holly, and Alexa pursed her lips. She refused to satisfy him by responding.

Holly sighed; now that enough time had passed, she felt bad over what she'd said to Alexa that morning, and wished she could clear the air between herself and her friend. However, Seamus's and Alexa's sniping was not helping matters. Holly was certain that if she ever got the two of them to have an actual conversation, they'd find that they had stuff in common. She was opening her mouth to suggest that they all move to the outdoor café for lunch when her cell *brring*ed loudly in her bag. Instantly, the nearest hypervigilant security guard appeared at Holly's side, scolding her for bringing a phone inside the museum. It was obvious that the guard had had the same showdown with one too many cell-addicted Hollywood types.

"Be right back," Holly muttered to Alexa and Seamus, turning to leave the gallery. She pressed the SILENT button on her phone, and checked the screen. It was Tyler calling. *Great.*

As Holly walked away, Alexa looped her fingers through the belt-holes of her slim-fitting Bermudas, willing herself to keep ignoring Seamus. She could feel him studying her with that same bemused expression. "You're an Arbus fan?" he asked, and Alexa was positive that he sounded surprised.

"Well, my favorite photographer is Robert Frank, especially his book, *The Americans*," Alexa replied, once again wishing she could stop being so forthcoming around Seamus. "But I guess Diane's a close second. Even if that Nicole Kidman movie was kind of weird."

"I wrote my thesis on Diane Arbus in college,"

Seamus replied. "My whole argument was that she was really a journalist, a photographer-journalist, in a way, and — whatever —" He cut himself off and shook his head, straightening his glasses. "I was such a dork."

"Well, not much has changed, has it?" Alexa retorted, shooting Seamus a sideways glance; in truth, though, Alexa thought the idea of writing a paper on photography sounded kind of cool, and she'd long dreamed of majoring in art history.

"You're a paradox, Alexa," Seamus replied, clearly unruffled by her remark. He gestured to the camera Alexa had kept around her neck, where it swung against the rose-colored tank she'd cinched in the middle with a big-buckled, bronze belt. "You spend the morning taking pictures, but then you put on heels and makeup. Not many true photographers play the part of a girly-girl so convincingly," he continued, his voice deep and thoughtful. "See, maybe the thing is, Alexa, that under that carefully constructed veneer, *you're* a dork."

Alexa's lips parted as her skin flooded with heat. *How dare he?* Not for the first time, Seamus reminded Alexa of Holly — of the way Holly could boldly pinpoint, as she had that very morning, Alexa's most secret, deep-down fears about herself. *Those two deserve each other*, Alexa thought venomously, wishing

Holly would return from her phone chat. But, through her fury, Alexa also felt the smallest shiver of joy; *a true photographer*, Seamus had called her, somewhere in between all those other insults. Those words gave Alexa a quiet jolt, the same jolt she might feel if a stranger shouted her name on the street. Like someone had recognized her.

"You can't presume to know everything about me, you arrogant jerk," Alexa finally replied, crossing her arms over her chest and narrowing her eyes. She saw no need for niceties.

To Alexa's surprise, Seamus nodded, looking sheepish. "Good point. After all, you don't know everything about *me*. Actually . . ." He paused and straightened his glasses again. "There's something I should have told you and Holly — "

"Alexa."

At the sound of Holly's voice, Alexa whirled around to see her friend reentering the gallery. Holly's freckled cheeks were very pink and her cell phone was clutched tightly in her hand. Alexa felt a rush of concern, wondering if the call had brought bad news from home.

"I think I need to go," Holly said, sounding more frustrated than upset as she neared Alexa and Seamus. "Tyler's being all weird. . . . We kind of got into this fight before, and he says we should talk when I can be *alone.*" Holly blew her bangs up with a sigh. "Tyler's my boyfriend," she explained, looking apologetically at Seamus.

Quickly, Alexa also glanced at Seamus to see if jealousy might be flashing across his face — she was still certain there was something brewing between him and Holly. But if Seamus was writhing in envy, he didn't show it. He merely nodded, furrowing his brow. "Do what you have to do, Holly," he said understandingly. "Thanks for coming to meet me in any case."

"You can stay if you want," Holly said to Alexa, her gray-green eyes wide. "I'm going to take the Hybrid back to *El Sueño* and call Tyler from there." Alexa noticed that Holly was twisting her new ring around and around on her finger, a sure sign she was worried.

For a second, Alexa looked back at Seamus — who was watching her with an unreadable expression in his eyes — and then at the photos she hadn't seen yet. *I can't stay*, she decided. Even though Holly had upset her that morning, Alexa still wanted to help her friend deal with what sounded like some potential drama. Alexa shrugged at Seamus by way of good-bye, and he shrugged back.

"I guess I'll see you girls," he said, lifting his hand in a wave.

No, you won't, Alexa thought as she turned to leave the gallery with Holly. Tomorrow would be their last full day in LA, and the girls wouldn't have time for any-thing but wedding preparations before the big event. Alexa felt a prickle of sadness at the realization; their visit was almost over.

When she and Holly stepped out into the sun-shine, Alexa glanced over her shoulder into the gallery, but she couldn't spot Seamus anymore. She guessed she would never find out what his deep, dark secret had been.

CHAPTER NINE
Shifting Gears

"Call him now," Alexa recommended as she and Holly breezed through the canyons, the late afternoon wind catching their hair. "It's obvious you want to." Alexa shot a sidelong glance at her friend, who was sitting tensely beside her in the passenger seat. Ever since they'd left the Getty, Holly had been clutching her cell to her chest. In Alexa's opinion, Holly was too attached to that phone. On all the trips they'd taken together, its presence had caused nothing but trouble.

"I don't know," Holly said, flipping open her phone to study the background — a close-up of Tyler, grinning after a lacrosse game. Her stomach twisting, she thought back to the quick, tense conversation they'd had on the Getty's terrace; usually Tyler got over their fights pretty quickly, but this time he'd seemed cold.

Holly assured herself that it was probably just a bump in the road of their relationship, one that would be smoothed over quickly. "He said I should only call him back when I was by myself," Holly added, looking up at Alexa.

"Please," Alexa snorted, easing the car over a speed bump. "I so don't count. I mean, you'd fill me in regardless, right?" Alexa peeked at Holly again, and smiled, deciding to forget about their own clash that morning — for now, anyway. "Speaking of which," Alexa said, turning the car toward the famous Mulholland Drive. "What *are* you guys fighting about? I thought everything was all peachy in Holly-Tyler Land." *Except for that bicker session at my mom's party,* Alexa added silently.

"So did *I*," Holly groaned. "Though I hope you don't actually think of us in those scary terms," she added, grinning at her friend, and suddenly grateful to have her there. "This morning, things got strange," Holly went on thoughtfully. "When I called him from UCLA, I was having a great time, and I sounded all giddy and maybe he was worried that —" *He wasn't the one making me happy,* Holly thought, surprised by her own thought.

"*You?*" Alexa teased, raising her eyebrows in mock shock. "Holly Jacobson, giddy about . . . *Los Angeles?*" Alexa smiled, watching the curvy road ahead, as Holly laughed in sheepish agreement. It had been increasingly clear to Alexa that Holly was actually sort of loving LA. Lately there had been a brighter sparkle in Holly's eyes, and a melodic, hopeful timbre to her voice whenever she spoke about the city. Alexa wondered if Tyler had picked up on the changes in Holly as well, which would explain his weirdness. Tyler Davis was not a big fan of change.

As Alexa steered the car along the twisting, cliff-like edges of Mulholland Drive, Holly sat up straighter, drew in a deep breath, and then pressed 1 on her cell phone to call Tyler. A blur of mansions and a dizzying view of the valley flashed by beneath them, and Alexa bit her lip, fully expecting I-hate-heights Holly Jacobson to have a panic attack beside her. But it was obvious that Holly was preoccupied with bigger problems at the moment. "Sweetie," she was saying into the phone, her voice taut. "What's going on?"

"Oh, thanks for calling right back, baby," Tyler said, his tone gentler than it had been a few minutes before. "Are you alone now?"

"Totally," Holly lied, shifting in her seat as Alexa helpfully turned down the volume on a vintage Red Hot Chili Peppers song on the radio. "Are you?"

"Yeah. I'm in my room," Tyler said, and Holly instantly pictured him on the edge of his bed — the bed she'd lain on so many times — surrounded by his posters of sports heroes, safe and secure in the home he'd always known, while she literally teetered on the brink of a cliff. But Holly realized that she didn't feel unsafe where she was. And she wasn't that homesick for Oakridge – or Tyler.

"So," Tyler continued, and the seriousness in his voice made Holly even more nervous. "I, um, felt like we ended things kind of abruptly earlier, and I wanted to explain a little more about why I – I kind of exploded like that."

Explain? Holly thought, gazing down at the stomach-dropping view. *Not apologize?* "That would be good," she replied cautiously, still unsure where this conversation might take them; it felt as unpredictable and dangerous as the road Alexa was driving along. "I had no clue that you've been sort of . . . pissed at me. . . ." she trailed off.

"I'm *not*," Tyler replied quickly. "It's just – I guess there's something I keep thinking about, and I guess it kind of came out in a weird way before. You know?"

"Not really," Holly replied truthfully, shooting Alexa a he's-being-confusing look. Alexa, keeping her gaze on the sharply zigzagging road, made a sympathetic face. "Tell me about it," Holly added. Her boyfriend could be so reserved, so reticent, that often she had to draw his thoughts out of him slowly, like cotton candy from a spinning machine.

Tyler let out a long sigh. "The thing is, Holly . . . I've had a lot of time to myself this week, with you being gone and all." There was a note of accusation in his tone, and Holly set her jaw, feeling a knot of irritation form in her chest. "And I haven't wanted to bring this up with you," Tyler went on, "because I know you've been having so much fun . . ."

"Tyler. Come on. I'm not having fun right now." Holly exhaled noisily, and out of the corner of her eye, she saw Alexa's lips twitch with a smile.

Tyler cleared his throat. "I keep thinking about that conversation we had the night of Alexa's mom's party — you know, before you left for LA? When you said you didn't want to make too many plans because you were feeling suffocated?" His words spilled out in a rush now.

Surprised, Holly held on to the bottom of her seat as the car bounced along a pebbly road; though she hadn't forgotten about that fight with Tyler, she hadn't had too much time to dwell on it, what with all the activity in LA. Closing her eyes, Holly called up Monday night in New York, which seemed to belong to another lifetime.

"I never said *suffocated*," she protested after a minute, opening her eyes. But as she spoke that word now, Holly realized that it perfectly described what she'd been feeling back home — as if all her obligations were pressing down on her like great weights, squeezing the breath out of her. Being away from that pressure this week, she'd almost forgotten the sensation.

"Maybe not," Tyler responded quietly and cleared his throat again. "But when I started talking about college and our future, you got this look on your face like you wanted to . . . escape."

And I did, Holly thought, looking out the windshield; she and Alexa were now approaching the Pacific Coast Highway, and the great orange orb of the sun was beginning its descent into the flat, shiny Pacific. In a rush, Holly realized how wonderfully free she'd been feeling in California. For once, her parents weren't breathing down her neck; there was no Coach Graham expecting her to show up at a track meet; and, if Holly was totally honest with herself, there was no homebody, play-it-safe boyfriend to dissuade her from going out to explore and dance and laugh.

At that last thought, Holly caught her breath, and felt a wave of something like fear wash over her. What was she *thinking*? What was happening?

"And," Tyler was saying into the phone, no hesitation in his voice now; Holly got the distinct feeling that he'd read her thoughts. "Ever since you've been in California, it seems like you're finally getting to do all those . . . *spontaneous* things you've always wanted.

Without me. You know, like hitting up big-time celebrity parties, and chilling with that guy Seamus —"

Oh, no. Tyler Davis had *not* just gone there.

"Hold on," Holly snapped, her face flushing so hot she felt *she* might explode. "Tyler, *please* tell me you don't think — Seamus is a *friend* — how could you —" Her indignation stole the words out of her mouth. She noticed Alexa glance briefly at her, braking behind a jet-black Porsche.

"Look, I'm not saying anything," Tyler responded swiftly. "But . . . well, I know sometimes when we're apart, you can get a little . . . crazy."

Another bolt of fury shot through Holly, and she gripped the cell so tight she knew her knuckles were turning white. She understood exactly what Tyler was referring to, and it made her throat close with hurt. Last month, not long after they had gone all the way for the first time, Holly had broken down and told Tyler about kissing Alexa's hot cousin, Pierre, in Paris. Tyler had been understandably upset, but his brooding had lasted for only a few days, and then he'd assured Holly that he forgave her. Still, Holly couldn't help but wonder if Tyler might begin to grow suspicious of her nonetheless. And here was living proof.

"Tyler Maxwell Davis." Holly spoke slowly and deliberately, even though her arms and legs were shaking. "If you knew me at all, you'd know I'd never do anything like that again. Just because you're — you're *jealous* or something of the fun I'm having on this trip, does not give you the right to . . ." To her growing frustration, Holly felt warm tears well up in her eyes. Alexa reached one hand out to rub her shoulder, but nothing could comfort Holly now. "Suspect me of . . ." she whispered, her voice breaking.

"Oh, God, Hol," Alexa murmured, not caring if Tyler heard her or not. It was obvious something major was going down between him and Holly.

Tyler tried to backtrack. "Holly, it's — it's not that I don't trust you," he began haltingly. "But I want you to tell me if you ever feel like I'm . . . holding you back or something."

As Alexa steered the car up the hill to El Sueño, Holly felt her chest shudder, even though she wasn't sobbing yet. "You're not holding me back," she murmured, all the while remembering how Tyler had talked about their living together at Rutgers, how he'd laid out the plan of their life as neatly as a grid. Holly was struck by an image of herself perched on a cliff above the ocean, ready to jump, while Tyler tugged on her arm, warning her of dangers ahead. "You're just . . . cautious," she added, fidgeting uncomfortably in her seat.

"You used to be cautious, too," Tyler replied, and

Holly knew the muscle in his cheek was jumping as he spoke. "You've changed."

Holly's Claddagh ring felt ice-cold on her hot finger, and she touched it, trying to stir up the joy she'd felt when Tyler had given it to her on Tuesday. But, thousands of miles away, it was hard to even envision Tyler's handsome face. And even though they'd spent spring break on different continents, Holly had never felt more distanced from her boyfriend than she did at this moment. "Why —" Her voice came out hoarse, and the tears hovered on her lashes. "Why did you give me the ring then, if you felt this way about me?"

"Wow," Alexa said under her breath as they approached Jonah's sprawling estate. She cast a sidelong glance at Holly; her cheeks were splotchy and her mouth turned down at the corners.

"Holly. Baby." Tyler's voice was heavy with worry in Holly's ear. "It's not like that. I just wanted to bring up this one issue. Things have been awesome between us —"

"No, they haven't," Holly snapped, fresh anger momentarily squelching her tears. *Awesome.* Suddenly she was sick of that word, of Tyler's need to always smooth matters over. "If they were," she continued, her voice softer, "we wouldn't be having this conversation." Maybe, for some time now, she and Tyler had been avoiding that very truth with apology hook-ups, with *sweetie*s, and *baby*s, and professions of love. Could it be?

A chill ran down Holly's backbone. She didn't know what to think. In a matter of minutes, her world had been split open, clean as a watermelon, and nothing made sense anymore. Her head was spinning in confusion as Alexa pulled the car to a stop in front of the guesthouse. "I can't talk anymore," Holly told Tyler abruptly. "I need to think. About everything."

"Okay," Tyler said softly. "Um, say hi to Alexa."

For a second, Holly wondered if her boyfriend — who was often more perceptive than he seemed — had known that Alexa had been at Holly's side the whole time. *Whatever.* She told him goodbye, slapped the phone shut, and promptly burst into tears.

"What happened?" Alexa cried, alarmed. She put the car in park, and then rifled through her denim Balenciaga clutch for tissues. "Did you guys break up?"

"No, of course not." Holly sniffled, and blew her nose in the tissue Alexa handed her. But suddenly she was thinking of the earlier talk she'd had with Tyler, back at UCLA. *Sweetie, I think we're breaking up*, she'd said when his voice had faded out. Holly swallowed hard. In a way, bad cell connections were like bad emotional connections — full of misunderstanding, distance, and frustration. As another shiver went through her, Holly wondered if she'd known something, deep down, during that conversation that she hadn't been able to admit to herself.

We're breaking up.

The thought was too impossible to bear, so Holly flung open the car door and leaped out, not caring if Jonah or Esperanza or *anyone* saw her in tears.

Which, of course, was precisely why Jonah Eklundstrom appeared at that very instant, coming out of the main house. He was trailed not just by Esperanza, but also by Margaux, her fiancé, Paul, a slender, dark-skinned man in a pink polo shirt talking on a cell phone, and a tall, broad-shouldered boy with curly brown hair and a mischievous look on his face.

A boy who eerily resembled — was it? — no — it *couldn't* be —

What would surfer Zach from the beach being doing here, at El Sueño? Had he somehow tracked her down to thank her?

Too distracted to care, Holly whirled around and sprinted for the guesthouse, faster than if she were running a race.

Alexa jumped out of the car, intending to follow her distraught friend. But she could see Jonah, Margaux, and their entourage advancing toward her, and she didn't want to cause more of a scene than necessary. Besides, the small stab of nerves she felt when she spotted Jonah kept her rooted to the spot for a moment.

"Alexa!" Margaux, who was clearly back from her ashram visit, waved both arms, her skull charm bracelet jangling. "Come meet Vikram, my wedding planner," she added, and gestured to the man in the pink polo shirt. It was obvious that Margaux had no idea what had happened between her brother and Alexa the night before.

Alexa snuck a glance at Jonah and felt herself relax. His dark brows were raised in a sweet, I-promise-I'm-not-mad-at-you expression. Alexa knew he *wasn't* pissed about her abrupt change of heart last night. In fact, something in those big blue eyes told Alexa that if she wanted another chance — a reshoot of the scene in the hot tub — he'd gladly give it to her. With the setting sun behind him, wearing a button-down periwinkle shirt untucked over board shorts, Jonah glowed. But the sight of His Royal Hotness failed to bring butterflies to Alexa's belly. Again, she wondered if she was missing some all-important love chip in her system.

"Yeah, join us," Jonah said, his tone warm but careful, as the rest of the troop headed for the waiting limo. "We're getting drinks at Daddy's, this low-key bar over on Vine."

Alexa's eyes flicked over to the others in the group,

and noticed that one of the guys looked insanely like the surfer Holly had rescued yesterday. *Random.* Thinking of Holly, Alexa waved back at Jonah, and shook her head apologetically. "I can't," she said, motioning to the guesthouse. "I need to . . . help Holly with something. But we'll talk at the wedding, right?"

"Right." Jonah smiled, holding her gaze for a moment, and then Alexa turned and flew down the flagstone path to the house, unsure as to how she should feel about their interaction.

She found Holly in her green bedroom, flopped across the circular bed with her shoes kicked off, her light-brown hair fanning out over a pillow, and a tissue pressed to her eyes.

"Hol?" Alexa ventured softly. "Do you want to talk about it?"

"I'm fine," Holly half sobbed, rolling over so her back was to Alexa. "Tyler and I had a stupid argument. You heard everything." Of course, Holly was not remotely fine. But even though she knew Alexa was throwing her a rope, a lifeline, she wanted to drown in her sorrows. She wanted to be alone with her swirling thoughts, to sob into her pillow, and come to terms with how she was feeling about her boyfriend.

"If you say so," Alexa murmured, backing out of the room and gently shutting the door. A blind girl could see that this *hadn't* been just another fight between Holly and Tyler. But Alexa knew Holly could be an intensely private person. She'd come around when she was ready. In the meantime, Alexa had enough to think about on her own.

"Tyler?" Holly mumbled an hour later, her eyes fluttering open. She'd been having the most vivid dream about her boyfriend, though she couldn't recall what it was. Instinctively, she reached one hand out, expecting to feel the warmth of Tyler's broad back. In Oakridge, Holly and Tyler had managed to spend a few nights sharing a bed, thanks to creative lies about slumber parties and a shared talent for tiptoeing past sleeping parents' bedrooms. Now, as Holly came to, she realized she was in California, and that the space beside her was empty.

Rubbing her eyes, she felt the dampness of her lashes, and then remembered everything: the phone call, the fight, and her crying jag. But Holly didn't feel like bawling now; sleep had given her a sense of clarity, and comfort. It was like those few times when she'd twisted an ankle on the track — getting a good night's sleep always dulled the ache a little.

As Holly slowly sat up, smoothing out her tousled hair, her dream came back to her in a rush. She'd dreamed that it was this past Tuesday morning, and she was saying good-bye to Tyler outside her parents' house. But instead of accepting his Claddagh ring, she was returning it to him, gently closing his fist around it. The dream hadn't been painful — rather, Holly had felt a sense of relief so palpable she'd assumed it had been real. Awake now, Holly even glanced down at her hand, and, to her slight surprise, saw that her ring was still in place, winking up at her through the moonlight streaming in through her windows. Her heart dropped in disappointment.

And that was when Holly knew what she had to do.

She swung her legs off the bed, trembling. Before she actually did anything, she needed to find Alexa, to finally talk things through.

But as Holly wandered through the silent, empty hallways, she realized that Alexa was never one to hang around a house on a warm Thursday night. Maybe she'd even rethought her Jonah decision and now the two of them were hooking up at some private, celeb-only club. With a sigh, Holly stepped into the kitchen, hoping to find some comfort food, but then a splashing sound outside the window startled her. At In-N-Out on Tuesday night, Jonah had told Holly and Alexa that he'd once caught determined photographers pawing through his trash can for mail or other kinds of illuminating garbage. Fearful of crazy, stalker paparazzi, Holly held her breath and peered out into the darkness.

But there were no stalkers outside — just Alexa. Holly saw her friend sitting on the edge of the pool, her blonde hair shining in the starlight as her feet kicked gently at the water. She looked like a mermaid contemplating whether or not to return home, and Holly smiled at the image. Without putting on shoes, she slipped out of the house and crossed the flagstone path to the quiet pool area. Alexa glanced up at Holly, her big blue eyes twinkling, but neither girl said anything. Holly sat beside her friend, also dangling her feet in the cool, chlorinated water. She thought about all the other times she and Alexa had sat side by side like this, not speaking, but being there for each other nonetheless.

"What were you doing all this time?" Holly finally asked, trailing a line through the blue water with her toe. She didn't feel like bringing up Tyler just yet.

"Thinking," Alexa replied, tilting her head to one side, "about our boy troubles." She paused. "And that I should cut my hair."

"Are you serious?" Holly demanded, forgetting Tyler for a minute. Alexa was always unpredictable, but this news was truly outrageous. Alexa's long, rippling, storybook hair had always been her trademark;

Holly hadn't known her friend otherwise. "Boy-short, like Margaux?" Holly added apprehensively.

Alexa shook her head, smiling at Holly's expression of shock. "To my shoulders, I think." Alexa knew she would miss her voluminous hair. It was her armor: She'd relied upon it to lure boys, make statements, and intimidate people. But now the time felt ripe for chopping and styling, for a look that was more grown-up, more New York, more . . . *new*. Maybe it was because she was still worried about her incapacity to fall in love – and felt that changing her look might change her outlook. Maybe it was because Jonah – the source of her love angst – had drooled over her "long blonde hair." She shrugged at Holly. "I just feel like shifting gears," Alexa explained.

Holly nodded, emotion rising in her again. "Change can be good," she agreed softly. *Shifting gears.* She thought about how natural it now felt to drive in LA, how she'd learned to be confident steering her way across unfamiliar ground. Holly took a deep breath of the salty-fresh air and looked up at the glistening stars. "I'm happy here," she murmured, as much to herself as to Alexa. It was the first time she'd articulated the thought out loud, and expressing it scared her a little, made it real.

Alexa remembered something Holly had told her in the car: *When I called him from UCLA, I guess I sounded all giddy. . . .* Alexa furrowed her brow, wondering if she should speak what was suddenly on her mind. For selfish reasons, she wanted to resist.

"Hol, didn't you . . ." Alexa began hesitantly. "Didn't you get into UCLA?"

Holly met Alexa's gaze, the expression in her gray-green eyes, understanding. "I did," Holly replied. Then she continued, her thoughts spilling out in a hurry now. "I applied on a whim — because Kenya had recommended it, and because of their great track program — but I didn't ever plan to go. It seemed so far away, so different." Holly looked down at her ankles disappearing into the water, then gave voice to the thought that had been lingering in her mind all day. "But being on the campus today felt so . . . right. Like . . . like I should be going *there* in the fall. And not Rutgers." Her cheeks flushed.

"Yeah," Alexa said softly, kicking up another splash of water. "I kind of got that vibe from you before." She felt an ache in her throat.

"Whatever," Holly said, waving her hand through the air as if to wipe the thought away. "I can't believe we're even talking about this! It's too late to do anything now, and it's not like I'd *actually* ever be able to withdraw from Rutgers and move out here, right?" Holly laughed, as if the idea were outlandish, but Alexa saw that the expression in her eyes was hopeful.

"It's not impossible," Alexa argued, still wrestling with herself inside. "It's only June — school doesn't start until September. And I bet your V.I.P. Assistant Principal mom could totally pull some strings with the admissions office." *What am I saying?* Alexa wondered. The last thing Alexa wanted was for Holly — her anchor, her rescuer, the one person on the planet who understood her — to move across the country. At the same time, Alexa had witnessed the new Holly blooming under the Malibu sun. It was as if all the changes Holly had gone through in the past year — becoming more confident, more lighthearted, more daring — had finally taken full shape here. Alexa would *never* have predicted it, but there it was, plain as day: Holly belonged in LA.

"This is where you should be," Alexa said firmly, looking at Holly. "I just feel it." Her heart broke as she said the words, but Alexa couldn't not be honest with her oldest friend.

Holly swallowed, glancing down at her hands. *Me, in LA?* She knew she'd never buy into the whole shiny-cars-and-fake-tans scene, but she'd been amazed to discover that there were people here — like Kenya, like Belle — who managed to exude California cool while still remaining down-to-earth. Here, Holly would have friends she could count on to mock all the shallowness with her while enjoying it at the same time.

But she wouldn't have Alexa.

When Holly looked up again, she saw Alexa watching her with a sad smile on her face; in the past, Holly had often wondered if she and Alexa were close enough to peek into each other's minds. "You'll be fine without me," Alexa whispered, tears welling in her eyes. "Better. You'll be saving boys from the ocean and going clubbing with Kenya —"

"Alexa, stop!" Holly gasped, reaching for her friend's hand. "Come on, I can't uproot myself like that — or leave *you* behind — and my parents would flip —"

Still, even as Holly stammered out her excuses, she knew, deep down, that she *wanted* to uproot herself. Needed to, maybe. Ever since her trip to South Beach last year, Holly had been struggling to prove to her parents that she was an adult, or at least on her way to becoming one. But Holly knew that if she remained in New Jersey forever — with her parents, with Tyler, even with Alexa, whom she'd always depend on for excitement — she'd never really grow up.

Rutgers, home, the safe, easy path she'd always followed . . . none of that compelled her anymore. She wanted to make her *own* excitement, to blaze her own trail. Holly thought of the American History class she'd taken that year, of the pioneers who'd headed west in covered wagons, plunging headfirst into uncharted territory. Now, maybe it was her turn.

"Just explain how you *feel* to Lynn and Stanley," Alexa advised, giving Holly's hand a squeeze. "They might put up a fight at first, but they'll understand. They'll have to."

At Alexa's words, Holly once again felt tears flood her eyes. "Well, I do need to call them anyway," she conceded, her voice catching. "Even if it will be an utter disaster."

"I know it's hard to believe, Hol," Alexa said, choking up even more as she thought of her own icy-cold mother. "But your parents want you to be happy." Holly nodded, squeezing Alexa's hand tighter. "And so do I," Alexa managed with a small smile. "Even if *I'll* be miserable going to Mayle and Bloomie's without you."

Holly shook her head vehemently. She couldn't yet deal with the fact that she and Alexa might be separated. After so many crazy ups and downs, the two of them had finally forged a true friendship, and now here she was, casting it off for California. "Hey, maybe you could come out here, too?" Holly offered, her voice trembling.

"No way," Alexa giggled, dabbing at her eyes. "If anything, this trip has reminded me that I'm a New York City girl at heart." Alexa's spirits lifted at the thought of New York: the grand museums within walking distance of Central Park, the hidden boutiques in the

Village, the vibrant community of artists and thinkers and fashionistas she'd soon be a part of. "Though being a cinematographer could be cool . . ." she added, imagining herself behind a movie camera. But then Alexa shook off the moment of self-absorption. "What about Tyler?" she added softly, glancing back at Holly. "He's not going to take this well. . . ."

"I know," Holly whispered, averting Alexa's gaze. Her toes looked blurry and distorted under the water; she knew Alexa would recommend she paint her toenails before tomorrow's wedding. "That's kind of what our fight was about before," Holly went on. "Even though I didn't flat-out tell him about wanting to go to UCLA." Up until now, Holly hadn't even admitted that desire to *herself*. "But I'm sure he sensed the change in me," Holly continued, staring down into the blue depths of the pool. "I've sometimes wondered if Tyler knows me better than I know myself. And maybe now he knows that it's time . . . time . . . for us . . ." Her throat closed. She couldn't go on. She couldn't finish that heartrending thought.

Alexa put her arm around Holly's shoulder as her own heart pounded. "For you guys to . . ." she prompted, not wanting to put the words in her friend's mouth.

"End things?" Holly phrased it as a question, but she felt certainty rise up inside her. It was agony to face. But she *knew* that if she and Tyler tried to stay together, and she went off to UCLA in September, the two of them wouldn't last longer than her first semester. She'd get caught up in her life here, and he'd begin to resent her — just like now. And, if Holly decided to stay at Rutgers, *she'd* grow to resent Tyler for, as he'd put it, holding her back. All of it was so inevitable, Holly was amazed that she'd never seen it coming before. "But," she added tearfully, thinking out loud. "It's so hard to picture myself without him."

"It'll only feel like that for a while," Alexa promised, stroking Holly's hair. "Especially if you know you're doing the right thing." Alexa had always assumed Holly and Tyler were perfectly matched, but now she saw that Holly was growing away from him. With a funny little tremor, Alexa recalled how *she'd* broken up with Tyler more than a year ago, unwittingly setting in motion the chain of events that had led her, Holly, and Tyler to where they were right now. Life was so weird.

Holly closed her eyes, remembering the light in Tyler's amber-colored eyes, the softness of his dark-blond hair under her hands. She replayed certain moments in her mind: the drizzly April morning of their junior year when Tyler had kissed her in school for the first time — right in front of her locker, his hoodie damp and his lips tasting of rain; the snowy

Valentine's afternoon in Tyler's bedroom when he'd traced a circle on her belly and whispered that he loved her; the two of them dancing to bad techno at the prom, laughing and sweaty as their classmates cheered them on. She felt like she was watching a film of someone else's life. Holly felt tears slipping out of the corners of her eyes and sliding down her cheeks. Tyler had been her first love. Her first real heartache. Her first *everything*. Holly had no idea how the script was supposed to go from here.

"Did you want to wait until we're back in Oakridge to, you know, do it?" Alexa was asking tentatively, as if she were referring to a mob hit.

"I think I'd lose my nerve by then," Holly replied, opening her eyes to stare at the cypress trees waving under the sky. "Besides," she added, turning to raise one brow at Alexa. "*You* wouldn't wait, would you? If there's anything you've taught me, Alexa St. Laurent —"

"Besides how to tell the difference between Chanel Glossimer and Stila Lip Glaze?" Alexa cut in. With a pang of sadness, she realized just how deeply she was going to miss her friend if things did work out with UCLA.

Holly managed a half grin. "Yeah, besides that, which, we *all* know is absolutely crucial. You taught

228

me that breaking up isn't always the world's scariest thing. I mean, look at what you did with Jonah —"

"No kidding." Alexa lowered her gaze. She didn't think now was the time to express to Holly her fear that, because of her impulsiveness, she'd never love again.

Holly planted a kiss on Alexa's cheek. "I'm sorry," she murmured.

Alexa glanced up, confused. "About what? You know I adore it when you pour your tortured soul out to me."

Holly shook her head. "About what I said this morning — how you were difficult with boys and all that? I didn't mean it, Alexa. You *will* make a guy happy someday. Of course you will. But it'll have to be a guy who really *gets* you."

Alexa gave Holly a small smirk. "Because there are so many of those around."

"You never know where one might turn up," Holly said as she got to her feet, wiping them off on the marble edge of the pool. She seemed to be composing herself for a moment, and then she cleared her throat. "I need to head inside and make those calls before it gets too late out there."

Alexa looked up at her friend. "Okay. Want me to come with?"

Holly remembered how, back in South Beach, Alexa had sat by her side during another very difficult phone call. Now, though, she knew she needed to go it alone. So she told Alexa good-night and headed back inside the house, her pulse tapping at her wrists. As she made her way toward her bedroom, where her phone lay waiting on her bed, she decided she'd make the calls in order of their difficulty: Kenya first, to ask some questions about UCLA; her parents next, to discuss the college decision; and, finally . . .

TYLER was flashing across the screen of Holly's cell just as she reached for it; she'd been so deep into her thoughts she hadn't even heard it ringing. Her heart in her throat, Holly clicked the phone on and brought it to her ear.

"Hi," she whispered. "I was just about to call you." *Kind of.*

"Holly." Tyler's tone was deep and sober. "We need to talk."

"That's putting it mildly," Holly murmured, unsure why she was joking. Then she realized that she *had* to make things a little lighter, or she and Tyler would be swallowed by their sadness.

"Ever since we got off the phone, I've been thinking," Tyler went on, his voice low with emotion.

"Me, too," Holly said, and sat on the edge of

her bed, studying the starry Malibu night through her drapes. "A lot."

"I love you," Tyler said.

"I love you, too," Holly whispered. "But . . ."

"But," Tyler replied, like a confirmation.

Holly felt the tears return, salty and familiar as they meandered down her cheeks. "So great minds think alike?" she managed to ask.

Tyler gave a half laugh. "God, Holly. I can't believe this is happening."

"I know," Holly whispered. "Except it . . . is."

Slowly, carefully, she and Tyler began talking, began unwinding a conversation that would flow deep into the night. Holly wasn't sure where their talk would carry them, but that was the thing about the future. It was unknown, and unknowable, but before you knew it, you were there.

CHAPTER TEN
Present Tense

All of El Sueño was in a tizzy. Photographers snapped shots of the main house while reporters swarmed the grounds, generating a constant humming sound.

When Alexa pulled up in Jonah's Hybrid the next morning, Miguel directed her to a parking spot behind a news van. As she pushed her sunglasses up and lifted two iced white chocolate dreams — The Coffee Bean's specialty — from the drink holders, Alexa thought she heard the faint slapping of a helicopter's blades overhead. *Insanity.* It was Margaux's wedding day, so either half the world was salivating for a glimpse of the handsome brother of the bride — *or* Holly had created a raging bonfire of Tyler's photos in the living room.

Stepping out of the car, and tucking the fat, glossy July issue of *Vogue* under her arm, Alexa saw that the guesthouse looked intact. *Whew.*

Last night, when Holly hadn't come back outside, Alexa had abandoned her post by the pool to go to bed; beauty sleep was a priority for the wedding. She'd been propped up on pillows, investigating LA salons on her laptop, when Holly had stuck her head into the room. She'd looked weary and wan, and her face was stained with tears, but she'd assured Alexa that she was coping, and that they'd talk in the morning. "Is it — over with Tyler?" Alexa had whispered from her bed. "Over," Holly had confirmed, her face crumpling slightly as she'd pulled the door shut. First thing in the morning, Alexa had crept out of the house to run errands at the Malibu Country Mart — such as dropping off her film, buying *Vogue*, and making an appointment at a chichi hair salon — so she hadn't seen Holly yet. But she'd been worrying about her friend the whole time.

Her Grecian sandals clicking against the flagstones, Alexa trotted past the main house, where Esperanza was standing on the sundeck, firmly telling reporters that Jonah wasn't home and that they should call his publicist for a quote. Alexa wondered what the scene was like at Margaux's house in the Hills — the site of the actual wedding. As Alexa let herself into the guesthouse, she felt a thrill shoot through her; in a matter of hours, she'd be in the midst of an honest-to-goodness Hollywood event. She couldn't think of a better way to kick off her summer — not to mention the rest of her life.

Humming contentedly, Alexa carried the iced coffee drinks to Holly's bedroom, expecting to find her friend watching the press outside her window. Instead, Holly was kneeling on the floor of her walk-in closet, wrapped in one of the guesthouse's fluffy white robes, her wet hair shielding her face — and looking absolutely miserable.

"Oh, *Hol*," Alexa murmured, leaning against the closet door and feeling a swell of sympathy. "I know it hurts." Even though Alexa had recently had her heart badly broken in Paris, she couldn't begin to guess at the raw pain Holly was dealing with. Alexa and Xavier had had a passionate fling, not the kind of together-forever relationship Holly and Tyler had shared.

"Huh?" Holly glanced up, blinking, and then shook her head when she saw the concern on Alexa's face. Despite her lingering pain over what had happened with Tyler, Holly felt a giggle rise in her throat. "Oh, God. It's not what you think."

Alexa raised one brow. Holly's gray-green eyes were round, but they weren't teary. "You're not crying over Tyler?" Alexa asked, passing Holly one of the iced drinks.

"Not now," Holly sighed, getting to her feet and taking a sip of the frothy-sweet concoction. "I think I successfully cried myself out last night." The dull ache in Holly's heart deepened as she thought back to the hardest conversation of her life. She'd once read an article in *CosmoGIRL!* that had equated breaking up with tearing off a Band-Aid. On the phone with Tyler last night, Holly had decided that the amputation of a limb would be a far better comparison. It didn't have to be a whole *leg* — maybe, like, a pinkie finger. Which, of course, still hurt like hell.

She and Tyler had opened up about everything — their frustrations, their differences, their desires. "I think we want opposite things out of life," Tyler had said at one point while Holly had wept into the phone. Tyler had sniffed hard — which was his way of crying — and added that he never wanted to be the person to keep Holly from achieving her dreams. "You've been so good to me," Holly had sobbed in response, knowing it was true. They'd finally ended the conversation by saying they'd talk again at gradu- ation. Afterward, an emotionally drained Holly had somehow found it in her to call her parents to discuss UCLA, a talk which hadn't been much easier. Then she'd tossed and turned the night away, sobbing into her pillow and repeating *I'm not with Tyler anymore* to herself. The words still sounded as if they were in a foreign language, but Holly wondered if, in time, they'd begin to make sense. To feel normal.

Alexa let out a breath of relief. She knew she and Holly would get into more detail on the Tyler subject later; she was just glad her friend wasn't completely falling apart over the boy. "All right," she said, taking a few steps back into the room. "Then why were you collapsed on the closet floor like Paris Hilton after a rough night?"

"I was figuring out which shoes to wear —" Holly pointed down to her beige sandals, beaded gold flats, Adidas, and jellies, stacked beside the new box of Bebe stilettos. "— to my interview with the dean of admissions at UCLA." Speaking the words, Holly felt a mix of eagerness and terror storm through her. She *still* couldn't fathom what she was about to do in less than an hour.

"An interview?" Alexa cried, incredulous. She sat on the edge of Holly's bed, too surprised to bring her iced drink to her lips. "How did *that* happen so fast?"

"With difficulty," Holly groaned, rolling her eyes. Last night, she'd gone through a battle of wills with her impossible parents. *Holly Rebecca*, her mom had chided, *it's not like you to be so impulsive*. Holly had wanted to reply that that was exactly the point, but then her father, sounding choked up, had jumped in to say that he'd hate to have his little girl thousands of miles away for four years. Holly was sure that the only reason she'd eventually triumphed was that her parents were too wiped out from their camping trip to give an absolute no.

"I got my mom and dad to agree that I should go in for a meeting," Holly elaborated, turning away from Alexa to pluck her A-line khaki skirt off a hanger. "But my mom flat-out refused to call the school and throw her weight around." Holly frowned as she noticed her prom dress dangling from a hanger in her closet — its shimmery skirt was wrinkled from being folded up in her duffel. Fortunately Holly had spotted an iron in the bathroom's linen closet earlier.

"Gosh, that sucks," Alexa said, glancing down at her *Vogue* to hide her expression from her friend. Last night, during their poolside heart-to-heart, Alexa had supported Holly's UCLA switch; now, in the light of day, she was secretly hoping that Holly would still end up back on the East Coast. Alexa felt as if the girls had only just cemented their friendship; it seemed a shame to let that bond go to waste.

"Yeah, but then I talked to Kenya this morning, while you were out," Holly was saying, carrying the khaki skirt to the bed and laying it out beside Alexa. "And it turns out that she worked part-time at the admissions office last semester, so she was able to set something up for me. Amazing, no?" Holly's pulse spiked at the thought of her UCLA future, which now seemed truly within reach.

As long as she didn't screw up the interview.

"Holly, you *do* realize it's not every day that colleges let people change their minds at the last minute?" Alexa asked, opening her *Vogue* to a Catherine Malandrino ad. "I mean, you're not *guaranteed* a spot in the freshman class, are you?" She shot a long, level look up at Holly.

"Thank you, O Voice of Doom," Holly replied, lightly jabbing Alexa's shoulder. "I thought you were *rooting* for me to live in Cali full-time." As Holly set her iced drink down on her bedside table and reached for her comb, she heard the cacophony of raised voices and ringing cell phones outside her window. The paparazzi may not have been pawing through the trash last night, but they'd sure made up for it this morning. Holly wondered, then, if this was what life in California would be like — until she reminded herself that she wouldn't be spending her college years on an estate in Malibu. Which was actually kind of disappointing.

"I changed my mind," Alexa said simply, then

sipped at her drink. "I want you close at hand in case I have any romantic crises at Columbia. Don't you know by now that I'm a selfish bitch?" she added, her eyes glinting as she grinned up at her friend.

"Listen," Holly said, combing out her damp hair. "Can you please do something *non*-selfish today and figure out what we should get Margaux as a wedding present? And we need to leave a gift for Jonah, too," she added as she scooped her gold hoop earrings out of her makeup bag. Holly knew her parents would never let her live it down if she forgot to give a token of thanks to her host.

"I guess," Alexa sighed, How was she supposed to shop for a guy whom she'd just rejected? Her favorite things to buy for boys — flannel boxers, crisp button-downs, designer aftershave — would feel *way* too loaded for Jonah, and besides, what was there that the actor couldn't already get for himself? "How about we divide and conquer?" Alexa offered. "I'll take care of Margaux, you get the goods for Jonah?"

"I don't think I'll have time," Holly protested as she pushed one of the hoops through her ear, and Alexa rolled her eyes. "I still need to ask Esperanza if there's a fax machine in the main house that I can use — I'm supposed to bring my latest report card to the interview. And then Kenya's coming to pick me up, and *then* I need to iron my dress before the wedding — " Holly paused as she felt her earring bang against the ring on her finger.

Her Claddagh ring.

Oh, yeah.

Her throat tightening, Holly reached down and tugged lightly on the ring. It slipped off her finger with little resistance. She held it in the warmth of her palm for a moment, sending it a silent good-bye, before she slipped it deep into her makeup bag. As she zipped up the bag, she found herself blinking back tears.

Now she really was ready for her interview. Ready to start anew.

"Hol?" Alexa said softly, feeling a pang of regret as she noticed how upset her friend was. Alexa reminded herself that, whenever she'd been distraught over a boy, Holly had dropped everything to comfort her. Alexa knew she *could* be ridiculously selfish, but maybe there was a way to alter that somehow. "Good luck with the interview and don't worry about the presents," Alexa added firmly as she reached up to squeeze Holly's arm. "I'll take care of everything. I promise."

Setting down her boxy shopping bags, Alexa sank into a free chair in the elegant Peach Grove salon. It was more than ninety outside, and hazy — not exactly prime weather for an outdoor celebration. Even in her strapless floral-print sundress, Alexa's collarbone was damp with sweat, and her thick hair was sticking to her back. *Not for much longer*, Alexa thought as she reached for an issue of *Variety*. She felt a beat of hesitation; did she really want to be doing this? Alexa wondered if Holly, at UCLA, was feeling similarly — looking forward to the change, but scared of it, too.

Alexa was rarely scared. But if this haircut got messed up, she'd have to deal with looking *less* than drop-dead beautiful in front of most of Hollywood — and, if E! turned their cameras on her, the *world. Maybe this is stupid*, Alexa thought, biting her lip. She remembered that crucial rule of facials — always leave three weeks between an avocado skin peel and an event. Who in their right minds scheduled a haircut on the day of the biggest wedding to hit LA in ages? To calm her nerves, Alexa opened *Variety* and flipped past an article on weekend box office predictions. Then she noticed a small blurb on Oren Samuels, who she remembered was Jonah's agent, accompanied by a photograph. Alexa was reading his client list — apparently, he represented Margaux and Paul as well — when she heard a voice above her.

"Alissa Sant Lauren?"

Alexa glanced up from *Variety* to see a tall, stunning

guy with mocha-colored skin and close-cropped, dyed-blond hair, wearing the salon's distinctive peach-colored apron over a black shirt and slacks. Besides Jonah, he was probably the hottest guy Alexa had seen yet in Hollywood, which made her forgive his name slipup.

Only she'd bet anything that he wasn't into girls.

"*C'est moi,*" she announced, standing up. "Alexa."

"Aramis," he replied, flashing a wide smile. "Come this way, sweetheart."

Scooping up her bags, Alexa followed Aramis through the salon, passing framed snapshots of Chloë Sevigny, Camilla Belle, and Margaux Eklundstrom herself. In between flowy peach drapes, pouty-lipped models slouched in black swivel chairs. Waifish stylists with Chinese-symbol tattoos on their midsections blow-dried and snipped and sprayed over a thumping soundtrack of Franz Ferdinand. Alexa settled down in one such swivel chair, and Aramis ceremoniously draped a gauzy peach cape over her. There was no going back now.

"Well?" Aramis asked, pouring a dab of scented oil into his palm and then lightly massaging Alexa's scalp. "What would you like to do with these gorgeous golden locks?"

Alexa gulped, watching her reflection in the tall

mirror. Beneath the mirror lay an array of scissors, clips, and combs — all weapons that would tear into her most prized possession. Feeling like she was breaking up with a beloved boy, Alexa let her eyes drift shut and remembered some of the best times she'd shared with her hair: all the high, sleek ponytails, the better to show off big dangly earrings; all the tossings over shoulders, the better to finish off a point she was making; all the sneaking into boys' mouths and hands during wild kissing sessions.

Then Alexa opened her eyes. It was time to let go of the past.

"I thought maybe . . . a change," she ventured, indicating with her hand the length she'd been envisioning. "Though not too *big* a change," she added hurriedly, meeting Aramis's sparkling eyes in the mirror. "And . . ."

"Yes, honey belle?" Aramis asked, the corner of his mouth lifting.

"I'm going to Margaux Eklundstrom's wedding this afternoon," Alexa blurted, her face growing warm. "So . . ." she trailed off, wondering if Aramis would even believe her.

"Say no more," Aramis said, running his fingers through her hair. "I understand the need for extreme fabulosity. You know," Aramis went on. "I used to do

Margaux's hair way back in the day, when she and her brother were two little runty kids growing up in La Brea. They still pop in here now and then."

"*Really?*" Alexa asked, intrigued by this slice of Eklundstrom family history. "What else do you know about them?"

"Oh, everything," Aramis sighed. "Including the fact that Paul DeMille's family is *loaded*, so he probably *is* marrying Margaux for love. And," he added, holding up a strand of Alexa's hair. "Aren't *you* the lucky one? I know for a fact that Baby Bear Jonah has a thing for blondes."

"So I've heard," Alexa sighed, rolling her eyes, and Artemis laughed.

"Alexa," he said decisively. "We are going to have fun today."

Alexa grinned in agreement, settling deeper into her chair. This was going to be the most entertaining haircut of her life.

Over in Westwood, Holly settled into the stiff chair outside the UCLA dean of admissions' office, her sweaty palms clutching the transcript her high school guidance counselor had faxed to El Sueño that morning. Holly had had just enough time to pick up the fax from Esperanza's office in the main house, before fighting her way through the reporters swarming outside and making it into Kenya's car.

"Gee," Kenya had deadpanned as she'd peeled away from the estate. "You'd think there was a wedding or something happening today."

Kenya had been such a soothing, funny presence on the drive to Westwood that Holly had wished her friend could accompany her to the interview, but Kenya had to attend a philosophy study session. Still, she'd assured Holly that she'd drive her back to Malibu, since Kenya had planned to spend her afternoon on Zuma Beach anyway. The notion that an afternoon in college could be whiled away on the beach had only reaffirmed Holly's decision. So had driving across campus observing the crowds on Bruin Walk, admiring the rolling green of the athletics fields. Holly had once again been enchanted by the spirit of the school.

Now came the tricky part.

Holly was a disaster at interviews. She got fidgety, blushed, suddenly had to pee, and forgot all the reasons as to why she was interviewing in the first place. In her opinion, phrases like "Tell me about yourself" had been invented by the devil; how was a girl supposed to sum up her entire existence in a few half-stammered sentences? Holly had managed to avoid having interviews with most of the colleges she'd applied to, but her parents had cajoled her into interviewing at Rutgers. In a suit, of course. Holly could still recall the choky feeling of the high-necked tweed jacket, the itchiness of the skirt, and her completely immature stuttering when the patient alum asked her why she'd chosen Rutgers. *Because my parents made me*, Holly had almost said — cursed, as always, by the honesty bug. Of course, she'd held back and mumbled something about a good academic curriculum, which was probably why she'd received that acceptance letter in April.

Taking a deep breath, Holly crossed her legs, studying the beaded gold flats she'd slipped on before leaving the guesthouse. She hoped they wouldn't come off as too flighty for such a serious interview. The rest of the outfit she'd cobbled together — the khaki skirt and a button-down blue shirt with short, puffed sleeves — wasn't quite the suit her mom would have recommended, either. When she'd first stepped off the elevator into the admissions office's elegant foyer, Holly had wished she'd bought something more formal back on Rodeo Drive. Especially when the department secretary had raised an eyebrow at Holly, and murmured, "Oh, yes, Jacobson. You're the one with the unique situation."

Holly hoped that "unique situation" wasn't code for "you've got no chance in hell, baby."

To distract herself, she picked up a copy of UCLA's alumni magazine and was skimming an article about how many movies had been filmed on the campus, when she heard footsteps behind the closed office door. Nervousness raced through her, and Holly instinctively reached down to twist her Claddagh ring — but there was nothing on her finger. *Right.* With a pang, Holly realized she had no one to rely on in that moment but herself.

And it was time to face the present.

The door to the office opened and an elderly man with a shock of white hair — Dean Brown, Holly knew — poked his head out and, to Holly's relief, gave her a warm smile.

"Come on in, Ms. Jacobson," he said in a deep, rumbly voice, pushing the door open all the way to reveal a sun-filled office hung with bright watercolors. "We've been expecting you."

We? Holly thought in confusion, until she walked into the office and saw the young, trim, auburn-haired woman seated at the dean's desk. She, too, gave Holly a broad smile as she stood and held her hand out.

"Holly, such a pleasure," the woman said. "I'm Olivia Farber, the coach of the —"

"Women's track team," Holly filled in, smiling herself now. "We spoke in January. You tried to recruit me?"

"That I did," Coach Farber said with a nod.

"With good reason," Dean Brown thundered, striding back to his desk as he motioned for Holly to take a seat. "We looked through your file again and saw a stellar letter of recommendation from your current coach, Ms. Graham. And your high school's assistant principal spoke very highly of you this morning."

Holly sat gingerly on the edge of the chair, her heart hammering away. "My — my assistant principal?" she echoed, glancing from the dean to Coach Farber.

"Yes," the dean boomed, accepting the transcript Holly handed him. "She called first thing today to ask that we make an exception for a student of your caliber."

"I — she *did*?" Holly asked, overcome. Her *mother*? Holly felt a swell of emotion; she couldn't believe her parents had actually come through for her.

"Yes," the dean said again, giving Holly a piercing look. "Of course, we have to take into account that she is, after all, your mother and therefore highly biased. You'll have to prove it to us yourself, Holly, that we should bend the rules and allow you into our freshman class."

"Okay," Holly said after a moment, pressing her hands together and sitting up straight. "I'll try."

* * *

Wearing boy shorts and a tank top that spelled out JE T'AIME in sequins, Alexa was sitting on the fake grass of the indoor golf course, painting her toenails Café Au Lait for the wedding. *This feels so weird*, she thought — not the do-it-yourself mani–pedi, of course, but the new sensation of cool air on her back.

When Aramis had unclipped Alexa's cape and announced that he was done, Alexa's heart had leaped in surprise at the sight of the shorter-haired blonde girl in the mirror. Was it really still her? But after driving back to El Sueño, walking past the stretch limo that was waiting outside to pick up Jonah for the wedding, dropping off her bags in her bedroom, and taking a long, hot shower, she was starting to suspect that this new haircut was very much her. The new Alexa — the college girl.

Alexa was blowing on her nails when she heard the front door open and slam. A moment later, Holly appeared, the expression on her face utterly unreadable and her hands behind her back as she crossed the green golf course toward Alexa.

"So?" Alexa cried, setting down her bottle of polish as suspense gripped her. "Are you in?"

"Oh my God, your hair!" Holly cried, marveling at her friend's sideswept bangs and shiny, flaxen hair cut just to her shoulders. "I love it, Alexa. You look . . . you look like a girl who works at *Vogue*." Suddenly Holly felt she was catching a glimpse of who her friend would really become: someone successful and savvy and so far beyond the shallow, self-centered Alexa of a few years ago. *We've grown up*, Holly realized, getting the slightest bit choked up. *Both of us.*

"Stop avoiding the subject," Alexa chided as she carefully got to her feet. "Am I looking at a member of UCLA's incoming freshman class or not?" She held her breath as she waited for Holly to respond. So much rode on the answer — including both girls' futures.

Her face still giving away nothing, Holly finally pulled her hands out from behind her back. She was holding up a thick manila envelope that was stamped with a bright blue-and-gold seal, and Alexa could make out the words THE UNIVERSITY OF CALIFORNIA. . . . She glanced from the envelope to Holly and noticed that her friend's eyes were shining.

"Oh, Hol!" Alexa squealed, opening her arms to hug her friend. Despite all the hesitations she'd had about Holly going to UCLA, she felt a bubble of joy rising in her. She wasn't sure *how* she'd survive without her best friend close by once college started, but this wasn't about Alexa now. It was about Holly seeing her dream realized — and Alexa had to celebrate that, no matter what.

Holly began to laugh, shaking her head back and forth as she returned Alexa's embrace. "It's the most surreal thing ever, right?" She knew the events of the day would feel more believable once she called her parents, and once she sorted through the envelope of registration materials that the dean had given her. But all that could wait. For the moment, she was enjoying the vaguely blurry, dazed feeling of happiness.

"*And* the most terrific," Alexa replied. "It's too bad we finished that champagne on our first night. If this doesn't demand a toast, I'm not sure what does."

"Relax – there'll be *plenty* of fancy drinks at Margaux's," Holly said, and she felt a surge of stress as she realized the wedding was a mere two hours away. "Well, what am I *doing*?" she gasped, taking a step back. "I need to shower – and paint my nails, right? – and my dress *so* needs ironing. . . ." Holly wasn't sure how she could cram everything in, unless she stripped right now and dashed straight into the waterfall shower, calling her parents and painting her nails as she ran.

"Stop." Alexa held up one hand, her eyes sparkling. "I almost forgot. Wait right here." Walking on her heels so as not to mess up her toes, she hurried out of the golf course room while Holly watched her go with growing curiosity. When Alexa returned, her face was glowing as she held a white Fred Segal bag out to Holly. Inside the bag was something wrapped in white tissue paper.

"What is this?" Holly asked, handing off her bulky envelope to Alexa to hold and hesitantly accepting the bag.

Alexa gave Holly a mysterious smile. "Something that I decided you need to make your trip complete."

Holly pushed back the layers of tissue paper. When she saw a sliver of papaya-colored fabric, she felt warm, then cold, then dizzy.

I don't believe it.

"Alexa — no," Holly whispered numbly, letting the tissue paper fall so she was left holding the too-beautiful-for-words Catherine Malandrino dress in her hands. Returning it yesterday, she hadn't thought for a second that she'd ever see it again. Which hadn't seemed like such a tragedy then, especially in the midst of all the UCLA and Tyler drama. But gazing at the dress now, Holly realized how much she'd missed it.

"I know you *had* to return it to have a clear conscience," Alexa was explaining with a smile in her voice. "Because that's just what Holly Jacobson does. But *I* felt like you were betraying the cardinal rule of clothes — never deny yourself something that makes you feel fabulous. So I stopped by Fred Segal today to correct your faux pas."

Glancing up at her friend, Holly smiled, too, even as a lump formed in her throat. "Because that's just what Alexa St. Laurent does."

Alexa bit her lip, feeling a tremor of worry. Had she been overstepping? "Uh-oh. Am I working the Little Miss Bossy thing too much?"

Holly laughed. "No . . . it's not that." She met Alexa's gaze again. "But I can't accept this, Alexa. I know how much it cost. And I can't repay you any time soon. . . ."

"Hol, it's a present," Alexa insisted, taking a step closer. "My graduation gift to you. It's high time I got you something to thank you for . . . " *Putting up with me*, Alexa thought. *Saving my ass so many times. And being a better friend to me than I ever was to you.* Alexa knew it was true; she remembered how cruelly she'd cast off Holly in junior high when Alexa had begun traveling in popular, fashion-y circles and Holly had remained steadfastly sporty. Maybe Holly was the strong one, Alexa realized. Maybe she'd been stronger all along.

"You don't owe me anything," Holly murmured, her eyes smarting. What with Tyler last night, and now this, she felt like a tear generator. "Whatever happened between us in the past, Alexa . . . that was *then*. Our friendship's so much better in the present tense, don't you think?" She gave Alexa a small smile, and then flung her arms around her friend once more.

"I do," Alexa agreed, giving Holly a quick squeeze. "That is," she added, stepping back and raising one eyebrow. "If you agree to *keep* the dress this time around."

Holly held the dress against her figure, loving the way it shone a paler pink in the late afternoon light. Really, wearing her prom dress now would just be *insulting* to Alexa, Holly assured herself. And she'd be saving time on ironing if she could just slip this number on after the shower. In some ways, she *had* no other choice. . . .

"Of course I'm keeping it," Holly finally replied, beaming up at Alexa. "If *you* admit that you got this for me because you wanted your wedding date to look presentable."

"*Presentable?*" Alexa snorted, rolling her eyes. "Please. By the time you and I are both dressed and ready, I think we'll be in serious danger of looking hotter than the bride."

"Isn't that really bad form?" Holly teased, slipping the dress back into the tissue paper and carrying it out of the room, close to her heart. "Oh, hang on," she added, remembering another detail of wedding etiquette. "What did you end up getting for Margaux? And Jonah?"

"It was so obvious when I thought about it," Alexa replied, feeling a flash of pride. "I'd just gotten my pictures developed, and there's this little store in Malibu that sells funky frames . . ."

"You framed two of your photos?" Holly asked, feeling a smile spread across her face as Alexa nodded, her cheeks flushing. "That's perfect, Alexa. I bet those will be the most unique gifts the Eklundstroms ever got."

Alexa returned Holly's smile, pleased by her friend's reaction. But the presents were more than unique; each carried a special meaning. She was giving Margaux the photo she'd taken of the Las Vegas strip during the daytime. The rawness of the colors, and the wildness of the desert, reminded Alexa of Margaux's own free spirit. And for Jonah she'd framed her close-up of the seashell, the one she'd taken yesterday morning in Malibu. She felt like that image captured the true Alexa — the photographer, the artist — that Jonah, sweet and earnest as he was, had never really *gotten*. Maybe this would be his chance to finally understand.

Before she headed out to go shower, Holly had another thought. "Alexa," she ventured. "Do you think you and Jonah might . . . make up? You know what they say about weddings," she added with a sly smile. "All that romance, and those boys in suits . . ." Holly, for her part, was realizing that it would be her first night in so long as a girl without a boyfriend. The thought was at once unsettling and freeing. As melancholy as she still felt about Tyler, there was a part of her that was a little excited to twirl around the dance floor in her new dress and meet the gazes of cute boys.

And even if she didn't end up doing that, she could always live vicariously through Alexa.

"No romance for me," Alexa murmured to herself, returning to her nails after Holly had departed. Yes, the possibility of seeing hot celeb guys gave her a tickle of anticipation, as did the notion of Jonah in a three-piece suit. But tonight would be all about dancing and eating and star-spotting: indulging in the Hollywood magic. And no boys — and the drama they inevitably brought — were going to spoil any of that.

She hoped.

CHAPTER ELEVEN
Fairy Tales

An hour, a shower, several swipes of lip gloss, a few smudged toenails, and two zipped-up dresses later, Alexa and Holly were stepping out of the guesthouse into the sultry Malibu evening.

Alexa was feeling similarly sultry in her teeny aquamarine dress, diamond studs, and silver teardrop necklace, but she was still a little self-conscious — a first for her — about her new hair. As Holly started down the steps of the sundeck, swinging her gold-studded black clutch (the one prom relic Alexa had allowed her), Alexa paused and leaned down to adjust the strap on one of her silver, pencil-heeled peep-toes. She realized she was stalling, as if trying to decide whether or not to go forward and face the evening. Maybe it wasn't about her hair, which she had to admit did look pretty nice with the dress on. It was more that she sensed, in her gut, that something at the wedding was going to change her life.

Which was just silly.

"Alexa? You coming?" Holly paused at the bottom of the steps and turned, struggling to stay upright in her skinny black heels. It was almost as if the friends had switched roles; usually, Holly was the one lingering back, questioning her hair and clothing choices. But now, the ruffled hem of her delicious new dress lifting in the breeze, her nails polished by Alexa, and her hair knotted in a loose bun at the nape of her neck, Holly felt more than ready to hop into the Hybrid and zoom up into the Hills.

Which was why, when Alexa finally tucked her silver clutch under her arm and began walking forward again, Holly made her suggestion.

"Want me to drive?"

Alexa blinked at Holly, astonished. Whenever the two of them drove anywhere, it was always Alexa at the wheel, steering their course and controlling the music — and Holly, never the world's most confident driver, had preferred it that way. But now, looking at her friend's determined face — her eyes smoky with shadow, her lips shiny with gloss, and her bangs full and straight with the rest of her hair pulled back —

Alexa understood that Holly no longer needed to remain in the passenger's seat.

And, suddenly, Alexa didn't mind trading places. She smiled, some of her nervousness dissipating. "Well," she pretended to deliberate, holding the car keys up between her thumb and forefinger as a grinning Holly came forward and snatched them. "You *are* moving out here, so you could probably use the practice. Just go slow when we're in the Hills."

"Isn't there some line from an old movie?" Holly asked, closing the trunk, where she'd placed Margaux's gift bag earlier, and unlocking the driver's-side door. "Something like, 'Fasten your seat belts, it's going to be a bumpy night'?"

"Bette Davis," Alexa laughed, sliding in beside Holly and obediently buckling up. "*All About Eve.* How fitting."

As Holly pulled away from El Sueño, the sky overhead changed from a dusky, heavy blue to a white-gray, and there was a distinct crack of thunder in the distance. "Oh, no," Holly groaned, guiding the car down the rocky path that led to PCH. "What if the wedding gets rained out?"

"I had the same thought earlier, when it was so gross and muggy," Alexa said, crossing her long, tanned legs and peering worriedly out the windshield.

"Naturally the weather's flawless every day we're here, and now tonight . . ." Alexa shook her head, dismayed at the thought of the girls' outfits getting wet. "How could Margaux do this to us?"

Holly sighed, checking the rearview mirror as she expertly changed lanes. "I guess there *is* something movie stars can't control."

A misty drizzle began to fall as the girls drove by the brightly colored mural of celebrities on the side of Hollywood High School ("Could you imagine graduating from *here*?" Alexa asked wistfully). But once they were climbing high into the Hills, joining the line of gleaming cars snaking their up way up toward Margaux's light-blue mansion, the sky turned a breathtaking rose-pink. It was still drizzling, but Holly dared to open her window a crack and breathe in the scent of lemon trees on the cool air. The Hills were all winding roads, thick-leaved trees, and quaint little nooks containing cottages that probably cost more than Holly's college tuition. Holly would never admit the childish thought to Alexa, but she felt as if they were driving through a fairy tale.

This sensation only intensified when the girls reached the circular driveway in front of the mansion, and a blue-jacketed attendant appeared to take their car. The marble columns lining the walkway of the mansion were twined with sparkling lights, and another path, leading behind the mansion, was strewn with black rose petals. As Alexa retrieved Margaux's present from the trunk, Holly shielded her hair from the drizzle with her clutch. Maybe it was because the talk with Tyler, and the UCLA interview, were both behind her, but suddenly Holly was feeling fairly chill about being at such a glamorous celebrity event.

Alexa sauntered over to join Holly, and for a second, both girls stood still to take in their surroundings. Slender legs ending in diamond-encrusted stilettos were emerging from white Hummer limos, and men in sleek black tuxedos opened umbrellas over the shiny heads of young women in silky-sheer gowns. Police cars, camera crews, and news vans were gathering outside the mansion, and security personnel ran by, barking into walkie-talkies as if, Holly mused, this were some international spy mission. Both girls spotted Jessica Alba, pouting prettily and murmuring into her cell phone. Brandon Routh was leaning against one of the columns, wearing sunglasses in spite of the rain, and was that Adrian Grenier stepping out of a Jaguar convertible?

Alexa sighed. It was Hollywood-stalker heaven.

"*No*, Alejandro, I told you, *don't* let the swans out of the pond — at least not until after the ceremony — well, of course they're trying to eat people's spinach puffs — but if that old bat in furs gives you trouble again, send her to me."

Alexa spun around to see Vikram, Margaux's beloved wedding planner. He was wearing a pink linen suit and barking into an earpiece.

Clearly through with Alejandro, Vikram glanced up and shot a don't-mess-with-me-honeys smile at Alexa and Holly. "I'm sorry, girls. I need to ask that you step right this way" — he gestured to a line of people that was forming before a burly guy dressed in a security uniform — "and give your names to Tucker. Then, you can follow the black rose petals to the garden." He paused and put a hand to his earpiece. "What, Alejandro? Did you say we're *out* of miniature quiches? That's it. I'm calling Wolfgang!"

"There's a *bouncer*?" Holly whispered incredulously as she and Alexa hurried away from Vikram and took their place in line behind an impatient-looking, Prada-clad Anne Hathaway. Seeing the willowy, fashion-diva actress, Holly felt some of her old shyness wash over her; maybe she hadn't changed *entirely* from that starstruck girl she'd been at The Standard.

"Hottest ticket in town." Alexa grinned at Holly, feeling herself ease back into her element. What had she been stressing about? She felt a rush of gratitude toward Margaux for inviting them into this enchanted world.

The bouncer — who had a tattoo of a bald eagle on his bald head and a permanent sneer — was finally crossing Anne Hathaway's name off the list and letting the actress pass through. Then he narrowed his eyes as Alexa and Holly stepped forward.

"Alexandria St. Laurent," Alexa announced confidently. "And one guest." She tried to toss her hair, but then remembered it didn't have the same effect with its new length.

Holly felt the tiniest morsel of dread as the bouncer's beady eyes scanned the list. She remembered how impulsively Margaux had invited Alexa to the wedding. Maybe the carefree actress had somehow forgotten . . . ?

"You're not on the list, blondie," the bouncer announced, looking back up at Alexa. "I can't let you *or* your guest in." He nodded at Holly. "Vikram will show you out."

"I'm — *what?*" Alexa stammered, stunned as a raindrop landed on her nose. "Of course I'm on the list — Margaux personally invited me — you have to check again!" A horrible thought occured to Alexa then: Had Jonah, in some weird act of vengeance, demanded that her name be taken off?

"Alexa," Holly urged as her friend's face turned purple. "Margaux probably spaced on putting you on the list." Holly began to take a few steps back, not wanting to cause a scene. She reached for Alexa's arm, but her fiery friend jerked away. "Come on," Holly added. "Let's get out of here — we'll go to the Chateau Marmont or something . . . get some drinks. . . ." Holly heard murmurs from the other people in line, which only made her panic deepen. Alexa raised one eyebrow as she and Holly held a silent discussion with their eyes.

The girls were still facing each other, both wondering how to proceed, when an elderly woman's voice suddenly emanated from behind Tucker, loud and imperious

"Where's Vikram?" she was demanding. "I want to speak to him about some disruptive *creatures* running around the wedding site."

"The guests aren't allowed to complain to Vikram," the bouncer replied, sounding pissed, and Alexa and Holly turned around slowly. "Who are you, anyway?" he added.

The woman — who wore her silver hair up in a bun, a diamond choker around her throat, and a mink stole over her black floor-length gown — put her hands on her wide hips. "How *dare* you? I am the aunt of the groom, Paul DeMille," she thundered. "I am Henrietta von Malhoffer!"

Henrietta von Malhoffer.

Alexa and Holly looked back at each other, their eyes huge. They would have recognized their old nemesis even if she hadn't spoken her name. They'd had dangerous run-ins with the volatile Henrietta in both South Beach *and* Paris.

Maybe she's following us, Holly thought, biting back a giggle and sidestepping behind Alexa as Henrietta continued to rail at the bouncer. Holly wondered what the fastest escape route would be; she'd hate for Paul's dear relative to recognize the girls who had once pretended she was *their* aunt.

Meanwhile, Alexa was having the opposite reaction. She was *thrilled* to see Henrietta. With the prissy *grande dame* screaming in his face, the bouncer was so distracted that he likely wouldn't notice if Alexa and Holly slipped right past him.

Which, after Alexa had grabbed Holly's hand and signaled the plan to her, they did.

Cool drops of rain battering their shoulders, the girls ran at full tilt toward the mansion, whipping past starlets and news reporters, who looked at them curiously. Holly wasn't remotely as fast as usual in her ridiculous heels, so she and Alexa kept pace with each other, hair flying and breaths catching. They staggered down the rose-strewn path, and then arrived, panting, in a sumptuous back garden.

With the drizzle letting up, the garden looked like a watercolor painting. In front of a glittering pond — on which downy-white swans floated serenely — stood a wedding canopy made of beech trees and gardenias. Rows and rows of white chairs with plush seats were set up before the canopy, and in the center of the garden was a grand white tent hung with small white lights. The sweet scent of roses mingled with Chanel perfume and peanut sauce wafting from waiters' silver trays. Tuxedoed musicians seated in a circle were playing Bach on their violins, and guests milled about, nibbling on chicken satay and sipping from tall flutes filled with champagne and wild strawberries.

They'd made it.

Holly glanced over her shoulder, but it seemed Tucker had more important things to deal with than chasing down two wayward girls. "I can't believe we got away with that," she whispered as she and Alexa hurried deeper into the crowd, passing a gaggle of good-looking young guys — groomsmen — wearing charcoal-gray, three-piece suits with silver silk ties.

"Why not?" Alexa asked as she gratefully accepted a strawberry-and-champagne drink from a waiter and grinned at Holly. "We, my love, are masters of breaking the rules."

Holly nodded and accepted her own champagne

flute. Maybe that was what LA had been all about — breaking with the past, inventing rules of their own. Mulling this over — and trying to keep her heels from sinking into the wet grass — Holly followed Alexa past streams of shimmering, laughing guests over to the white-draped gift table, which was laden with giant boxes wrapped in gilt-and-cream paper.

"It's gorgeous," Holly sighed, meaning not only the gift table, but everything. She sipped from her champagne, tasting the fresh strawberry, and glanced around her to survey the garden. *I'm really here. At Margaux Eklundstrom's wedding.* Holly spotted a woman with abundant auburn hair wearing a flowing blue gown, standing under the wedding canopy with her hands clasped. A few guests were starting to fill the white chairs, grumbling slightly over the rain. "I think it's going to start soon," Holly added, feeling a pang of anticipation and setting down her unfinished drink; she would be driving back later that night.

Balancing her champagne flute in one hand, Alexa was busy trying to fit her flowered gift bag onto the jam-packed table. When the bag slipped from her grasp, the tissue paper, card, and photo of the Vegas strip landed face up in the damp grass at Alexa's feet.

Shit.

"That's a beautiful photograph," someone commented in a slightly raspy voice. A pair of leather black shoes came to a stop before the photo. "It's a shame to see it treated like that."

Alexa let her gaze travel upward, over a pair of dark gray pin-striped trousers, a well-fitted gray suit jacket, a gray silk vest and tie, a half-smiling, full mouth, and then slicked-back blond hair, high cheekbones, and bright hazel eyes behind black-framed glasses.

Alexa's heart stopped. She forgot all about the photograph. Disbelief shot through her as she tried to absorb the insane fact that she was looking right at . . .

"Seamus?" Alexa gasped, feeling Holly freeze beside her. With his hair combed back, he looked different, and Alexa wondered if the boy who had tormented her on their road trip had a twin brother who knew the Eklundstroms — and looked damn sexy in a suit.

"Hi again," Seamus replied, and gave a wide, easy grin.

"Seamus, what are you *doing* here?" Holly demanded, feeling light-headed at the sight of him. How had *he* gotten past the bouncer?

Alexa, who was wondering the same thing, took that moment to notice that Seamus was dressed exactly like the other groomsmen who'd been milling about. He obviously *wasn't* crashing.

What on earth . . .

Seamus gave a bashful smile and lowered his head, putting his hands in his pants pockets. "Remember, at the Getty, how I said I had something to tell you?" he began, and then he lifted his head to meet Alexa's gaze.

The weirdest thing happened then. Alexa felt her heart give a kick, and her cheeks flushed as she studied the depths of Seamus's hazel eyes. In them she saw kindness and intelligence and — something else. Something that made her heart beat even faster.

"Shay! What up, brother? You want us to start the wedding without you?"

A guy in a black tux appeared at Seamus's side. He was short and stocky, with salt-and-pepper hair, and Alexa immediately recognized him as Oren Samuels, the agent she'd read about in *Variety*. Oren thumped Seamus on his shoulder, then pointed across the grass. "Jonah's looking for you — it's almost showtime."

Still stunned, Holly looked over to where the other guy was pointing. Next to a grove of lemon trees, all the groomsmen were gathering alongside the bridesmaids, who wore pale-blue gauzy dresses and garlands of violets in their hair. Holly could make out Jonah, handsome and grinning as he posed for a photo with another groomsman.

"I have to go," Seamus said unnecessarily as Oren

led him away. "I'll find you girls after the ceremony." Then Seamus glanced at Alexa. "The photo —" he said, gesturing to it.

The photo had slipped Alexa's mind as surely as it had slipped from her hands. She knelt down to retrieve it but kept her eyes on Seamus. "Yeah?" she replied cautiously.

"That's the one you took in the car, right?" he asked, giving her a half smile. "I remember."

Alexa nodded, her heart going to her throat. *Seamus knows*, she realized, the thought springing to her head before she could stop it. *He knows* me.

Flustered, Alexa restored the contents of the gift bag, found room for it on the table, and hurried with Holly over to the rows of white chairs, which had been wiped dry by Vikram's staff. The rain began to let up as the girls breathlessly sank into the last two remaining seats. They were sitting behind Esperanza, who looked as prim as ever in her white suit and high, tight bun.

"I can't believe Seamus lied to us," Holly was fuming as she set her gold-studded black clutch in her lap.

"Well, I guess he didn't technically *lie*, since we never *asked* him if he'd be here," Alexa argued, twisting around in her seat to look at the groomsmen. She didn't see Seamus, but she spotted Jonah standing at the head of the line, self-assuredly smoothing back his dark hair. Alexa thought about waving to him, but she decided she'd wait until after the ceremony. Besides, she had other things on her mind now.

"Since when are *you* Seamus's defender?" Holly asked. She could feel a mischievous smile tugging on her lips.

Alexa whirled back around to face her friend, her cheeks pinker than Holly had ever seen them. "I'm *not* – I just –" Before Alexa could finish, the musicians struck up a tune on their violins (Holly recognized it as the Beatles' "Here Comes the Sun," which she thought was a cute choice) and the processional began.

Down the aisle came the adorable, towheaded child actress Nevada Giroux, wearing a tiny replica of the bridesmaids' blue gowns, and scattering fresh violet petals from a woven basket. *Oohs* and *ahs* followed her, and then faded as beaming, dressed-to-the-nines parents and grandparents took their turns, nodding graciously as camera flashes went off. Next came the groomsmen and bridesmaids, walking two by two. Jonah, the best man, led the way, beside a curly-haired redhead who had to be the maid of honor. Up ahead, Holly noticed the crew from E! filming, and helicopter blades were whirring overhead, as they had that morning at *El Sueño*. In that heart-jumping moment, it fully dawned on Holly that she was at an event that would be major pop-culture news for at least a week.

Thank God she hadn't worn her prom dress after all.

A hush fell over the crowd, and all heads turned to see Margaux and Paul, arm in arm. Alexa gasped at the genius of Margaux's Paz Ferrara–designed bridal gown: It was very eighties-retro, short and strapless with a bubble hem — and it was fuchsia. She wore it with high-heeled, strappy, fuchsia sandals, carried a bouquet of black roses, and wore a wreath of the same flowers in her short hair. Her tear-filled dark-blue eyes darted from side to side, and then she smiled.

She was stunning.

Scandalized murmurs shot through the crowd. Now the camera flashes went off with a vengeance, and Holly was so blinded by them that she only caught a quick glimpse of Paul, who looked almost clean-cut in a black tux that hid his tattoos. The couple stopped under the canopy, facing the auburn-haired woman in the blue gown.

"Welcome," the woman said into a microphone, her voice strong and melodic. "My name is Bluebird Wasserstein, and I am a certified Kabbalah Minister of Love and Peace, practicing only within the city of Los Angeles."

"That's a surprise," Alexa snorted, and she and Holly covered their mouths to muffle their giggles. Esperanza glanced over her shoulder, arching one dark eyebrow.

"Today," Bluebird went on, smiling serenely at the crowd. "We — I say we, because a wedding is at its essence a communal affair — will wed Margaux and Paul in a truly beautiful ceremony combining Buddhist, Jewish, Christian, and Wiccan traditions."

"Is this for real?" Holly whispered to Alexa.

Up front, through the bustle of the crowd, Alexa thought she saw Seamus cough into his fist in order to disguise a laugh, and she grinned.

After Bluebird had chanted a few indecipherable prayers blessing the bride and groom, Margaux and Paul turned to each other to exchange the rings and speak their vows. Suddenly Holly felt some of her silly mood subside. A seriousness bloomed in her as she watched the couple gaze lovingly at each other. The rain had stopped completely, as if in deference to the ceremony, and as the sun set behind Margaux and Paul, the sky layered itself into shades of violet, yellow, and pink — like the hint of a rainbow. The whole garden seemed to glow.

A director couldn't have set up this scene better, Alexa mused with a smile.

"Paul," Margaux said into the microphone, her

voice throaty with tears. "My heart, my rock, my reason for living. Whatever adventure life takes us on, I know you will be beside me, holding my hand as we skydive out of that plane, drive backward down Hollywood Boulevard, and dance naked on the roof of the Roosevelt Hotel." Nervous titters echoed through the crowd. "Or whatever," Margaux amended, grinning.

Alexa was chuckling at Margaux's overdramatics, but Holly bit her lip, thinking of Tyler. Her hand strayed to her now bare ring finger just as Paul slid the gold band onto Margaux's. Everything Margaux had said, crazy as it was, defined what Holly had wished she and Tyler could have been. She wanted a fellow adventurer, someone who'd urge her to take risks when she was feeling her most cautious. Holly hadn't exactly doubted her decision about Tyler before, but now she felt certain about what she'd done — even if that certainty was colored with sadness.

The sun was disappearing behind the hills, and the first stars were appearing overhead, as Paul stomped on a glass wrapped in fabric, the crowd erupted in cheers, and the newlyweds started kissing in a totally inappropriate, get-a-room way. Even Alexa felt herself blushing at the sight. *God.* It had been so long since someone had kissed her like that — and suddenly she craved that kind of reckless passion. Almost unintentionally, Alexa searched the wedding party for Seamus, but she couldn't make him out between the blinding camera flashes.

As Margaux and Paul, hand in hand, darted laughing up the aisle, a woman sitting behind Alexa and Holly cleared her throat. "I give them three months," she remarked snidely.

Holly sighed and began to clap for the couple. Despite all of the skepticism, irony, and fakery in Hollywood, and despite Holly's own recent love woes, she was still determined to believe in romance. And no matter how long she stayed in Los Angeles, she knew she always would.

The cocktail hour was held inside the tent, which was decorated with gold fairy lights and black-and-white snapshots of Margaux and Paul. Each of the fuchsia-draped tables, which were arranged in a heart around the dance floor, was scattered with black roses and marked with different movie titles, such as CASABLANCA and GONE WITH THE WIND. While Holly went off to find their place cards for dinner, Alexa rose up in her peep-toe shoes and scanned the masses for Seamus again. She wanted to see if she'd feel that funny, heart-pounding way in his presence again.

Scoping out the golden-hued tent, Alexa spotted more famous, chiseled faces, including Charity Durst, who was talking to Belle Runningwater. Jonah and several groomsmen were laughing and getting down in the middle of the shiny dance floor, even though the stage — which was set up with drums, a keyboard, and a microphone — was lacking musicians. And then, with a jolt, Alexa saw Seamus, standing in line at the bar and chatting with one of the giggly brides-maids, who was clearly throwing herself at him. But Seamus kept glancing around the tent as if he, too, were searching for someone.

"Guess what?" Holly grunted, reappearing with a sour expression on her face.

Alexa glanced at her friend, feeling her stomach sink. "We don't have place cards," she replied flatly. *Thanks, Margaux.*

"This is so cruel," Holly groaned, tucking her clutch under her arm. Delicious smells of olive oil, roast chicken, and basil were wafting over from the back of the tent; she was ravenous. "What are we going to do?"

"Don't panic," Alexa recommended as a stream of guests maneuvered past her on the way to their tables. "We just need to get resourceful and —"

"Could I be of any help?"

Alexa turned her head to see Seamus holding two glasses of white wine, a sheepish half smile on his face.

"Um," Alexa said, uncharacteristically floored. She wished she weren't blushing.

"Well," Holly jumped in, putting one hand on her hip. The table situation was making her feel bolder than usual. "You could help in one way, Seamus — by telling us how and why you're at this wedding."

Seamus sighed, holding out the glasses of wine to the girls like peace offerings. "I'm sorry, you guys — I wanted to explain a couple times before, but we kept getting interrupted."

Holly felt herself softening as she noticed the sincerity in his hazel eyes. "So . . . you must know Paul? Or Margaux?" she prompted, taking one of the glasses and passing it to Alexa.

Seamus ran a hand through his thick blond hair, unintentionally mussing it. "I've known Margaux all my life," he replied with a smile. "'Cause Jonah Eklundstom is my best friend."

"*What?*" Alexa and Holly asked at the same time, glancing at each other.

Seamus nodded, looking a little amused by their surprise. "The three of us grew up together — right down the street from each other in La Brea, and we went to school together, too. Jonah and I used to play soccer in my backyard, and I'd help him study for English tests. . . . He wasn't always world-famous, you know." Seamus's voice carried a hint of nostalgia.

"Oh, I know," Alexa said, thinking back to the stories Aramis had told her about the sweet, airheaded, teenage boy who'd flunked half his classes at Santa Monica's Crossroads High School. She was still astonished by Seamus's revelation, but at least it was starting to make more sense.

"And when I moved out east for college," Seamus added, "we stayed in touch, and Margaux and Paul visited me a lot when they were filming *Grit and Gravel* in Brooklyn. Margaux thought it would be cool to have a childhood friend in the wedding party."

Alexa felt a shiver of realization go through her as she remembered something Jonah had said that night at The Standard: *My best friend lives in New York. . . .*

"I know it's kind of dumb," Seamus continued, anticipating Holly's next question as she opened her mouth. "But I don't like telling people that I'm Jonah's friend. Not even my college buddies, let alone people I meet for the first time." He glanced from one girl to the other, his tone impassioned. "I couldn't be more different from the whole Hollywood scene, and I always feel like I'm showing off or something when I mention my connection to it, so — I don't." Seamus lifted his shoulders, looking apologetic, and Holly knew his regret was genuine. "I should have said something in the car," he continued. "Especially when I dropped you guys off at El Sueño. But . . . I just couldn't. In a way, it embarrasses me, you know?" Holly nodded, well understanding Seamus's mixed feelings about Hollywood.

Then Seamus looked at Alexa, his hazel eyes bright with mischief. "And, since you didn't seem like my biggest fan in the first place . . . I thought I might come off as really arrogant."

Alexa returned Seamus's gaze, feeling her cheeks warm up again. "You came off as arrogant anyway," she retorted almost automatically, but she found herself thinking: *He cared what I thought about him?*

Seamus laughed, holding Alexa's gaze. "You won't let me off the hook for a second, will you, Alexa?"

"Never," Alexa swore, and as she and Seamus continued to look at each other, she felt an electric spark pass between them, so intense she had to catch her breath.

Seamus seemed to feel strangely as well, because he cleared his throat, adjusted his glasses, and looked swiftly back at Holly. "Look, I'm sure you girls have your own seats," he began. "But any chance you'd want to sit at the wedding party's table? Oren's ducking out early to meet with a potential client"— Seamus rolled his eyes at this —"and it's way past the flower girl's bedtime, so we've got two empty spaces." He flashed them both a contrite grin. "What do you say?"

"Oh," Holly replied lightly. "I'm sure our table will understand if we desert them."

Within seconds, Seamus was leading Alexa and Holly through the crowds toward a table marked GUESS WHO'S COMING TO DINNER? Alexa noted that Jonah wasn't one of the groomsmen present — he was seated with the Eklundstroms and Paul's family at a long table marked THE GODFATHER. Seamus introduced the girls to the spiky-haired Buzzkill Smith, a fellow grooms- man who was a music video director, and Buzzkill's girlfriend, Sugar, the redheaded soap opera actress who'd been Margaux's maid of honor.

Just then, Belle Runningwater appeared tableside, looking ravishing in a long violet Bodarte gown, and excitedly greeted Holly. As the two of them caught up, Seamus got into a heated debate with Buzzkill over which comic book hero would make for the best movie adaptation, so Alexa was left to make small talk with Sugar, who seemed even flakier than Margaux.

"You know, you could almost be an actress," Sugar was saying to Alexa as the waiters came around to serve bowls of chilled watermelon and blueberry soup. "You have that . . . air about you. Don't you think? I could put you in touch with my agent."

"Thanks, Sugar, but I'm kind of busy now," Alexa

replied, digging into her soup and barely processing the fact that she had, in a sense, just been discovered. "I'm starting college, and to be honest, I find the moviemaking process kind of . . . funny sometimes."

"Funny?" Sugar echoed, clearly confounded, and Alexa noticed Seamus, who was sitting across from her, watching her with a smile on his lips. She was wishing that he would swap places with Sugar so she and he could talk, but then there was a sudden twang of guitars from the stage.

"Check it out, it's Blue Dog Babylon — these guys are phenomenal," Seamus told Buzzkill, gesturing toward the stage. "Jonah and I found them on Myspace and then heard them play at a club in Silver Lake."

Alexa glanced up to see the band: four hot young guys, decked out in tuxes but wearing battered Converses on their feet. "Hey," the lead singer, who had curly brown hair and big brown eyes, said into the microphone. "We're so psyched to be playing here tonight. . . ."

Alexa set down her spoon, struck by a sense of recognition. She turned to Holly, whose face was already crimson. "Hol, isn't that —" Alexa began as Sugar glanced from one girl to the next in confusion.

"Zach," Holly managed, looking back at the stage in wonder. So it *had* been him she'd seen yesterday with Margaux and Jonah. Of course. *My band, Blue*

Dog Babylon, he'd told her that day on Zuma Beach. What were the chances? Holly felt a wave of shock wash over her that recalled the cool ocean waves against her skin. It seemed like it had been only moments ago that she'd pulled him from the water, but yet there he was, alive and well onstage.

First Seamus, and now Surfer Boy, Alexa thought dazedly as Zach said something into the mike that made everyone laugh. "Are we in some freaky alternate universe?" Alexa whispered into Holly's ear.

Holly grinned, her eyes on Zach. She remembered the feeling she'd had earlier, that she and Alexa were entering into a fairy tale. "Yes, and it's called Hollywood," she whispered back.

"Please give a great big welcome to Mr. and Mrs. Paul DeMille!" Zach was calling into the mike, lifting his arms above his head and grinning in a way that made Holly melt a little. "And as my grandpa would say, 'Mazel tov!'" Thunderous applause greeted Margaux and Paul as they flitted onto the dance floor in a black-and-fuchsia blur, and Blue Dog Babylon struck up a raucous, punk-rock version of The Ronettes' "Be My Baby." Holly cupped her chin in her hands, forgetting her soup as she watched Margaux and Paul move across the floor in perfect tandem, and listened to Zach's rich, strong vocals. His voice was confident but not showy, with just enough scratchiness to sound badass.

When the waiters had cleared away the soup, Belle returned to the wedding-party table — she was stranded over at CASABLANCA with Charity Durst and her cronies — to summon Holly onto the dance floor. The band had started playing a new song — something about surfing blues — and Margaux and Paul were swallowed up by a blur of beaded minidresses and black tuxes.

"I've seen how you can shake it," Belle said, her black eyes flashing as she pulled Holly to her feet. Holly felt a knot of nervousness; what if Zach saw her from the stage? Would it be weird? Though she supposed she *could* try to accept his thanks and not act like a freak this time. She blew Alexa a kiss as Belle led her out onto the dance floor.

A second later, Sugar and Buzzkill got up to dance as well, and the rest of the wedding party followed suit, until only Seamus and Alexa were left at GUESS WHO'S COMING TO DINNER?, facing each other across the black rose petals and wineglasses. Alexa could almost hear her pulse tapping in her throat.

"So." Seamus gave her a teasing half smile. "You've clearly got a talent for photography, but how are your moves on the dance floor?"

Alexa tried to glare at him, but then she broke into laughter, realizing how Seamus's compliments always gave her a little thrill. "I'm awful," she joked. "And I've got on dangerous heels, so I'm a real threat."

"I'll take my chances." Seamus pushed back his chair and stood, extending one hand toward Alexa. "Shall we dance?"

The old-fashioned way Seamus posed the question made Alexa's heart flutter. She accepted his hand — which caused more fluttering — as he led her onto the crowded dance floor. It was strange; there was still the same mocking, barbed vibe between the two of them, but Alexa sensed something else simmering beneath the surface — a deeper emotion that might have been there all along, if Alexa had only opened her eyes.

Closing her eyes, Alexa rested her head against Seamus's shoulder as he put one hand on her waist and moved with her across the floor, his steps confident. She could feel his heart beating rather quickly through his silk vest, and that made her knees go kind of wobbly. Blue Dog Babylon was playing a slow, sweet song, with lyrics about finding love where you least expect it.

"You lied," Seamus said after a minute, and Alexa felt the vibration of his chest as he spoke. "You're not an awful dancer at all."

"No, *you* lied," Alexa shot back, opening her eyes and pulling away slightly, but Seamus kept a steady hold on her waist, his eyes sparkling. "Or, at least, you kept the truth from me. How can I ever trust you again?" Her tone was light; Alexa knew she *could* trust Seamus — with everything. How had she never before noticed his insight, his thoughtfulness?

"My apologies." Seamus leaned Alexa backward in a dip, and she couldn't help but laugh at the dramatic gesture. When he brought Alexa back up, he grinned and added, "But fine, fair enough. Feel free to ask me anything you want about myself and my secret, evil motives."

Alexa stared up into his hazel eyes, overcome by how much she suddenly wanted to know about Seamus Kerr. *What's your favorite book? Are you an only child? Have you ever been to Paris? Why is that you can get a rise out of me when nobody else can?* Her tongue quivered with the desire to speak these questions, to find out about the boy she was dancing with. Alexa wasn't sure she'd ever been so curious about another person.

"Here's a question," Alexa finally said, coming to her senses. "If you and Jonah are so buddy-buddy, why weren't you at the Standard party on Tuesday night?" *And more important, did he tell you about me?* she wanted to add, but she held back.

Seamus paused in their dancing, and reached into

his jacket pocket to pull out his cell phone. Flipping it open, he revealed a picture of the most adorable baby boy Alexa had ever seen. "My nephew," Seamus explained with a crooked grin. "My sister, who lives near my parents in La Brea, just had her first kid, so I was doing a lot of family stuff this week — even watching my nephew some nights to give my a sister a break. I was bummed to miss Jonah's party, but, as you can see, this little guy is sort of hard to resist."

So are you, Alexa thought before she could stop herself. Guys who were good with kids never failed to make her melt. Alexa was about to ask Seamus more about his nephew, when someone touched her arm. Turning around, Alexa saw the petite, dark-haired Paz Ferrara, wearing her trademark thigh-high boots with a short red dress cinched in the middle with a fat satin ribbon. "Gail's daughter, *si?*" Paz asked, grinning up at Alexa as if she hadn't totally ditched her at Gail's party on Monday. "I did *not* know you knew the Eklundstroms," Paz added, her eyes wide.

Alexa brushed at her glossy new bangs, relishing her new hairdo as she returned Paz's smile. "Oh, Margaux and I go *way* back," she sighed, feeling Seamus's amused gaze on her. "Her dress is to die for, by the way," she added truthfully — that, she couldn't deny.

"Thank you!" Paz bubbled, giving Alexa an approving once-over. "You have — how you say? — a good eye. Your mother, she told me you are an excellent photographer and that you will be interning at *Vogue*. Would you have interest to work with the photographer who will be shooting my line?"

Alexa felt the warmth of excitement race through her. She hadn't even dared hope for an opportunity like that this summer. "I — I'd love to," she stammered. And what warmed Alexa even deeper than Paz's offer was the knowledge that her mom had recommended her as a photographer. She couldn't wait to tell Holly.

"I will talk to Anna," Paz said, referring to *Vogue*'s famous editor-in-chief, as she walked off, waggling her fingers at Alexa. "*Ciao, querida.*"

Alexa turned back to Seamus, knowing her cheeks were flushed and her eyes were shining. Seamus's eyes were shining, too, as he looked at her. "That's so cool, Alexa," he said softly, his voice full of admiration, and Alexa was suddenly grateful that he had been there to hear the news. "I *knew* you had to be a good photographer from the moment you took that picture in the car in Vegas."

Alexa shook her head, bewildered by Seamus's confession. "Seamus, I thought you couldn't stand me on our road trip. I thought it was Holly you preferred."

"I like Holly," Seamus said, and Alexa felt his arms

draw her in closer. "But I'm not dancing with her now, am I?" Alexa was holding her breath, barely able to believe what Seamus had said, when suddenly he glanced over her shoulder and his face broke into a grin. "If it isn't our resident Oscar winner–slash-heartthrob," Seamus called with a wave, and Alexa's stomach dropped.

"Shay! Haven't seen you all night." Jonah came forward and gave Seamus the typical boy-hug: a couple of fast slaps on the back and a vigorous handshake. "Can you believe Margaux's old and married?"

As the two friends bantered, Alexa glanced from one boy to the other. Jonah was still outlandishly gorgeous, but he was lacking the fire — the energy — that made Seamus who he was. Now Alexa could see why Jonah didn't give her butterflies. Seamus was neither a celebrity nor a hot French painter . . . he was just a New York writer-guy. But studying him now, Alexa felt an unmistakable pulsing in her belly. It was *him* she couldn't take her eyes off — not the movie star.

Jonah was in the midst of telling Seamus something about *The Princess and the Slacker* when he glanced in Alexa's direction — and went bug-eyed. "Alexa, I didn't recognize you!" he exclaimed. "You changed your . . ." He reached out, as if to touch Alexa's hair, then seemed to think the better of it.

From the way his brow furrowed, Alexa could tell that Jonah wasn't loving her new cut, and for some reason, that made her want to laugh. *Of course*. Someone like Jonah *would* prefer girls who had traditionally long hair; it took a guy with more edge, and more imagination — a guy like Seamus — to see why a different style might work.

Alexa nodded at Jonah, and any tension she might have felt around him began to fade. It seemed like ages ago that they'd kissed on the rooftop and in the hot tub; so much had happened between then and now, including the haircut. Alexa knew that Jonah *had* cared for her — at least, in his actor-y way — but she sensed that he was letting go of those romantic feelings, even as they stood there together. Maybe it was her hair.

Jonah looked from Alexa to Seamus and back again. "You guys know each other?" he asked, and though there was a note of jealousy in his voice, Alexa sensed that Jonah was pleased to see his friends mingling together. He certainly wasn't going to call Seamus a traitor, or insist that he take his hands off Alexa. As much as Alexa secretly wished she'd be the catalyst for some nineteenth-century-type duel, she had to concede that the festive, sparkling party energy was keeping everyone in good spirits.

"Yeah, we just met," Alexa spoke, meeting Seamus's

knowing gaze. In a way, it felt as if they had — as if tonight was the way they should have met all along.

Jonah nodded, then put his hand on Alexa's arm; to her relief, the gesture felt more friendly than anything. "Seamus is a great guy," he said, smiling at her, and Alexa smiled back, knowing Jonah was right, and knowing that, in his way, he'd given her his blessing.

Either that, or the actor was spacey enough to miss out on the total chemistry between Alexa and his friend.

As Jonah made his way back into the teeming crowd, Alexa watched him go, feeling a sense of closure. When Seamus took her hand and pulled her near once more, she breathed in his aftershave — a heady bay-rum scent — and they started slow-dancing again. Blue Dog Babylon was playing a fast song, but neither she nor Seamus seemed to care.

"Hmm," Seamus said into her ear. "I didn't know Jonah was so taken with you."

"Not anymore," Alexa protested, feeling the laugh build in her throat. "I don't think he likes my hair."

"Really?" Seamus raised one eyebrow, and then, as Alexa's skin tingled, he ran his fingers through her bobbed locks. "I'm a fan. Very sophisticated. Then again, it's not how you look that captivates me."

Alexa felt her head swimming, her heart bursting.

"It's not?" She slipped her arms around Seamus's neck to keep herself steady.

Seamus shook his head, watching her intently. "It's something in here." He moved his fingers over to her forehead, caressing her ever so slightly, and then let them trail down, over her collarbone, to rest lightly against her heart. "And here."

Alexa felt wonderfully dizzy. *So this is why I thought this night would change my life.* "You have a really weird way of showing how you feel, Seamus."

"I've been a jerk." Seamus offered her an apologetic smile. "You *confused* me, Alexa. At first I thought you were like so many other girls I'd known, but then when I got your sense of humor . . ." He stopped dancing for a minute. "I knew there was more to you than meets the eye."

As they stood pressed close together, their faces inches apart, Alexa desperately wanted Seamus to kiss her — but was also afraid that he would. She was worried that if they gave in to the sexual tension simmering between them, Seamus would become nothing more than another hook-up. Whatever they had would lose meaning. So Alexa pulled back, and, in doing so, happened to spot Holly across the dance floor. In her pink dress, with her hair pulled back, she could be one of many lovely starlets flitting about the party; only her eyes — wide and sparkling with warmth — gave her away. She was talking to Jonah and Belle, and Alexa wondered what the three of them were discussing.

"Hope you girls are loving life right now," Jonah was saying to Holly and Belle, playing the part of hospitable best man to a hilt. "Let me know if there's anything you need," he added, and then glanced around the tent. "By the way, have either of you seen Esperanza? I need to ask her where she put my cell phone charger."

Holly shook her head, fanning her hot face with one hand; she hadn't seen Jonah's stuffy assistant since the ceremony. And she'd been far too busy in the past half hour getting her groove on — and sneaking peeks at Zach — to really look for anyone. As Jonah was saying something else to Belle, Holly did scan the dance floor — and immediately noticed Alexa shooting her a huge smile. She and Seamus were dancing, their arms lightly draped around each other, and Holly was filled with elation — though not much surprise. Nobody bickered as much as those two did unless they were meant for each other.

"Charity was looking for you," Holly heard Belle saying to Jonah. "I think she . . . misses you, Jonah."

Intrigued, Holly turned back around to see the actor give Belle a kiss on the cheek, wave to Holly, and trot off in search of his once and future leading lady.

"Oh, wait – *there's* Esperanza," Belle exclaimed after Jonah had gone. Holly followed Belle's gaze, and then her jaw dropped.

Jonah's assistant had finally, *finally* let loose. She was dancing in a far corner with one of the groomsmen, sipping from a miniature bottle of pink champagne. Her hair, appropriately, was out of its ever-present bun, and swung down her back in abundant, dark waves. She'd also shed her white suit jacket to reveal a silky white camisole underneath. Holly would never have thought it, but Esperanza was pretty . . . *hot*. The groomsman seemed to think so, too, from the way he was dancing with her. Holly prayed Alexa was getting a glimpse of this action.

"Wow," Belle commented with a yawn. "That's what happens when you work for a high-maintenance actor twenty-four-seven, and then get the night off." She shook her head, and nudged Holly. "I'm getting tired just watching her. Want to take a break?"

Holly hesitated, glancing up at the stage. The whole time she'd been dancing, she'd alternated between hoping that Zach would, and wouldn't, spot her. At moments, it had seemed like the lead singer's eyes had strayed in her direction, but he gave no indication that he either noticed or recognized her. Holly didn't really mind; it was pleasure enough to listen to his unique voice, to watch from afar as he moved along

293

the stage, sinuous and confident, a rock star in Converse sneakers. "He's so sexy," Belle had said at one point, and Holly had simply blushed in agreement, keeping their connection to herself.

Now, Belle was watching Holly expectantly, but before Holly could look back at her and say that, yeah, a break sounded good — after all, her spice-rubbed chicken, mango sauce, and wild rice dinner was waiting — Zach was stepping up to the mike and undoing his bow tie.

"Folks," Zach called, wiping sweat from his brow. "We're gonna take a quick break and let the DJ — we've got Samantha Ronson here tonight — do a turn. See you again soon." He lifted his guitar up over his head and set it down by the drum set. Her face heating up, Holly watched as Zach also removed his suit jacket and then went over to say something to his drummer. To Holly's disbelief, both Zach and the drummer looked right in her direction, and Zach's face broke into a huge grin.

"Guardian angel?" he mouthed at her, his brown eyes sparkling, and Holly gave a small nod, feeling Belle's inquisitive gaze on her.

And then Zach and his drummer hopped off the stage and were weaving through the crowd. As the drummer — a cute, short guy with long-ish brown hair — began chatting up Belle ("You must get this all the time, but aren't you Pocahontas?"), Zach stopped in front of Holly.

"I don't know if you could tell, but I kept checking you out all night," he finally said, after they'd both studied each other for a moment. "And not in a sketchy way. I wasn't sure it was *you*."

Holly smiled shyly. "What tipped you off?" she asked.

"Your eyes." Zach shrugged. "They were the first things I saw when I came to the other day, on the beach. They're unmistakable."

Holly wondered if it was possible to catch fire from the warmth of her own skin. She looked down, trying to come up with a response. She thought about telling Zach that his eyes were unmistakable as well, and that he looked adorable tonight, with his white shirt untucked and his brown curls framing his flushed face. But she thought the better of it.

"You know, you never told me your name," Zach spoke, clearly not put off by Holly's awkwardness. "I like Guardian Angel, but I'm guessing that's going to get old after a while."

Holly couldn't help her laugh. "Holly — Holly Jacobson," she said, holding out her hand, and her heart jumped a little when Zach shook it.

"Zach Rose," he replied, holding her hand for a beat longer than necessary. His fingertips felt calloused from the guitar playing, but in a pleasant way. "Terrific to meet you, Holly." He paused, then rolled up his white sleeves, revealing the nicely toned arms Holly had admired on the beach not too long ago. "I should have known you'd have celeb connections," Zach went on, smiling at her teasingly. "Running off all mysteriously when I tried to thank you . . ."

"I know, I'm sorry," Holly told Zach, raising her voice over the thumping music. "But I don't *really* have celebrity connections. I just got kind of embarrassed on the beach the other day and —" A Panic! At the Disco song came on then, drowning her out.

Zach leaned close to her, close enough for Holly to make out the freckles on his nose again. "Do you want to get out of here for a second?" he asked. Holly nodded, ready to leave behind the close, sweaty crowd for a spell.

After fighting their way through the throngs, and pushing past the gauzy blue curtains leading outside, Holly and Zach walked into the chilly, star-sprinkled night. All traces of the earlier heat and rain were gone, and Holly took a deep breath of the fresh mountain air.

"Nice, huh?" Zach asked with a grin. "Hard to

believe the beach is so close. I guess there's a little bit of everything in California."

"There really is," Holly replied, thinking of all that had happened in the short space of time she'd been in LA. She stopped to slip off her black heels, and soon she and Zach were strolling along the garden path, the grass cool and damp beneath Holly's feet. As the sounds of celebration floated out from the tent behind them, Holly explained to an attentive Zach about Alexa's run-in with Margaux in New York and the girls' subsequent, impromptu journey to LA. "Which is what brought me to Zuma Beach that day," she summed up.

"Therefore saving *my* sorry ass," Zach filled in with a grin. Holly laughed, and Zach added, "It's pretty dope, though, how you picked up and came to Cali at a moment's notice. That's *exactly* what I would have done."

He and Holly came to a stop at the edge of the hill, overlooking the houses and trees below that were illuminated by the moonlight. "I feel like life's too short *not* to be spontaneous," Zach went on thoughtfully. "There's so much to see in the world — so much to taste and experience —" Zach paused, then glanced at Holly, running a hand through his dark curls. "Sorry. I get kinda carried away sometimes."

"No, I know what you mean," Holly replied softly, dangling her shoes from one hand. It was the funniest thing, but Zach reminded her a little of Alexa — he had the same appetite for adventure, the same spark of daring that never failed to inspire Holly. *That's the kind of person I need in my life*, Holly reflected. *Someone to remind me that things aren't as scary as they seem.* "For example, I always hated flying," Holly continued, staring into Zach's deep brown eyes. "But then I realized how much I love to travel — so I learned to like airplanes. Somewhat."

Zach chuckled, his eyes sweeping over Holly's face. "Traveling's my passion," he replied. "Well, after music — and surfing. Over winter break, I swam with dolphins in Australia, which was amazing. I've spent most of my life in California but I'm definitely moving to Italy or Spain sometime."

Italy, Holly thought with a sigh; she'd always dreamed of visiting that country. She was starting to ask Zach more about his Australia trip, when a sudden crackling sound overhead interrupted her. Thinking it was thunder again, Holly looked up at the sweeping sky.

Over the distant hills, green, gold, and red bursts were exploding and then showering down. "Is that for the wedding?" Holly asked. She'd read in *People* of movie stars getting fireworks to go off in sync with their celebrations.

"No, I think it's the Hollywood Bowl," Zach replied as he gazed out at the fireworks. "It's this great concert space built right into the Hills" — Zach took a step closer to Holly and pointed — "and every summer you can bring a picnic dinner and listen to music and look out at the Hollywood sign. At the end of some shows, they have fireworks."

Holly nodded, picturing the idyllic place. "If I get out here at the end of August," she ventured, glancing away from the fireworks to look at Zach, "we could go."

Zach smiled at her. "I'd like that," he said. "And it'll be my treat. I never *really* thanked you for saving my life the other day."

"Oh, that's okay," Holly said nervously as Zach took a step closer to her. She waved a hand. "There's no need —"

"Can I try now?" Zach asked softly, and before Holly could respond, he put his hands on her shoulders and kissed her softly, his lips lingering as the fireworks boomed overhead. It was bizarre to think that Holly had held her mouth against his once before — this time, it felt very different. It felt spontaneous and tender and more than a little hot.

When Zach drew back, Holly put a hand to her tingling lips. "I — I just broke up with my boyfriend," she told him, her pulse racing. "I don't think I can . . . I need some time . . ."

"It's okay," Zach said, kissing Holly on the cheek. "Don't worry. That was just something I wanted to do right now. Live for the moment and all, you know?"

"I know," Holly whispered, smiling up at Zach. Sometimes a kiss didn't have to be anything more than a fun, dazzling moment — like fireworks going off.

And sometimes, Holly decided, it was okay to have a crush. Even if that crush only lasted for one magical night.

"Zach! We're back on in two seconds!" One of Zach's bandmates was standing outside the tent, waving his arms. "Get over here!"

Putting his arm across Holly's shoulder, Zach led her toward the tent. Before he took the stage again, he walked Holly back to her seat, and they exchanged cell phone numbers, promising they'd be in touch when Holly returned to LA. Swaying by her table, Holly watched as Zach stepped up onstage, slung his guitar across his body again, and brought the microphone to his mouth. "I want to dedicate this next song," he said, his eyes holding Holly's, "to someone who saved my life. It used to be called 'Diving into the Deep.' But tonight I'm officially changing the title to 'Holly.'"

"Did you hear that?" Alexa cried, pulling back from the circle of Seamus's arms when she heard the surfer boy speak Holly's name. Alexa looked around for her friend and saw her by their table, her face lit up as if by candles. It made Alexa's heart buoy to see Holly so content, especially after her tears yesterday. "Isn't that the most romantic thing ever?" Alexa added, turning back to Seamus.

Seamus chuckled. "What happened to you?" he asked, glancing down at her with mock seriousness. "Since when did you stop being such a cynic?"

Since we started dancing, Alexa thought. But instead of saying the words, Alexa decided to finally surrender — and do what she'd been wanting to do the whole night.

She rose up in her peep-toes, put her hand against his lightly stubbled jaw, and kissed Seamus Kerr on the lips. His mouth was warm and inviting, tasting of blueberries, and as he began to kiss her back, softly and sweetly, Alexa knew that this wasn't just another meaningless makeout. She could feel in Seamus's lips, in the intensity of his kiss, how seriously he was taking this. Alexa remembered the dream she'd had on the way from Vegas — a dream about a boy holding her, a boy who'd filled her with warmth. Now, in her mind's eye, that boy had a face. It was, without a doubt, the boy she was kissing now.

"That was weird," Seamus whispered, wearing a blissful smile as his lips brushed against hers.

"What was?" Alexa whispered back, her arms around him. She *was* a little off-kilter from their kiss, but it had also felt so natural. So inevitable.

"That it *wasn't* weird," Seamus explained, smiling even bigger, and then with one hand he slipped off his glasses while he drew Alexa in even closer with the other.

Alexa let out a sigh of pleasure, admiring his beautiful hazel eyes, which looked different now without the glasses. There were so many things she hadn't seen about Seamus, but she felt as if she were waking from a long, long sleep. And as Seamus tilted his head and started kissing her again, long and deep, Alexa understood that she *was* capable of being in love. Or being in like, to start small. Her previous hook-ups and heartaches didn't matter, not when she was close to Seamus like this. Maybe it was time to let her past fall to the ground, like hair snipped by scissors. *Boys don't* always *cause drama*, Alexa realized. Sometimes, they could even help a girl get over hers.

Resting her head on Seamus's shoulder once more, Alexa scanned the glowing tent. Zach was on the stage, singing his heart out to Holly, who looked overjoyed. Alexa did a double take when she saw Esperanza in the far corner, kissing a groomsman with wild abandon. Nearby, Jonah was twirling around a contrite-looking Charity Durst, and Alexa wondered if the two of them would end up back together. And Margaux and Paul were in the center of it all, dancing and kissing, oblivious to the world.

Holly had been right: There *was* something about weddings. . . .

Alexa lifted her face to kiss Seamus again. She wasn't sure what the next day would bring, but for the moment, in this rose-strewn tent under the starry Hollywood sky, things felt pretty close to happily ever after.

CHAPTER TWELVE
Life, Camera, Action

The word DELAYED flashed on the computer screen, hurting Holly's bleary eyes. According to the slightly blurry True West website, the airline strike was over, but Alexa and Holly's eleven A.M. flight to Vegas was delayed until later that night.

This was all Holly's sleep-deprived brain was able to process as she sat on the guesthouse's living-room floor in her boxers and tank, Alexa's laptop balanced on her knees. Fuchsia bags of wedding swag — which each contained a gift certificate to a Malibu spa, a box of Godiva chocolates, and, lamely, a pre-released *Grit and Gravel* DVD — were on the floor beside her, and her and Alexa's shoes lay in a tangle by the door. The scent of wild strawberries and roses lingered.

It was eight in the morning, and both Holly and

Alexa had totaled about a half hour of sleep. Margaux's celebration had raged until a pale-pink dawn broke over the Hollywood Hills, with Blue Dog Babylon playing set after set. As the crowd thinned out, and the snooty industry types began to flit off to their mansions, the mood in the tent became even more vibrant; everyone — even Seamus and Alexa — had swapped partners and danced until practically no one was wearing shoes. Zach had taken a few more set breaks to dance with Holly — though they didn't kiss again — and Holly had worked up the nerve to ask Jonah to autograph a napkin, which she'd save as a souvenir for her mother.

When Zach, giving Holly a see-you-soon wave from the stage, had finally packed up his guitar, and Belle's admiring drummer had packed up his drums, Holly had dragged herself outside to pick up the car, leaving Alexa and Seamus a private, good-bye-until-New-York moment. Alexa had dozed most of the way home and Holly had stayed awake by admiring the gold shadows in the morning sky, and by sucking down the espresso Vikram's staff had passed to her, and each guest, as a parting gift.

"St. Laurent!" Holly called hoarsely from the living room, too beat to actually get up and cross the cool marble floors to Alexa's bedroom. "Update — our flight's not until nine tonight!"

"Thank God!" Alexa called back, lying half-comatose on her bed, still in her aquamarine dress; it carried the bay-rum scent of Seamus's aftershave, and it seemed she could still feel his warmth through the silky material. If Alexa had had her druthers, she would have kept dancing with him, even after the band left, even after the sun rose, their arms wrapped around each other, their lips touching, their eyes meeting in quiet understanding. *Seamus*, Alexa repeated to herself as a small thrill raced through her. *Seamus Kerr*. She knew she was wearing the biggest, goofiest smile on her face as Holly appeared in her doorway.

"What do you mean 'thank God'?" Holly asked, hands on her hips.

Alexa sighed, lifting her head from the pillows. "Do I *look* like I'm packed?" She pointed one bare toe toward her floor, which was covered with open suit-cases, a jumble of shoes, and heaps upon heaps of tunics, jeans, and footless tights.

"But Alexa!" Holly cried, picking her way through the mess toward her friend's bed. "Graduation's *tomorrow* at nine A.M. sharp." Just last week, Holly's own mother had herded the senior class together for an assembly to remind them that nobody could be even a minute late to the ceremony — or they would run the risk of not walking with their class. Holly plopped down on the edge of the bed, giving Alexa's leg a shake. "That was why we wanted to leave early today, remember? We'll have to take the eleven P.M. red-eye out of Vegas, then we won't be in Newark until seven in the morning! That gives us only two hours —"

"Which is *plenty* of time," Alexa yawned, contentedly settling back against the pillows. Nothing could bring her down this morning. Sunlight was pouring through her drapes, and Alexa knew that if she drew them back, she'd be gazing out at a landscape of crystal-blue sky and bluer water, ringed by the greenest of palm trees. She appreciated Los Angeles even more now, knowing it was Seamus's hometown. "Besides," she added, grinning devilishly at Holly. "This allows us to see our boys again today if we want."

"Zach?" Holly asked, her cheeks flushing. "No, I'll let him sleep his night off. I probably won't call him until the fall anyway," she added pragmatically. Though Holly had had a blast with Zach at the wedding, she knew it would be healthy for her to take some time to really be single. She still needed to heal from Tyler, to feel as if things were tied up with him, before she moved on. But there was still something tantalizing about knowing that Zach — and other adorable boys like him — waited in LA.

"I knew you guys were going to end up together somehow," Alexa said with a self-satisfied smile, watching Holly. "When you pulled him from the water that fateful day —"

"Oh, please." Holly rolled her eyes, still blushing. "You're only saying that because on our way home this morning, *I* told you that I saw your Seamus hook-up coming from a mile away." Holly had noticed the spark between Alexa and Seamus while watching them spar like crazy at the Getty. Meanwhile, even though Holly and Seamus got along famously, it was purely platonic. "You know what?" Holly mused, tilting her head to one side as she recalled her first impression of the smart, practical boy. "I just realized that Seamus kind of reminds me of . . . me."

"He reminds me of you, too," Alexa laughed. "Because he never hesitates to call me on my divaness." She sighed fondly, then raised her eyebrows at Holly. "And I have to say that Zach, who is *clearly* a total ham . . ."

"Is basically Alexa in boy form," Holly giggled, nodding at her friend. "Isn't that freaky?"

Alexa shook her head, reaching over to tug on Holly's ponytail. "Not at all. We balance each other pretty well, don't we?" The girls exchanged a quick glance, and they both realized at once that graduation would mark the beginning of their separation. Within a couple months, they'd be living on opposite coasts. Apart, for the first time in eleven years.

Before either girl could get emotional, Holly got to her feet, announcing that she was going to make use of their extra time and go for a run. Kenya had mentioned Runyon Canyon in the Hollywood Hills as a great spot to jog — and celeb-stalk, if one so desired.

After Holly left to change, the buzz of Alexa's cell phone on her nightstand told her she had a text message. She wondered if it was Portia, whom Alexa had texted on the way to the wedding yesterday — just to remind her friend of how Alexa was spending *her* Friday night. But when Alexa flipped open her phone she saw the words: have u changed ur mind and decided u hate me again?

So Seamus wasn't sleeping either.

Her heart brimming, Alexa texted back: i hate u so much i want to walk with u on the beach later and hold ur hand.

Grinning, Alexa closed her phone. She'd been half fearful upon waking that the wedding had been some champagne-induced dream: that Seamus didn't really like her, and hadn't really kissed her, that it had been some other boy she'd danced with all night. Now, shutting her eyes, Alexa decided to drift off and dream about Seamus, the boy she knew was real and awake and thinking about her on the other side of town.

Meanwhile, Holly was feeling surprisingly peppy

as she left the guesthouse in her Sauconys, shorts, and racer-back tank, armed with a mammoth bottle of Fiji water, her iPod, and her cell. El Sueño was still and serene this morning, with the birds chirping, and Jonah likely fast asleep inside the main house. "Miguel?" Holly called, waving to the gardener, who was sitting by the pool, typing on a laptop. "Do you know the best way to get to Runyon Can — wait," Holly said, shielding her eyes from the sun. "Isn't Saturday your day off?"

Miguel nodded. "I came here today to work on my screenplay," he said, gesturing to the laptop. "Mr. Eklundstrom lets me borrow one of his computers to write it. He's very supportive of my ambition. Oh, you know, this is Hollywood," Miguel added, clearly seeing the bemused expression on Holly's face. "Everyone has some crazy dream."

And mine is to live here for four years — and see what it's like, Holly thought, smiling to herself as Miguel gave her the directions and she turned and headed for the car. Of all the crazy dreams in the world, that one didn't seem too bad.

"I know it's crazy, but I wish I didn't have to go back today," Alexa sighed, her hand in Seamus's as they stood on the beach across from El Sueño, their toes sinking into the butter-soft sand. "Just when we're finally learning to tolerate each other . . ."

Seamus laughed, his hazel eyes gleaming behind his glasses, and his straight blond hair whipping across his forehead. In his jeans and faded Loops & Pluto shirt, he looked much more like the casual Seamus whom Alexa had first met, instead of the dapper Seamus of last night — but he made Alexa's stomach flip just the same. They'd had lunch at a fun Caribbean place on Santa Monica Boulevard called Cha Cha Cha, and then Seamus had driven Alexa back to Malibu. Every moment had been filled with energetic talk and debate, from the topic of Jonah (whom Alexa had confessed to going on a date with) to the issue of New York City versus Los Angeles. Alexa hadn't wanted the afternoon to end. She still didn't.

"Well," Seamus said, turning to her and putting his hands on her waist. "We can keep on tolerating each other when I'm back in New York in two weeks." He smiled, and then leaned down to kiss both of Alexa's cheeks. "I was thinking of something when I couldn't sleep this morning. I'll be doing some writing and reporting for *The Observer*, but I'd love to try photography as well. Would you be interested in being my private tutor?" His eyes twinkled with mischief.

It had occurred to Alexa that morning that she

would only be starting college while Seamus was starting his first *job*. But she could tell from his expression now that he saw her as his equal in every way. Alexa felt a flood of gladness; suddenly, life on the East Coast without Holly didn't seem nearly as bleak. "I have to warn you that I'm very strict," she replied, standing on her tiptoes in the sand to kiss the birthmark beneath Seamus's ear. "There may be some punishment involved if you don't do your homework," she added teasingly, slipping her hand beneath the collar of Seamus's shirt, and he pulled her tighter against him, laughing into her hair.

"I don't think I realized before," Seamus said, wrapping his arms around her. "We're both journalists, Alexa. No wonder we're always butting heads." Gently, Seamus rested his forehead against Alexa's, making her pulse race. Here was a guy she could butt heads with forever, and never find boring or predictable. She was angling her head for a kiss when she heard Holly shouting from the hill above the beach.

"Alexa, we need to pack and we *can't* miss this flight!" Holly hollered in her most responsible voice. Alexa saw she had changed out of her running gear into her Seven jeans, a white tank, and long green beads. "Oh, hi, Seamus," she added, waving.

"Hey, Holly!" Seamus grinned at her. Then he turned back to Alexa and took her face in his hands.

"Congratulations, graduate. Call me right afterward tomorrow, okay?" As he brought his lips to hers, Alexa realized that even though she was kissing a beautiful boy on a Malibu beach and the late afternoon sun was reflecting off the water, she *didn't* feel like she was in a movie. She felt like she was in her life. And that was even better.

When Alexa returned to the guesthouse, she found Holly in a packing frenzy, making organized piles of her clothing in her room. "I called my parents from Runyon Canyon," Holly reported, carefully folding her new dress in tissue paper. "My mom has to be at the school, like, two hours in advance, but my dad and Josh can come get us from Newark and zip us over." As Holly picked up her makeup bag, the glint of something gold inside caught her eye. *My Claddagh ring*, Holly realized, sifting through the tubes of clear gloss to remove the ring. Holly felt the familiar ache in her throat, and she quickly tucked the ring into the pocket of her jeans. She felt it would be her good-luck charm for the plane.

"I'll miss *El Sueño*," Alexa was sighing, trailing her fingers along Holly's floor-to-ceiling windows. "I'll even miss Esperanza." The sight of Jonah's assistant going wild last night had really improved Alexa's opinion of the woman.

Holly chuckled as she zipped up her duffel. "I'll

bet anything she's too hungover this morning to remember *either* of us."

As if Esperanza had heard them from the main house, the hallway intercom buzzed right then. When Alexa answered, a sheepish-sounding Esperanza asked if the girls were in need of the Hybrid that day. "Mr. Eklundstrom was planning to drive Ms. Durst home in it," she explained.

Aha! Alexa thought, intrigued. So Charity had won over her costar after all. Suddenly, Alexa wondered if she could ever read *Us Weekly* again. Now that she knew the truths behind the gossip, it all seemed less exciting somehow — though she couldn't *wait* to read about Margaux and Paul's Icelandic honeymoon.

After Alexa assured Esperanza that they no longer needed the Hybrid — but asked if they could have the limo to take them to the airport — she retrieved the photo for Jonah from her bedroom and placed the gift on the kitchen counter, where Jonah had left *his* welcome gift. She attached a note leaving Jonah her cell number. She wasn't sure if the actor — or his impulsive sister — would ever really stay in touch with her, but she hoped Jonah might hang out with her and Seamus when he was in New York to film his favorite romantic comedy.

By the time Alexa and Holly had cleaned up the

guesthouse and sufficiently shoved all their belongings into their bags, the limo was waiting outside.

"Our last time in a limo," Holly said wistfully as she and Alexa slid into the soft leather interior.

"Speak for yourself," Alexa laughed, closing the door. "Though then again, *you're* the one who's moving back here. Maybe you'll end up a big-shot director one day."

As the limo drove down the Pacific Coast Highway, the ocean flashing by the windows, the girls were silent, each remembering her experience in the golden city.

"Who knew one week could change so much?" Alexa started to ask Holly as they approached LAX, but then she noticed that her friend was sleeping, her light-brown head resting peacefully against the seat. Alexa reached out to pat Holly's arm, remembering how their one week in South Beach had also altered the course of everything. She and Holly could certainly get a lot done in a short amount of time.

Including make it to graduation — if they were lucky.

After their two uneventful flights, Alexa and Holly were standing impatiently in line to exit the plane at Newark Airport.

"It's almost seven thirty," Holly moaned, checking her watch. Back in Las Vegas, their flight had also been delayed and they'd taxied down the runway in Newark for what seemed like hours. Holly knew her dad was waiting in the arrivals area, tapping his watch while Josh complained about how Holly was always late to stuff. That — combined with the knowledge that she'd be seeing Tyler very soon — made Holly's stomach twist with anxiety. She seemed to have lost her California mellowness somewhere over Kansas.

Alexa had been feeling absolutely Zen the whole flight, mentally composing a music mix for Seamus, and reading all the inaccuracies about Margaux's wedding in the *New York Post*'s Page Six. Now, as the line finally inched forward, she was starting to worry. She did like to arrive fashionably late to certain events, but she knew fashionably late wouldn't fly at graduation.

After making it through a hellish wait at the luggage claim, the girls finally burst into the arrivals area, bags in hand, stumbling a little as they ran. Holly's father, wearing a navy blue suit, his dark bushy eyebrows raised in expectation, was waiting for them, while Josh slumped into a chair nearby. Her brother looked surprisingly handsome in a suit, Holly thought, but, predictably, he was scowling at her. She knew her family way too well.

"I'm sorry!" Alexa cried guiltily as the girls flew

toward Mr. Jacobson. It was now after eight o'clock — and the drive from Newark to Oakridge took about an hour. *If* there was no traffic. "It was my fault!" she added as Holly threw her arms around her dad. "I thought they lost one of my bags — the Prada one, actually — but by the time I went to ask security, it was coming down the carousel and Holly grabbed it. . . ."

"It's okay, it's okay," Mr. Jacobson said, patting Holly's hair with his free hand. "I'm just glad my wandering girls are back. At least for a little while," he added, smiling down at Holly, who smiled back at her dad, relieved to be home — for a little while.

Meanwhile, Alexa watched the two of them silently, feeling a pang of envy; she didn't get to experience that kind of parental affection too often.

"Now, let's go," Mr. Jacobson said, turning businesslike again. "Your mortarboards and gowns are in the car — Alexa, I stopped by your dad's this morning to pick yours up, since I figured you wouldn't have time to go home and change."

"We can't put our gowns on over *jeans*!" Alexa exclaimed, gesturing down to her True Religions. She shuddered to think how Paz Ferrara or Margaux Eklundstrom would react to such a fashion atrocity.

"Well," Holly said, looking at the collection of luggage at Alexa's feet. "We have skirts and dresses in our bags, don't we?" She glanced at her father pleadingly. "Dad, if Josh can bring in the gowns, it'll take us, like, two seconds to run to the ladies' room, and change and fix our hair —"

But Mr. Jacobson was already striding across the sunny airport, carrying as many of the girls' bags as he could. "You can change in the car," he announced over his shoulder. "Come on, Holly. Get up, Josh. Your mom is going to kill us."

"Ugh, *gross* — I can't believe my sister is changing right behind me," Josh was groaning fifteen minutes later as Mr. Jacobson tore down the highway, and Alexa and Holly were shifting uncomfortably in the backseat, trying to give each other enough space — *and* to tug off their jeans without flashing the world.

"Shut up, Josh," Holly grunted, creatively sliding feetfirst into her drawstring white skirt, but almost falling off her seat in the process. When her Claddagh ring tumbled out of the back pocket of her jeans, Holly reached down to retrieve it.

"Yeah," Alexa said, attempting to wriggle into her strapless floral dress and slip in her dangly silver earrings all at once. "If you're going to be a suburban teenage boy, you'd better get used to girls being half-undressed in your backseat. Sorry, Mr. Jacobson," she added quickly when Holly's father shook his head reprovingly.

As Alexa and Holly stuck their arms through the long sleeves of their black gowns and did speedy makeup fixes in their compact mirrors, Mr. Jacobson drove the car as fast as he dared down Oakridge's quiet, tree-lined main drag. Alexa, her tube of Chanel gloss poised above her lips, looked out the window to see Suzy's Salon, the redbrick library, and the pizza parlor flash by. It felt strange to be so abruptly thrust back into small-town Oakridge after five glittery days in La-La Land, but Alexa smiled at the familiar sights; no matter how fabulous the destination you were leaving behind, there was always something comforting about homecoming.

"Jeez, Dad," Josh commented as Mr. Jacobson made a sharp turn, wheels screeching, and Oakridge High came into view. "You're gonna get arrested." Glancing over his shoulder at Holly, Josh added, "That would be the most exciting thing to happen to the Jacobsons in years, huh?"

I've had enough excitement to last me a while, Holly thought, holding her breath as she saw the numbers on the car's digital clock switch to 8:58. A second after her dad squeezed into a parking spot in the Oakridge lot, she and Alexa tumbled out of the backseat,

319

adjusting their gowns around their knees and carefully fastening their caps on their heads.

"Is it just me, or is this the most unflattering piece of headgear ever invented?" Alexa asked, as she flicked the braided gold tassel out of her face and tried to straighten the boxy mortarboard. With Josh and Mr. Jacobson leading the way, the girls hurried across the hot parking lot, Alexa's sling-back sandals clicking on the cement. The school's football field, where the ceremony was being held, loomed in the distance. "What, you *like* mortarboards?" Alexa asked Holly when her friend didn't answer right away.

Holly stopped for a minute before they reached the field, shading her eyes to look at Alexa. "No . . . it's just that . . ." The sight of her friend, standing before her in a long black gown, with the black mortarboard cockeyed on her blonde head, was at once strange and wonderful. "We're really *graduating*," Holly said, shaking her head in amazement. The whole morning had passed in such a whirlwind that she hadn't had time to fully process where she and Alexa were rushing off to. In a way, Holly was glad that they'd just come from California; if she'd had the night before to prepare for graduation, she probably would have been a sobbing nervous wreck right now.

Alexa sized Holly up as well; her childhood friend looked adorable in her cap and gown — though, if they'd had more time, Alexa would have recommended that Holly wear her strappy black sandals instead of her beaded gold flats. But whatever. "That we are," Alexa said, adjusting the strap of her Nikon camera on her arm. She was *so* ready to wrap things up.

"Girls!" Holly's dad was hissing, waving them over to the entrance of the football field. "You *won't* really be graduating if you don't get over here now! They're starting!"

Oh, right.

Running into the stadium, where Holly's mom was already up at the podium, Holly went left and Alexa went right. Both girls apologized in loud whispers as they stepped over legs and feet on their way to their assigned alphabetical seats. Meanwhile, Holly's dad and Josh took their seats in the back with the rest of the families. "Today, you are about to begin the rest of your lives," Holly's mom was intoning as Holly, her heart pounding, took her seat beside Eliot Johnson, who'd been Alexa's first real boyfriend.

Holly looked over her shoulder to study the sea of students, each of whom she associated with a different memory. There was Meghan, her dark eyes wide and hopeful, and Jess, who was watching the proceedings with a skeptical expression. Then she saw Tyler, and her heart beat faster; he was facing forward, looking incredibly serious, and she wondered if he'd seen her dash in late. She began to stress about how things would be between them once the ceremony was over — until Holly caught sight of Alexa. Her friend flashed her a thumbs-up sign — and then crossed her big blue eyes, a gesture that never failed to make Holly laugh. And she did laugh then, bringing her hand to her mouth, and feeling her fears ease.

With that, she faced forward and waited for the rest of her life to begin.

It's over! Alexa thought, jubilant, as she elbowed her way into the packed gymnasium, her rolled-up diploma under her arm, and her camera bag on her shoulder. She'd endured two sweltering hours of countless speeches ("It's up to your generation to save the environment!" some congressman had chirped while Alexa had fought to stay awake), streams of graduates marching across the field to collect their diplomas (Alexa had fairly flown over the grass to get hers), and finally, a happy shower of black mortar-boards in the air. Now, as relieved graduates and proud parents met up in the gym, it seemed the only reward was . . . fruit punch and sugar cookies?

Alexa shook her head, regarding the lame spread on the table under the basketball hoop. Of course, less than twenty-four hours after Margaux

Eklundstrom's lavish affair, pretty much anything would seem pathetic. But this was truly depressing. Alexa was concocting a plan to throw her own graduation party at her house that night — maybe she'd invite Holly, Portia, Maeve, and some of Holly's track friends over for guacamole and icy Coronas — when she spotted not one, but two, familiar faces across the gym.

Her parents.

Yes. Alexa's father was there, as she'd assumed he'd be. But so was her *mom*. Impossible as it seemed, Gail Wilson-St. Laurent-Feldman had remembered her daughter's graduation.

Alexa hurried through the crush, passing her friends Tabitha and J.D., waving to Portia and Maeve, who looked as if their LA curiosity was killing them, and noticing Holly standing off to the side with Meghan and Jess. When Alexa finally reached her mom and dad, she paused, gripping her diploma. Socially at ease with almost anyone, Alexa often found herself tongue-tied around the two people who'd known her the longest.

"Félicitations, chérie," Alexa's dad finally said, handing Alexa a bouquet of daisies and kissing her on each cheek while Gail looked on, a wry smile on her lips.

"Merci, Papa," Alexa replied, answering in their

native French because she knew her father would appreciate it. "Mother, you made it?" she added, not bothering to disguise her surprise.

Gail ran a bejeweled hand over her tight blonde bun. "I snuck in while that dreadfully boring congressman was rambling on," she sighed, rolling her ice-blue eyes. "I nearly fell asleep."

"Same," Alexa laughed, feeling a flush of pleasure. She hadn't expected her mother's presence at graduation to mean this much to her, but Alexa felt suspiciously lighthearted. Maybe she'd needed to travel all the way to California and back to realize she *did* care what her mother thought of her. "By the way," Alexa added. "Thanks for putting in a good word for me with Paz."

Gail beamed, and extended one arm to envelope Alexa in a quick, let's-not-wrinkle-my-silk-blouse hug. "Of course, darling. You know I'm very proud of you." She pulled back, glancing at Alexa's dad, who was smiling and looking misty-eyed. "We both are."

Alexa gave a happy sigh, clutching her flowers and diploma to her chest. It was beyond weird to see her long-divorced parents standing side by side. But she also sort of enjoyed the feel of the three of them grouped together for the first time in years — like an actual family.

Meanwhile, on the other side of the gym, Holly

was too busy dealing with Meghan and Jess to search for anyone in *her* family — or for Tyler.

"Okay, you are so busted, Jacobson," Jess was saying, hands on her hips as she and Meghan stood before Holly, blocking her path of escape. "When Tyler told us you were in LA for the week, we were sure he was bullshitting us — until Meghan called me last night, freaking out."

"I saw you on E!" Meghan exclaimed, her brown eyes taking up half her face. "What were *you* doing at Margaux Eklundstrom's wedding?"

"It's a long story, you guys," Holly sighed, running her fingers through her bangs, which had been squished by the cap. "And I'm sorry I didn't tell you about it before I left. It just all happened so fast. . . ." *Wait until I tell them I'm going to UCLA!* Holly thought, shaking her head. At least her friends weren't as pissed at her as she'd feared.

"We saw you *dancing* with some cute guy!" Jess interjected, sounding both scandalized and monumentally jealous. "He looked very into you. Does Tyler know?"

"Do I know what?" Tyler asked, appearing behind Meghan and Jess, looking handsome and scholarly in his cap and gown.

Holly gulped. She hadn't expected Tyler to catch her so off guard; she'd wanted some time to prepare before seeing him, to compose herself and rehearse a speech in her head. Now, that didn't seem like a possibility as Meghan and Jess went off to find their parents, calling back to Holly that she owed them a full report on her mystery trip.

"So," Tyler said to Holly once they were alone — well, as alone as they could be in the middle of a jam-packed gym.

"So," Holly replied, nervously twisting her hands together inside her long sleeves.

Tyler scratched the nape of his neck, then glanced up. "Holly, look, I —"

"Tyler, we should —" Holly was saying at the exact same time.

They paused, and, to Holly's relief, both laughed. After their last phone conversation, Holly didn't think the two of them could ever laugh together again. Now, standing with Tyler, gazing up into his familiar face, Holly felt a deep warmth toward him. Not the warmth of romance — even though she knew she'd forever miss how sensitive he'd been as a boyfriend. It was the warmth of friendship. She and Tyler had always been true friends to each other, along with everything else. Holly was sure that foundation would remain.

Tyler slowly, haltingly, reached out one hand and rested it against Holly's freckled cheek. "I think we did the right thing," he said softly, a sadness in his amber-brown eyes. "Your parents told me about your transferring to UCLA. I had a feeling. . . ."

Holly couldn't help but smile up at Tyler. "I love that you heard the news from my parents and not me." Holly realized that Tyler getting along with her family as well as he did made him feel more like a brother than anything else. She wondered if, in the future, she'd try her hand at dating guys who her parents might not approve of as readily. Why not? It could be . . . fun.

As Holly reached up to clasp Tyler's hand in both of hers, both she and Tyler felt the cool band of Holly's Claddagh ring against their skin. Holly drew her hand back, looking down at the ring; out of instinct, she'd slipped it back on in the car, with the heart pointing inward, as before.

"You kept it?" Tyler whispered, his voice catching. "I thought — maybe — you . . ."

"Threw it into the Pacific?" Holly teased. "Never." Taking a deep breath, she slid the ring off her finger, and turned it around, so that the delicate gold heart faced outward. Easing the band back onto her finger, she glanced up at Tyler, knowing her eyes were bright with tears. "See?" she whispered. "Now it symbolizes friendship."

"Like magic," Tyler whispered back, the corner of his mouth lifting in a smile. Then, taking Holly's hands in both of his, he leaned down and kissed her very lightly on the lips — for the last time, Holly knew. When he pulled back, he was smiling down at her tenderly. "You were my first love," he said quietly, so quietly Holly wasn't sure if she'd heard right. But she knew she had when she felt her heart contract in her chest.

"You, too," Holly whispered, holding tight on to Tyler's hand. "And nothing will change that."

They gazed at each other for a long moment, saying more with their eyes than they could any other way, when Holly heard a loud, excited whoop go up right behind her.

"Holly! Bubaleh! I come all the way from Miami to see my beautiful granddaughter and what does she do? She talks to boys!"

"Grandma Ida!" Holly cried, turning away from Tyler and dabbing at her tears. Her grandmother — short red hair aflame, cat-eyed, leopard-print sunglasses atop her head, her trim figure clad in a long sundress printed with flamingos — came bounding toward Holly, surprisingly spry for a septuagenarian.

"Go ahead," Tyler said, putting a hand on Holly's shoulder, and she glanced back at him gratefully. "We'll talk later," Tyler added, waving good-bye. Holly nodded, then turned and immediately flew into her grandmother's arms.

"I'm so glad you came," Holly whispered, squeezing her grandmother tight and breathing in the familiar scent of her Estée Lauder perfume. Over Grandma Ida's shoulder, Holly saw Miles, the sweet elderly gentleman whom Grandma Ida had recently married in an impromptu ceremony on the beach. Holly and Alexa had been bummed that they couldn't attend the wedding, since it had been during finals.

"Are you crazy? How could I miss such an event?" Grandma Ida asked, pulling back to look Holly up and down. "My *goodness!*" she gasped. "You *have* grown up since I last saw you in South Beach."

Holly was reminded of Kenya, also sizing her up back in Hollywood. "It's been a busy year and a half," Holly admitted, leaning down to kiss Grandma Ida's wrinkled cheek. In that moment, Holly's parents and Josh appeared. Holly's dad was scolding Josh about something or other, but Holly's mom was looking right at Holly, a smile playing on her lips.

"Look who's back," Holly's mother said, putting her hands on her hips. "So . . . how was Jonah?" And Holly could tell, from the gleam in her mother's eyes, that she'd decided not to care that Holly had shown up late to graduation. And Holly knew her mom would care even less when she gave her Jonah's autographed napkin.

Holly was hugging her parents and Josh when she

heard Grandma Ida exclaim, "My favorite spitfire! You've grown up, too."

Holly knew before she even turned around that her grandmother was embracing Alexa. Holly was eager to pull her friend aside to fill her in about Tyler – and the fact that they'd been on E! The Jacobsons and St. Laurents gathered together, making the usual parental small talk, while Miles and Josh began discussing baseball. Exchanging an understanding glance, Alexa and Holly linked arms and slipped away, heading over to the table laden with punch and cookies.

"How were things with Tyler?" Alexa asked carefully, filling two glasses with punch.

"Intense," Holly sighed and touched her Claddagh ring, unfamiliar in its new position. "But okay, I think. I'm sure we'll talk off and on during the summer." Taking a sugar cookie off a tray, Holly looked back at her family chatting with Alexa's. "How are you dealing with your mom being here?"

Alexa rolled her eyes dramatically. "It's hard, getting used to your parents paying attention to you."

"Oh, come on," Holly said, smiling at her friend. "I knew she'd show up. You need to have a little faith in people, you know?"

"Yes, Ms. Optimist," Alexa grinned, then handed

Holly one of the glasses of punch. "To . . . our grand finale," she added, lifting her glass.

Holly shook her head, giggling. "You mean to our grand *beginning*," she corrected.

"We never can agree on anything," Alexa said as the girls touched their plastic cups, both of them missing their champagne flutes from El Sueño.

The girls drank, watching each other over their brims. Thinking of all the random toasts she and Holly had shared, Alexa felt her throat tighten. *We've been through everything together.*

"I know something we can agree on," Holly said, finishing her punch and wiping her lips with a napkin. She took Alexa's hand, turning it over as if she planned to write something in her palm. "That we'll IM, e-mail, and write each other on MySpace and Facebook every minute of every day when we go away to college." She could hear her voice starting to tremble.

"Um, you forgot the *phone*," Alexa pointed out, and she and Holly burst out laughing – the kind of laughing that was a few heartbeats away from crying. "And," Alexa added, smiling through the threat of tears. "First long weekend I can get – I am going to Cali, babe. We never *did* get to go to the Chateau Marmont, did we?"

Holly rolled her eyes. "I *knew* there was something we forgot to do out there." Then she reached out and wrapped her arms around Alexa, and the two old friends hugged tight, not letting go for a long time.

"We'll be fine without each other, right?" Holly asked, tears running down her cheeks now as she pulled away.

"Oh, sure," Alexa sobbed, not caring this time if her mascara was making lines down her face. "You basically live in my head anyway – whether I want you there or not." Alexa thought of all the times Holly had been the disembodied voice of reason that had stopped Alexa from making some ridiculous decision.

And you'll be in my heart, Holly thought, knowing Alexa would snort at the cheesy sentiment. But it was true: Holly always relied on Alexa to help her sort through her emotions.

"Love you, Hol," Alexa said, taking Holly by surprise. Alexa's blue eyes regarded Holly with fondness as she slung an arm around her friend's shoulder. "You're my forever friend, no matter what coast you're on."

"Love you, too," Holly replied truthfully, sliding her arm around Alexa's waist and swallowing back her tears.

The emotional moment was broken by the girls' families appearing at their sides, Holly's mom clucking about lunch reservations in Saddle River, and

Alexa's mom muttering something about running off to a facial in Manhattan.

"Would you girls like a picture?" Alexa's dad was asking, holding Alexa's Nikon aloft; Alexa had handed the heavy thing over to him to carry moments before.

"Oh, God, yes!" Alexa exclaimed, realizing that, during their whole time in LA, she and Holly hadn't taken a single photo together. "How should we pose?" she added, glancing at Holly.

"Just like that," Alexa's dad replied, bringing the camera to his eye. "With your arms around each other." He paused, turning the lens. "Okay, what do you they say in Hollywood? 'Life, camera, action?'" Mr. St. Laurent's heavy French accent, combined with the incorrect phrase, made both Holly and Alexa crack up as the camera flash went off.

"It's *lights*, camera, action, Dad," Alexa groaned, taking the camera back from him. Though she had to admit that substituting the word "life" kind of made sense, too. After all, what did cameras record if not life in action?

"That's such a perfect picture," Grandma Ida was commenting, clapping her hands together. "You girls should always be laughing like that."

And we will, Holly thought. It lifted her spirits to know that she and Alexa, tearstained but happy in their graduation outfits, would always exist that way in that picture. She'd be sure to ask Alexa to print doubles, so that there'd be one copy of the photo in Holly's California dorm room, and the other on Alexa's desk in New York City.

"You do realize," Alexa said, turning to Holly as their families began to make their way out of the gym, "that this — our being on opposite sides of the country — gives us the best possible excuse to do more traveling. I mean, there's always winter break. . . ."

"So, where to next?" Holly laughed as the girls started walking toward the exit. "Australia? Hawaii? The Italian Riviera?"

"Hmm," Alexa said, flashing a dazzling smile at her best friend. "I'm not sure, Hol. But we'll figure something out. We always do."

DON'T MISS

Breaking Up

A fabulous and fashionable
new graphic novel
written by *New York Times* bestselling author
Aimee Friedman
and illustrated by Christine Norrie.

TURN THE PAGE FOR A SNEAK PREVIEW!